HER SIXTH SENSE

Imelda Megannety

HER SIXTH SENSE

By the same author

Song without Words
Kaleidoscope
Return to Moineir
The Last Exit
Kilshee

With grateful thanks and appreciation to
Stephen for all his invaluable help

Cover from oil painting by Marie-Claire Keague
www.marieclairekeague.com
ISBN 9798645003043

Chapter 1

Mavis was doing what she really enjoyed, driving on the motorway without a care in the world. She loved the silence and long periods where she could think clearly and plan her life and compose the music and psalm responses that she used in the church choir. Her life was orderly now and she felt in control. After a long life as a loving wife and attentive mother, she felt that this was her time now and relished her freedom. As she turned off the motorway, she switched from her favourite classical music radio progamme to the national news to hear what was happening in the rest of the country.

Nothing much but the usual political talk that bored her to bits. Two political parties that were all the same to her and she could not, for the life of her, understand why they just did not amalgamate and have done with it. She switched off the radio and concentrated on entering the traffic laden lanes which brought her out of the city area and onto the south side. Her daughter Rosemary always worried about her travelling on her own, but she was sure of herself and thought that she would know when it was time to stop driving. She was only seventy for heaven's sake. Nowadays, that is not old, is it?

Smiling, she pulled into the drive of the semi-detached house in the old area she knew so well.

,

She rang the bell and hoped her sister-in-law Maureen, would like the silk scarf that she had bought for her. She was surprised when her niece, Jenny, opened the door.

'Hello, my darling! How lovely to see you! I didn't know that you would be here too.'

Only then did she register the surprise on her niece's face.

'Aunt Mavis! I was not expecting you. How are you.' She hugged her aunt and kissed her on both cheeks.

As Mavis came into the kitchen, her mobile phone pinged. Before she could say anything, Maureen's voice shrilled over the phone, 'Where on earth are you? Lunch is ready and waiting. I thought you would be here by now!'

Mavis frowned, and looked at Jenny. 'It's your mother,' she mouthed. Only then did she realise she was not in Cork at Maureen's house but in Dublin. How did she do that?

Jenny took the phone from Mavis and said, 'Yes Mother, Mavis has just arrived.'

There followed a long tirade and Jenny just listened patiently, then handed the phone back to Mavis.

'Oh Maureen, I am so sorry. I took the wrong turn onto the motorway and went north instead of south.' She started to laugh and rolled her eyes at Jenny.

Her sister-in-law's voice was shrill, and Jenny could also hear the strident voice of her mother.

'I've cooked an organic chicken and all the trimmings, what am I supposed to do with it now? How could you have forgotten?'

Mavis tried to quietly tell Maureen that she had not forgotten, just taken the wrong turn and ended up in Dublin at her niece's house instead of down in Cork. Surely anyone could understand that error. They were the two places she visited most often, so as far as Mavis was concerned, it was an understandable mistake.

'What about the food I've cooked? What do I do with it now?'

Mavis bit back an inappropriate suggestion and gently asked if she could go down to Cork tomorrow instead? She did not think she would be up to travelling down to Cork now, after already having driven for two hours.

'No! Tomorrow I have my flower arranging class and then I lunch with the girls in the book club.'

Mavis thought about the 'girls' as Maureen called them, not one below the age of sixty-six, the same age as herself.

'I apologise again Maureen, let me ring you later in the week and we'll sort something out. Perhaps you can freeze the chicken when it's cold?'

'You know I don't agree with freezing cooked food, Mavis. I am disappointed in you. Do you think you should see a doctor?' Then she hung up.

Mavis sighed and looked at Jenny. 'Oh dear, now I have upset my only sister-in-law. Now it'll be six weeks of tiptoeing around her and checking every sentence I utter.' She started to giggle and soon Jenny had joined in and the two of them laughed until Mavis had to wipe her eyes.

'Jenny, do you think I should see a doctor, because of this mistake?' She watched to see how she could read Jenny's expression but saw nothing there out of the ordinary.

'Mavis, I don't think you are doddery, you made an understandable error. So what? I am glad that you did. Now let's go out and have a nice pub lunch, will we?'

On the return journey, Mavis went over things in her mind. Was she failing? What other mistakes had she made? She tried to think. Surely if she were able to remember them and know they were mistakes, she could not be suffering from dementia, could she? She decided she would have a quiet word with her doctor, John O'Dea, a great family friend and the one who had treated her darling husband. She recalled the mistake she had made a couple of months ago when she was making custard for her friend's grandchildren at their house and had absentmindedly added gravy powder instead of custard powder. It had caused a lot of consternation at first but then they all saw the humour and it ended brilliantly, everyone laughing their heads off. That would now go into the family archives, she knew. She sighed sadly. She had friends who were beginning to fail, and it saddened her a lot. She did not want to go like that. She thought of her friend Sadie, a wonderful generous and loving person who had helped her so much when her darling husband Dennis had died. She had helped her to come to terms with her loss and encouraged her to try to rediscover her hobbies and interests. Sadie had been partly responsible for her having recovered her self-confidence that had gradually eroded over the years as a stay-at-home mother. Dennis had not wanted his wife to work once they had married. She was his second wife and looked after his two little children as though they were her own. Their mother, Sylvia, had been her best friend and she had been devastated when she died shortly after giving birth to Rosemary. He thought his wife's going to work, would reflect badly on him, in his friends' eyes. After all, he was now a successful businessman, self-made and moved in important circles, as he said himself. He loved showing off how successful he was and liked his wife to dress well, always look well-groomed, perfect hair and nails perfectly manicured: a tribute to his wealth. She loved him, and she knew that at heart, he was the same impetuous man she had married and that he was unfailingly kind and generous. He was just a little boy who had never grown up and she did not object to pandering to his wishes. While married to Sylvia, he had not been as wealthy, but his hard work had paid off.

Her thoughts strayed to Frank, their son. She thought of both children as hers, as they had been so young when they lost their mother; she never even thought of them as her stepchildren as she, being so close to Sylvia, had stepped into their lives to help, eventually marrying Dennis a couple of years later. Frank was four then and Rosemary, two years old. He was now thirty-five and seemed happy in his life, seemingly prosperous. He had his father's impetuosity and she worried that he took risks easily without proper consideration. He had taken over his father's car dealership and had diversified into other fields. All she could be sure of, was that he seemed to be doing well. He had his own apartment in Dublin, a flashy car which she felt must have cost a lot and a lifestyle that most men of his age could only dream of. So why was she worried about him? He did not confide in her and she felt his relationship with her had changed when his father died ten years ago.

Rosemary was another worry. At thirty-three she lived at home and did not seem to have any ambitions. She was too dependent on her, Mavis felt. She did not have as much self- confidence as her brother, and he was quick to take advantage of that. He could be quite cruel at times, she knew. Frank was tall, athletic looking and very handsome and unfortunately, he knew it. Rosemary had a problem with her weight and was always on one diet or another. Mavis tried to encourage her to be more active and she would try for a time. Then she seemed to give up and lose interest again. Frank would pass remarks which could only hurt anyone as sensitive as Rosemary, and Mavis told him off on so many occasions that he stopped doing it in her presence, but she knew that he still did it when she was out of the room. She could read Rosemary's face perfectly and see the hurt.

She sighed as she turned off the motorway and wondered if Rosemary would ever meet the right man who could make her happy and confident. She also wondered whether Frank had met anyone yet that he was serious about. His life was full of parties and business dinners and lunches.

As she parked her car, she was surprised to see Frank's car there too. It was a pleasant surprise. They did not see enough of him and she missed his presence. There was always drama assured when Frank was there, that and lots of laughter. She missed the laughter a lot. Dennis had a keen sense of humour and they enjoyed each other's company so much. When the children were at school and later at college, it was just the two of them and they acted like a couple of mad teenagers at times and life was so good. She knew that she would never stop missing Dennis and was appreciative of her faith which gave her strength and hope, and she knew in her heart that she would see him again. A lot of her friends did not believe in the hereafter she was shocked to learn and often wondered how they coped with serious illness and death.

When she entered the house, she could hear their voices coming from the kitchen below. She walked swiftly down the stairs to the basement kitchen which Dennis had made into a bright and wonderful room with the garden area almost like another room, surrounding it. She cheerfully announced her arrival, with a loud 'Hello'.

Frank rose from his seat rapidly and hugged his mother. He took a long look at her and told her she looked very well. Mavis returned the compliment. He then suggested they all have a drink in the sitting room until dinner was ready. Rosemary had a casserole in the oven, and they left the kitchen for the cosy sitting room upstairs on the ground floor. Mavis always had a drink before dinner, usually, but not always, a gin and tonic. As they sat chatting, Mavis took in her son's appearance. He dressed so well and looked fit and healthy and yes, even prosperous. A man of substance, she thought. He was like his father and good at business. He was lucky of course in inheriting the family business and was a hard worker. His father would be proud of him, she knew. She felt proud of both her children as she looked at them this evening. She looked at Rosemary and thought she looked a bit subdued. She hoped that Frank had not been making any nasty comments. She wished her daughter could give as good as she got, but she seldom retaliated and suffered any hurt or insult in silence.

Chapter 2

Rosemary was a schoolteacher and taught English at the girls' secondary school in Greenways, which was only a five-minute drive from where she lived with her mother. She had shared a house once, while in teacher training college and later when she qualified. The girl she shared with then, took a break to travel and Rosemary came back to Ravenswood. She could have afforded the rent alone, if she had dipped into the trust fund which her father had set up for her, but she was nervous of being alone and had missed her mother a lot. She knew she lacked self-confidence; all her friends were in their own apartments or houses by now. She felt she would never be like them. She liked to socialise but had never met a man who attracted her, and anyone that did, was either married or not interested.

She loved her work and was good at it, of that she was certain. In the classroom she blossomed and was confident and self-assured and had no problems there at all. She really put out for her students and most of them appreciated that and felt that they had an ally in her and could talk to her about anything that was troubling them. She was one of the volunteers who stayed on each day to supervise the pupils who stayed late to do their homework. It was usually just after six when she got home each evening, except for Fridays, when all pupils left at the usual time.

Today was Friday, and she was home by four o'clock. She was in the kitchen looking in the fridge to decide what to cook for dinner. She knew her mother was visiting her aunt Maureen in Cork and would be home around seven. The phone rang and she answered it. It was Maureen, and Rosemary got an earful of her disappointment at having cooked a meal that Mavis had not turned up for. Rosemary was surprised to hear that her Mum had gone to Dublin instead. On hearing Maureen's story, she became worried. Maureen was serious in her suggestion that Mavis might be suffering from dementia. It was up to the family, her aunt said, to see to things and not let them progress. On putting down the phone, Rosemary sat and thought about it. Was her mother failing or losing her marbles, as Maureen said? Anybody can make a mistake, surely? Her mother was very active and always bustling about and had a lot on her mind. But the seed had been planted and Rosemary began to imagine life without her mum. Tears began to roll down her cheeks. At that moment, Frank had walked in and found his sister subdued and sad. He checked the sarcasm that immediately sprang to his lips and listened as Rosemary told him about the phone call. He made his sister a cup of tea and they both sat sipping tea and talking about their mother. He asked his sister whether she had noticed anything about their mother that was out of the ordinary recently and quizzed her about any other 'mistakes' she had made. The only thing Rosemary had noticed was the difficulty sometimes her mother experienced in getting a name out or a word to describe something.

'But Frank, she was always like that. Calling us the wrong names or searching for a word she said was on the tip of her tongue but could not recall. She still does her crosswords and flies through them, doesn't she? And what about her music? She still plays the piano quite well, although she does say that if she does not practice her 'serious' pieces daily, she forgets them, but then, those pieces are by memory and she doesn't read music for them.'

Frank sat, deep in thought, his chin in his hand. 'I think we should keep an eye on her, Romy, just in case there is something going on. I'd hate for something bad to happen her. We would never forgive ourselves if we had sat back and had done nothing to prevent it.'

They sat in silence for some time. Then Frank got up and stretched himself. He looked at his sister and said, 'Cheer up sis, it's not the end of the world and I'm sure the Mater will be alright. In fact, we should start thinking of the future. Would you be happy living here in this big house all alone, when Ma pops her clogs?'

This was the sort of conversation that Rosemary hated. She shook her head and silently wished her brother would not continue.

'Think about it, Romy, you would be better off in a smaller house with less work and maintenance. Look at the size of this property, you could easily build three bungalows on the land here, good sized ones, too. Planning permission might not be such a big problem either, if you know the right people. Think of it, Romy! By selling this place, there would be plenty of money to build the other houses.'

Rosemary shook her head. 'I don't think Mum would ever agree to leaving here. She loves it and it holds so many memories, don't forget.'

Frank spread his hands out and said impatiently, 'Memories! What memories will she have if she is losing her mind, eh?'

Rosemary was spared responding to this as they heard their mum's shoes tapping of the wooden floor and her big happy 'Hello'.

Dinner was served in the kitchen. They only used the dining room at the weekends or if they had company during the week. Talk flowed and Mavis recounted her surprise at arriving in Dublin at Jenny's house instead of Cork.

'Of course, Maureen will take ages to get over that!' she exclaimed cheerfully. 'Jenny and I could not stop laughing about it. Poor Maureen and her cooked chicken!'

The way she told it was so funny that Rosemary started to laugh too. Only Frank, it seemed, was not amused. After Rosemary had cleared away the dishes and served an apple tart that she had bought, Frank announced that he had very exciting news for them. They looked at him expectantly and he poured more wine as he relayed his news.

'You don't mind if I take up temporary residence, do you Ma? It is necessary as I am going to sell my apartment.' He paused and took a sip of wine.

'Of course not, Frank. It will be lovely to have you around again, even if only for a while. But why are you selling your lovely apartment? I thought it was your pride and joy.'

'Ma, if I sell now, I stand to profit by around a million or more. The property market is at the highest ever, and Dublin is where the action is. I only need to redecorate the lounge and it will be as good as new.'

Mavis thought about the stunning apartment she had been shown four years previously. She had been struck dumb at the luxury and décor of the place; marble floors in the bathrooms and granite worktops, solid wood floors, to say nothing of the modern furniture. At the time, she felt he had got to the top too fast and hoped it would last.

Rosemary was staring at her brother in a confused way. 'Where will you live, if you sell it, are you moving out of Dublin?'

Her brother looked at her in exasperation, 'Of course not! Dublin is the only place to live in. No, I have other properties of course, but they're all rented out. One and two bed apartments are really the best money makers. You steer away from families, at all costs!'

Mavis sipped her wine and smiled at Frank, 'As long as you know what you are doing, love.'

'I do indeed Ma. And, I have news that will interest you, I hope. I have contacts in the stock market business and financial institutions, also other friends like various estate agents, who have slipped a few facts my way.' He tapped his nose and winked at them as he made this statement.

Rosemary hated this habit of his, it made him appear shifty and dodgy in her eyes.

'Don't roll your eyes, Romy, until you hear my news! The market is set to crash in about six months and what a fall it's going to be! Worse than the last recession I've been told. That's why I want to sell my fancy apartment, which I bought as an investment anyway. Then when the prices tumble, that's the time to start buying again. Who knows? I may be able to buy the same apartment back at less than the original price I paid for it!' He grinned around at them proudly, looking like a little boy who expected to get a treat for his cleverness.

Mavis looked at Frank and said, 'Well, I suppose that is interesting news, for the people who are going to profit, not so good for the unfortunates who will lose out.'

Frank leaned forward and leaned his arms on the table. 'This is why it will interest you Ma, and you too Romy,' he nodded at his sister. 'If you sell Ravenswood before the crash you will make a killing and, with all the land that Ravenswood is on, you could build a lovely modern, easy to manage and well insulated bungalow for yourselves. You would not need to sell any of the land, only the old house, with the gardens.' He leaned back and searched his mother's face eagerly.

Mavis was stunned and could not speak. 'I would have to think deeply about this, Frank. It's not an idea that I have ever entertained before now. I suppose as I get older, I will need a smaller place, won't I? It is tempting to think of a smaller and modern house, but I have years yet, before I need to do such a drastic thing. What do you think of this, Rosemary?'

Her daughter looked into her mother's eyes and said, 'Ma, when the time comes, you will know. Only then, need you consider moving.' She glared defiantly across at Frank.

Undaunted, Frank again turned to his mother. 'It's not only you, Ma. Romy should have her own house by now, shouldn't she? There would be room enough to build two houses here. That way she would be independent and be on the property ladder.'

'All one hears about, is this property ladder,' said Rosemary sullenly. 'With you it's a bloody scaffolding you're on! Just be careful you don't fall off!' She rose from the table and strode out of the room.

Frank's laughter followed her all the way upstairs to her room.

Later, Mavis and Frank watched the news on television. When it was over and Mavis was ready to go to bed, Frank again brought the conversation around to the house and its selling potential. 'It's Romy I worry about,' he confided to Mavis. 'She is too dependent on you Ma, and what is to become of her when you go, hoping of course that you have years left in you. You are remarkably healthy and fit of course, but Romy is getting older, and it worries me. In fact, she confided in me recently that there is no way she could ever leave you, that you would never manage without her, so even if she met someone, she feels obliged to stay. Don't say anything to her, it was said in confidence.'

Mavis sighed. She worried about Rosemary too but was shocked at Frank's disclosure about Rosemary's attitude. She had never realised that she might be a hindrance to her daughter's future and happiness. 'Let fate decide Frank, don't worry.'

Upstairs, alone in her bedroom, she sat down at the small writing desk she had bought herself recently and upright chair that went with it and took out her notebook. She had always kept a notebook of her daily activities. It was not a diary as such, just a place to jot down her activities in the garden mainly, her choir practises and what she planned to do next. Writing it down helped her to remember ideas that came to her during the day. Tonight, she jotted down her mistaken journey to Dublin. She made a note to contact Maureen in two or three days, to give her time to simmer down. Must contact Sadie too, she wrote, the poor woman would be back from Dublin and the tests she had to endure since her dementia started.

Looking up she gazed at the photograph of Dennis on her desk. She remembered when that photo was taken and went into a reverie. She smiled at him and as usual said out loud, 'I miss you, my darling, I wish you were here, but be happy wherever it is you are in the spirit world.' He was taking care of her she knew. She never spoke to anyone about her strange experiences, not that they were strange to her, to other people they would be. She was always elated and full of joy whenever she experienced these 'happenings', as she thought of them.

They had begun years ago, maybe when she was a child, she could not remember. The first time that she vividly remembered was before Sylvia died. There was the same surreal feeling before it happened. It was this familiar sense of the unreal that she remembered and knew that it had happened before Sylvia, but she had never taken any notice of

18

it then. After Sylvia, she was more aware. They had been shopping for Sylvia's honeymoon clothes and the strange feeling descended as they were chatting. Mavis and Sylvia had been happily looking through rows of pretty nightwear and underwear. Looking up to attract Sylvia's attention, the shop seemed to have altered, for a moment she did not know where she was, Sylvia was gone and there were lots of women milling around who had not been there when they had entered the shop. Looking around, she began to panic. Where was she and where was her friend?

It had only lasted a few seconds but at the time, it seemed ages before she had spotted Sylvia at the end of the row of clothing and everything looked the same again, just as when they arrived at the shop. There were no crowds of women around, only them. She had felt a bit disturbed then and wondered if there was something going on in her brain. Maybe she had an incurable tumour or something!

The other time, while Sylvia was still alive, it happened at Rosemary's baptism. She had been asked by Sylvia if she would be godmother and was delighted and of course said yes. Sylvia could not be present at the church, being still ill in hospital. At the baptismal font, she was holding the baby Rosemary when the feeling came again. Suddenly there nobody there except her, holding the baby, who suddenly turned into a little girl about seven and who stood beside her, looked up at her and called her

'Mum'. She had smiled at the child who was no longer a baby in her arms. Then the 'happening' passed and the baptism was proceeding normally. She joyfully thought she was given a vision of her own daughter who would appear in her life sometime. She was not disturbed by that 'happening', at all. The opposite in fact.

She had not had a 'happening' now for a while, unless she counted the times Dennis came into her dreams, usually when she had something on her mind. The problems then always had a way of being solved; she thought that Dennis had something to do with it in some way. She had never spoken of these things, how could she? It would come across as extremely strange sounding to any ordinary normal person and she was vain enough in not wanting to be called a 'mad hatter'.

Chapter 3

Frank moved back into his old room and after a few weeks the women got used to his coming and going. It did not affect the routine of their lives. He left early in the morning and was usually late home. Mavis continued with her choir work and her visits to Sadie. Recently she had started teaching piano again although in a limited way. During her marriage to Dennis, she had persuaded him to let her continue in a small way, her music teaching. First it was her own two children and then a few of their friends. Now it was a couple of retired friends who were at a loose end. She enjoyed her renewed talent, and it satisfied a need in her life. One such adult was James Regan. His wife had died two years ago, and it had left him battling. He had left the choir and all his other hobbies to nurse his dear wife and now was left feeling empty and depressed. Mavis met him one day and persuaded him to return to the choir and to take up the piano as well. He had been quite a musician in his day, and he began to thrive again.

The choir practice took place in the local church, one morning a week. Another practice was later added, after the choir expanded, for the members who could not attend the early morning practice. This second practice took place in her home, in the large reception room at the front of the house, where she had her baby grand piano, a wedding gift from

Dennis. They usually practiced every Monday night for an hour. Rosemary would make dinner and loved listening to the choir as they went through their repertoire. At eight sharp they would finish, and the two women would eat their dinner, have a glass of wine and discuss the various members and the music they were doing.

James Regan came on Wednesday afternoon, although that could vary, depending on their various duties and availability. One afternoon Rosemary came home early from school. There was a hockey match between her school and another local school, and the afternoon study was cancelled. As she took off her coat in the hallway and went down to the basement kitchen to make a coffee, she would hear a version of Debussy's "Golliwog's cakewalk" drifting down. She knew it was not her mother playing and wondered how her mother could bear to hear music being massacred! She smiled to herself. She brought her coffee up to the small sitting room where the television was and sat down. Suddenly she heard her mother shouting, 'No, no, no, James!' Startled she put down her cup. She had never heard her mother shout before. She tiptoed over to the door and listened.

'You must lighten up James! Relax your body, you are too tense. Come here, get up and I'll show you what you must do.'

There followed a lot of commotion, running movements and her mother singing, 'Dah da, da dah da.' There followed more running movements and her mother laughing. 'You can do it James, you can!'

Rosemary must have made a noise outside the door because suddenly the door was flung open. Her mother stood there, her hair a bit dishevelled and her face flushed.

'Good, there you are Rosemary, just the girl I need. Please come and help me here.'

Rosemary stared at her mother and then at James, standing awkwardly in the middle of the room. Mavis explained what she wanted Rosemary to do, and Rosemary's mouth gaped open.

'You want me to dance with James? Ma I can't dance, you know that.'

James nodded and said, 'Neither can I, and she insists I must, to be able to play that piece.'

'Come on, now,' said Mavis. I am going to play the music and I want you to guide James around the room, just letting yourselves move to the music, anyway you want. He must lose his woodenness.'

She sat down at the piano and started into the lively piece of music. James and Rosemary stared at each other helplessly. Mavis stopped playing and sighed. 'For heaven's sake James, made the effort, will you? I am too old for jumping about, that first time nearly killed me.'

,

She started playing again and Rosemary took hold of James' arms and said, 'There will be no peace until we try, I know my mother.'

They started walking around the room. The music stopped and Mavis, got up and went over to Rosemary and took her hand and put her other hand on the girl's waist and launched into a mad gallop. After a round of the room, she stopped and said, 'That's what I'm after. Do it!'

They started again and the music was furious and compelling. Suddenly Rosemary began to laugh and got into her stride. She had to pull James at first, and he was indeed very tense, she thought. Then the jazziness got them, and they let themselves go and really enjoyed it. Mavis shouted as she played, 'Loosen up, move whichever way the music takes you, you're like soldiers. Swing! Sway! You can slow down at the slow part.'

After the music finished the two dancers collapsed on the sofa, breathless and laughing. Mavis beamed at them. 'That's the way you must play James, with soul, like you are dancing, man. Understand what I am saying? Oh, by the way, this is my daughter, Rosemary. This is James Regan, Rose.'

James nodded helplessly, still grinning. 'You are an awful woman, Mavis. I came to play the piano, not take dancing lessons. Sorry Rosemary that you were dragged into this.'

Rosemary stood up on shaking legs and said, 'I need a drink to recover from this, and I don't mean coffee!' She left the room still smiling. Dear Lord, she thought to herself, my mother *is* mad! She giggled again. Mad in a good way, she thought, not insane mad. What would Maureen say if she had witnessed that scene? She sat down and looked at her cold coffee, then went over to the sideboard and poured herself a glass of red wine. From the front room drifted the sound of Debussy again, but a much better version than the first time. He had obviously benefited from the physical lesson. How had her mother known that that was what he needed, to understand the music?

Frank returned in time for dinner that night and not in a good mood. Rosemary decided not to relay the hilarious afternoon she had spent in the front room. Mavis asked Frank how the decorating was going and received a grunt and a shrug in reply. Pressed, he admitted that the painters were not the professionals he was promised and that he had dismissed them and hired a different firm. He was worried that the place would not be finished in time for the first viewing next week. Rosemary went out later to the cinema with a friend. When he was alone with his mother, he suddenly asked Mavis if he could borrow some money to sort out the decorating. She was surprised although she did not show it and asked how much?

'Oh, not much. About five thou, Ma. Cash flow is a bit slow just now, you know. A lot tied up in the other properties. It will just be until the end of the month.'

Mavis was a little shocked. It had been a long time since he asked for a loan. For someone who lived the life he did, it seemed to her that five thousand was not so much. Of course, she would lend him the money, she would never begrudge her children anything, it was just so unexpected. Again, she wondered how things really were with him.

After agreeing and giving him a cheque, she left to go to bed. As she got to the door, he asked her whether she had given any further thought to the idea they had discussed about selling the house. Mavis admitted that she had not thought about it as she was busy but would do so in the coming months.

He smiled at her and said, 'That's the spirit, Ma, you must come to terms with the future, which could be very bright for you!'

Mavis climbed the stairs to her room and felt for the first time, alone and anxious. How she missed Dennis now. He always knew the right thing to do, and he would be a good advisor to Frank. What did she know about business anyway? Money never bothered her. She was able to live on the pension that Dennis had left her. Anything she had, would be going to the children anyway and the charitable institutions she supported. Getting into bed, she recalled the afternoon with James and Debussy. She started smiling again and spoke to herself as she often did, out loud. 'Mavis girl! Get a grip! Frank is a grown man, not a child and you are a young woman at heart and enjoying life.'

Frank was still watching television when Rosemary returned from the cinema. She told him a bit about the film and then realised he was not listening. As she turned to leave the room he suddenly said, 'Romy, have you not tried to convince Ma that selling here, would be good for you both?'

'I think she will come around in a while, Frank. It needs a lot of thinking about, plus, she needs to feel that it would be right for her. That has not happened yet as she is so busy and active in her life. Don't press her about it.'

Frank persisted with his argument, 'And what about yourself, don't you ever wish you had your own place? I could find you such a smart little apartment around these parts. It wouldn't use up all your trust fund at all. There would be plenty left over, don't worry.'

Rosemary shook her head. 'For the moment I am fine. I know that I can buy a place of my own anytime I like. Mum probably feels the same.'

'If she waits much longer, she will have missed the boat! Does she not realise that prices are going to drop? A place like this might prove unsellable later.'

'She is our mother Frank, and I am not going to pressurise her and cause her distress. She is happy in the place she is in, right now.'

'Oh! Like you are happy in the place you are in right now? You will soon pass your sell-by date Romy and end up a dried-up old maid! I could fix you up with a half decent bloke who is not too fussy, if you would just lose a bit of weight and glamorise yourself, even a little bit.'

Rosemary left the room without replying. Later in bed she wept silently.

Chapter 4

It was Friday and Maureen had contacted Mavis the week before to arrange another meeting. She had regretted her outburst with her sister-in-law and knew that the real cause of her anger had been her own fault. She had offended another old friend of hers and now was realising that her tongue got her into a lot of trouble. She must learn to curtail her impatience and not fly off the handle so readily.

Mavis had agreed to meet Maureen in Cork city and they both wanted to visit the English Market and stock up on delicacies of all sorts. Mavis had a substantial breakfast after a leisurely bath. She checked the doors and got her bag, all ready to leave for the day. When she went to lock the front door, she realised she did not have her keys. She looked in the drawer in the hall table, where she always put them. They were not there. Puzzled, she checked her bag and then went down to the kitchen to check the dresser, all the time knowing that she never put them there. After thirty minutes of futile searching, she knew that she would be late for her meeting with Maureen and risk her wrath again. Cursing under her breath she went back to the kitchen and climbed on a chair to retrieve the spare car key that was on the top shelf of the dresser. She decided to ring Maureen to prepare her for a thirty-minute wait. She did not elaborate on why she was running late. Now she had to leave the hall door unlocked and she prayed there would be no break-in. She put the house alarm on and left in a more confident mood. The keys would turn up.

Rosemary met some friends the same afternoon. She had been feeling energetic all week for some reason and when Susie asked her to go swimming in the town pool, she had readily agreed. Normally she was not an exercise girl, walking was alright though. Today she really enjoyed the swimming and swam about ten lengths, which for her, was something. In the changing room Susie suggested going for coffee to the new hotel nearby, she had heard that they had a salad bar, something quite innovative in this town. Nothing but salads served, she told them. The other three girls thought that the idea would never take off but were willing to give it a go.

It proved to be a great success. They were delighted with the diverse salads and many combinations, plus the fact that you could make your own dressing. All the ingredients were provided and very small bottles into which you put your choice of olive oil plus whatever you fancied, closed the lid and then shook the bottle to mix up and pour over your salad. Rosemary was very impressed. She was able to make her favourite dressing of Dijon mustard, Irish rape seed oil and white wine vinegar.

'My mother would love this,' she told her friends, 'I must bring her soon.'

Susie told them all that she had started a new exercise regime, could they guess what it was?

They all suggested whatever new fad was in vogue, but Susie shook her head.

'No, I'll tell you now! It's held here in this place. All next door to the swimming pool. It's line dancing!' She beamed around at the other three.

Aine shook her head, 'Ah, that's old hat, Sue. That was the rage about thirty years ago. My granny would probably have done that!'

'It's back girls and I'm doing it. The workout is only amazing and afterwards I go into the pool to cool off. You'd never believe how exhausting it is. Will you try it?'

Only Rosemary was interested and asked what she had to wear. The important thing was comfortable shoes, or would wreck her feet, she was told. Susie wore tracksuit bottoms and a cotton top as it was so energetic the sweat poured off you.

After discussing the merits of movement to music, followed by a swim, the other two decided it might be worth a try. They agreed to try it the following Friday at six, when the class started, have a swim and then eat in the salad bar.

Rosemary reached home around six-thirty and was disturbed to find the front door unlocked. She knew her mother was in Cork and would be home around seven or thereabouts. She felt a bit nervous entering the house but soon realised that all was well. The alarm had been set and as she disarmed it, she knew that nobody could have broken in. Mavis would have had a decent meal in Cork so there was no dinner to prepare. Rosemary felt remarkably full after the salad and realised that today had been a most pleasant day and her mood was quite elated and positive. She wondered if she would be in the same mood when Frank came home and started on at her. She was very fond of him, but he could be hurtful especially if he did not get his own way. She wondered again about why he was so keen to get her to buy a property and why he wanted Ravenswood sold. He wanted them to make money, she supposed. She thought about her life and how content she was teaching, how she had everything she needed. Of course, it would be nice if she had a male companion to share her life with. She remembered how happy Mavis and Dennis had been. They were always laughing, it seemed to her. There were arguments sometimes, but they were generally light-hearted, and laughter always followed. If she could find a partner like her Dad, she thought, life would be complete.

Mavis reached home at seven thirty. She was tired after walking around Cork and looked forward to having a drink and just sitting in front of the telly. She called 'Hello' and went to the kitchen to put her perishable goods in the fridge. Rosemary was in the small sitting room watching the news and had a bottle of wine open, ready for her mother. The room looked so welcoming, three lamps in corners lit and a fire burning merrily. Oh, she so loved her home and there was her lovely daughter sitting waiting for her! Shortly after she joined Rosemary, Frank arrived and putting his head around the door, asked what was for dinner? The ladies looked at him blankly and told him they had already eaten, and Rosemary apologised and said that she had quite forgotten that he would be there. Mavis told him to go down and have a root in the fridge.

'You will find something, I'm sure. I brought back lots of lovely things from the English Market,' she said. 'Put on the kettle while you're down there, a cup of tea would be welcome.'

Frank looked a bit put out. 'Oh, you went visiting Maureen, did you? I forgot about that.'

He took himself off and the ladies grinned at each other. 'With all his money, wouldn't you think he would get a meal in Dublin, before coming home?' Mavis sighed. 'I think we must have spoiled him a bit, somewhere along the way.'

Rosemary remembered about the hall door and mentioned it casually to her mother. She did not want her to think that she was beginning to doubt her competence but felt she should mention it. Her mother nodded and told her daughter about the thirty-minute scramble, to try and find her car and door keys. She had forgotten about it until Rosemary brought it up. Rosemary said she would look for them tomorrow, being Saturday and not needing to go anywhere. They must be somewhere they agreed.

When Frank came up bearing a plate with bread and cheese, he found the two of them discussing the salad bar in the new hotel, and the new/old fad of line dancing. He sat down and turned up the television, looking a bit bad tempered at his lack of dinner. Rosemary got up and after a few minutes returned with a tray with three cups of tea.

Mavis asked him how the decorating was going and was relieved to see him smile and nod his head. It was all coming together nicely; the first viewers were coming Monday morning and he was pretty sure the apartment would not be on the market for long. He said he had to return to Dublin in the morning for a meeting with some top executives and did not expect to be home until quite late. He planned to go golfing on Sunday with some old school friends.

'Who do you still keep in touch with?' his mother wanted to know.

'Oh, just the usual three. Paul Kavanagh of course and the Moloney brothers.'

'What does Paul do?' his mother wanted to know.

'He has a partnership in a car dealing outfit, north of Dublin. He still spends a lot of time down here when he is not travelling. In fact, he has offered me a partnership in another company of his. Not sure if I will take it. It involves a lot of travelling, which might be a drag.'

'Sounds as if he is doing alright for himself,' Mavis remarked. 'Are any of your friends married yet?'

'Well Paul was. He is separated now, and the two brothers are married to two sisters. Both have two children.'

'Have you not found any one to take you on, Frank?' Rosemary asked mischievously. 'She would have to be someone who was not very fussy, don't you think?' She smiled at him, superciliously.

He glared at her. 'My girlfriends have all been highly educated and sophisticated, all well-groomed and attractive. No overweight country schoolteachers tolerated!'

Mavis was shocked and upset by this exchange between brother and sister and for once was silent. She was too tired to get involved with this unpleasantness. She rose and said that she was going to bed.

'Good night Mum. See you in the morning and I'll help you look for those keys, don't worry.'

'What's up with the keys then Ma, forgotten where you put them? I spent most of my youth searching for Dad's keys when he couldn't remember where he left them.' Frank yawned and stretched his arms out. 'Oh well! The joys of old age, I expect.'

Rosemary got up then and both mother and daughter exited the sitting room. They climbed the stairs together and kissed each other goodnight.

Mavis was so tired. Walking around a city was so different to walking in the countryside. The pavements were so hard on the feet and even though she had worn comfortable shoes, her feet were aching. She decided that she would soak them in the footbath, which Rosemary had given her one Christmas. It was useful and very soothing. She took her cholesterol tablet first then put it away in her bedside locker and took out her blood pressure tablet to take in the morning. She had learned that the best way of remembering, if she had taken her tablet, was to put them away after taking one and taking out the next tablet needed. She knew that doing routine things absentmindedly could lead to confusion and she made the effort of doing things in a mindful way. She sat with her feet in the hot water with a drop of lavender essence and closed her eyes. Her mind strayed again to the misplaced keys. She had forgotten all about that episode until Rosemary had mentioned it. She slowly went over her movements of the previous day. What time had she returned home? She tried to visualise her movements from coming in the front door. The trouble with routine was, that it did not provoke any memories, unless something happened to make you remember.

After some time, she woke with a start. She dried her feet and undressed for bed, then washed her teeth and put some face cream on. She looked at herself in the mirror and wondered when had she become so old looking? Did it happen so gradually that she did not notice? It must have done. She had not looked like this when Dennis was alive, she knew. Maureen had not been a great help there, either. She had looked at her sister-in-law critically today and asked if she had been ill, or was she on a diet? She then expounded on the dangers of dieting at Mavis' age and how it always showed on the face. 'Nothing ages like a diet,' she had said.

Mavis did not bother to reply and turned the conversation around to the coming elections. That led Maureen off on another rant about the ineptness of politicians in general, the shocking state of the country and the total immorality of the young, the lameness and stupidity of the judiciary, never mind the awful weather and terrible traffic. All Mavis had to do was stay silent and look at the shops as they walked along the pavements. She silently wondered if Maureen had anything good to say about anything or anybody. Had she always been so negative, she wondered? Maureen had once been married. Her husband had been a gentle creature, interested in the arts and literature but too quiet for Maureen, who had bullied him terribly and publicly made fun of him and his dated ideas and quaint ways. On his fiftieth birthday, he simply left her and went to live abroad in Spain. The shock had silenced her for all of six months. After that, she was back to her usual boisterous and self-opinionated ways.

She decided she should read a bit before trying to sleep. All the day's commotion was roiling about in her head and she knew that she would have trouble dropping off, despite having fallen asleep with her feet in the footbath! She picked up her latest library book. It was a small book on positive thinking, with different chapters with such titles as; 'Peace and calm', 'The absence of sound', 'Soothing Words', 'Listening to running water', and other such ideas. At first glance she had dismissed the book as idiotic, but after reading a couple of pages, she decided to give it a go. She was glad she did. No effort was needed to comprehend the ideas behind the various chapters and after two or three pages, her eyelids would droop. Now she turned to a new chapter, 'Living in the now'. After a few pages, sure enough, her eyes began to feel heavy. Then that familiar 'feeling' suddenly and quietly happened. She was standing in a strange place, on a drive leading up to a very big building. Although she had not been there before, she just knew that it was a prison, and she was going to visit someone there. Mavis slept as the small book slipped out of her hand and fell on the floor.

,

Chapter 5

Mavis slept so well that night that she felt years younger when she awoke. She sang as she made her bed and went about getting ready for the day ahead. She usually woke with a song in her head ready to sing. She thought it very normal and was surprised when her friends noticed and laughed at her. It was usually on holidays with a few close friends, that comments would be made about the morning singing. She thought about those friends now. It had been a year since they went anywhere for a holiday. She did not count the two or three days away walking as a real holiday, they were just "breaks". Now she felt like it was time for a holiday and new scenery. She promised herself that she would ring Norma that weekend to try and arrange a week somewhere.

Frank had already left when she went down to make her breakfast. She felt relieved and then felt guilty for feeling that. Why did his presence recently bring a tension and atmosphere that she did not enjoy? Well, it probably would not be for much longer. He probably did not like living at home either, having been used to his freedom and independence. She prayed the apartment would sell soon and that he would find another place to move into.

She sat at the island in her kitchen and drank her tea and ate her two slices of homemade soda bread which either she or Rosemary baked. She might go out and do a little bit of tidying in the garden today. She would practice the programme for tomorrow's church service later. She hoped all the choir members would turn up.

Rosemary came down as she was leaving the kitchen. They smiled at each other and Rosemary asked, 'Did you sleep well Mum?'

'Like a baby, Rose, and did you?'

Her daughter nodded, but Mavis noticed the dark circles under her daughter's eyes and said nothing. She knew that having Frank back at home was unsettling for Rosemary. She went into the utility room and put on her gardening boots. As she walked around the garden, she felt uplifted seeing how everything was thriving. She loved Spring and the changes that came in the garden. Suddenly life would return, and growth come, shyly at first then boldly and then rampantly. She went into her tunnel and decided she needed to give the inside a good wash to remove any of the green growth that came with the icy weather. The onion sets and garlic which went in during November were showing a sturdy growth. She planted them in holes made in black plastic bin bags. That cut out the need for weeding and she always had a good supply of onions, which she kept stored in her garage. Her sturdy plastic troughs outside both doors of the tunnel were full of rainwater and she had added seaweed, brought back from her trips to the seaside. She opened back the tunnel door and took a watering-can of water and watered the onions and garlic. She had spread old newspaper and sheets of cardboard over the other beds to keep down the weeds. Her days of digging were coming to an end. Her back complained after too much time bending over and she was beginning to understand what 'pacing yourself' meant.

As she turned towards the house, she saw Rosemary coming up the garden path with a cup of tea in her hand. She held something up in her other hand, grinning madly.

'Guess what I found,' she sang. Mavis' house and car keys dangled from her hand. 'What is the reward for this, Mama dear?'

'Oh, my goodness! Where did you find them, darling?' Mavis was so thrilled and relieved. She had forgotten all about them again.

'Mum, they were in the hall table drawer, right at the back. You must have missed them.'

Mavis paused in thought as she took the bunch of keys. 'I'm sure I searched the two drawers thoroughly Rose. Am I going senile?'

Rosemary shook her head and smiled at the older woman. 'No Ma, definitely not senile. You were probably in such a hurry that you didn't see them at the back.'

'Well, I am certainly relieved to get them back. I must put a spare house key in a jar and keep it in the tunnel, just in case. I did not like leaving the house open like that.'

Rosemary asked her if she would like to go for lunch to the salad bar which she had told her about. Mavis loved salad and agreed readily.

They had a leisurely lunch which Mavis enjoyed very much and then she proposed a trip to the garden centre to see what was new. She could never resist buying something for the garden whenever the opportunity arose. While there she bumped into her farmer friend Marie, who supplied her so generously with her chicken's manure. Mavis once told her that she was her own personal gold mine. Marie called her aside to look at a plant she was interested in. She knew that Mavis had them in her garden.

'What is the name of this blue one, Mavis. You have lots in the front garden, haven't you?'

Mavis looked and knew them immediately. She frowned as she gazed at the plants and tried to think of the name of them. She could not remember! She looked at Marie and shook her head.

'I know them perfectly well, but the name won't come to me, damn it!'

She called Rosemary over and asked her if she could remember what they were called.

'They are Hostas, Mum and the other blue ones behind are Agapanthas.'

'Of course, they are, why on earth could I not get the names out? So annoying.'

'Mavis, if that's all you have to worry about, you're lucky. My memory is faulty and a lot worse than yours. Last night I was at a meeting and had to introduce two people who did not know each other. Lord, I was so embarrassed! I couldn't remember either of their names, and they are as familiar to me as my own children. What they thought of me I don't know.'

Mavis laughed. 'My friend Sadie says, that as long as I don't end up in the wrong bed, I'm alright. She told me that she knew of someone staying in a hotel at a wedding who mistakenly went into the wrong room and got into bed with someone whom she thought was her husband. Luckily the fellow was not quite asleep and jumped out very smartly and put her right! Imagine if she fell asleep and the man was asleep, what would be the reaction in the morning? Heart attacks all round, I imagine!'

They all laughed at the story. Rosemary giggled and said, 'Well, depending on their ages, it could have been very difficult to explain to others. Imagine if the fellow's wife had come up later to bed, to find someone in her place! Could have been a couple of divorces there I'm sure.'

The three left the garden centre still smiling and for once, Mavis did not buy anything at all. She was still annoyed at not remembering the plant names.

They drove home and Mavis thought she might have a nap. Rosemary had work to do on a project she was going to introduce to her pupils. She and Susie were going out for a drink tonight. As they drove up the drive, they could see a strange car parked to the right of the house. There were two figures in the distance coming down from the 'paddocks' as the two fields were called.

The women sat in the car and watched in curiosity. As they came nearer, they recognised Frank. They did not recognise the other man. Mavis and Rosemary got out of the car as they neared the front of the house. Frank saw them and waved. Rosemary went into the house, and Mavis remained standing, waiting for them to come nearer.

'Paul this is the Mater. Ma this is my friend from school, Paul. Do you remember him from way back?'

Paul stepped forward and proffered his hand. Mavis took it and looked up at him. She smiled and said, 'No, I can't say I remember you Paul, but then you would have been a little boy and not the very tall man I see before me.'

He agreed and said that it had been a long time. 'It's still the same beautiful place that I remember. Nothing has changed here, has it? The ponies are long gone I expect.'

'Oh yes, they were there for a short time, until it became a chore to look after them, isn't that right Frank?'

44

Frank smiled and nodded. 'Animals are fine, but they need a lot of attention and care. Paul and I are going to the greyhound stadium later and I just thought I would show him the place while we are filling in time.' They refused the tea offered by Mavis and left shortly after that.

Mavis joined Rosemary in the kitchen, and they talked about Frank appearing with Paul and without warning. 'Surely he could have brought the fellow in for a cup of tea. That would have been mannerly, wouldn't it?'

'What on earth were they doing up in the paddocks? The ground is still quite soft from that rain we had.' Rosemary sat with her elbows on the table, hands under her chin as she gazed out the window, up towards the fields. She felt suspicious of Frank and his motives. He was too interested in Ravenswood and for all the wrong reasons. She wished he would move out and that they could get on with the lives they had enjoyed before he came back.

Mavis went off to the piano to practice her church music for tomorrow and Rosemary went upstairs to the study, which was her father's, on the first floor. They had not changed it one bit; the same worn furniture and desk which had been there when he was alive. She loved the sameness of it and could almost smell her father's presence there and the lovely tobacco smell from the old pipe he used to smoke. She took out her laptop and began to work.

She worked steadily until she had finished and then saw the clock. It was six thirty. Time to think about dinner she thought and closed her laptop. She could not hear any music from the front room and wondered if her mother was napping. On entering the kitchen, she got the lovely smell of curry and found her mother humming away and creating an aromatic and delicious dinner. One thing they shared was their love of spicy and exotic food. They took turns in cooking dinner and loved experimenting. Mavis had a lot of Indian friends from her time abroad and loved to recreate the food she had learned to love and cook while she had been in England. They loved all foods but especially Middle Eastern which was so subtle and not just about heat. They had recently found the new Japanese restaurant in town and made regular trips there. Rosemary loved sushi and Mavis the dumplings and vegetables in tempura.

'No wonder I have a problem with my weight Mum, your dinners are just too delicious.'

Mavis smiled as she placed the bowls of curry and rice on the island and put out plates and cutlery. 'There is no way I can live without spice my girl, and I do not believe this food is fattening really. It's good healthy stuff, no additives and does not come out of a packet.'

When Rosemary had gone out with her friend, Mavis decided she must make a few phone calls. They were more satisfying than texting, which was alright for quick messages. She could only ring Sadie anyway, her reading skills had sharply declined with the onset of dementia. Firstly, she rang Norma, her walking friend. She wanted to discuss any ideas that might have come up about a holiday. There were four of them and the holidays worked out very well. After the walking, they would all go to dinner and then come back to the hotel and play bridge with a bottle of wine handy. They seldom stayed a full week, which was alright by Mavis. She just did not like travelling a long distance to stay only for a night or two. It was tiring for her nowadays. Their walk on the Camino was for about a week. That was three years ago. She was not sure whether she would be up to that again. There was a lot of walking but the weather had been cool so there was no problem.

Norma loved planning trips and she eagerly got stuck into suggesting places and hotels. Mavis just listened. She followed where she was brought. A trip to Cape Clear was mentioned but that would only be for two nights away at most, maybe just one. Mavis loved the idea of seeing the island. There was something about islands that pulled at her imagination. Then Norma mentioned the Scottish islands and Mavis' heart jumped at that. The friends agreed to meet soon and discuss things further and have a chat with the other two women to see how things were with them and fix a date when all would be free. After saying goodbye, Mavis rang Sadie.

The conversation was as usual, a bit disjointed but alright. Sadie was glad to hear from her and Mavis gave her any news that she had. She did not ask too many questions as she did not want to put any stress on Sadie if she got stuck for words. Enough to say that she would be down to see her very soon. Sadie was happy and said she looked forward to seeing her.

Again, Mavis thought about her not being able to recall those familiar plant's names and wondered if there was an exercise she could do, to help her brain cells. She made a note to ask John O'Dea when she saw him next. Then she reached for her notebook and entered that idea in it. From now on, she would write down anything that happened to her memory and see if that helped. She also wrote down the word "keys". She then took out the tablet she hardly ever used and started to research the symptoms of dementia. She looked at ten early signs and could identify, she thought with some of them. Her short-term memory was certainly not so good; struggling for familiar words was another; forgetfulness where one was supposed to be on a certain day, misplacing things like keys. She sighed as she switched the thing off. She sat and counted the things that she had failed in; going to Dublin instead of Cork; not remembering the familiar plants; her missing keys.

,

Her mood was always good, optimistic rather than apathetic, she could still play the piano reasonably well, her focus was good. She decided that the things she was failing at, were not that important after all. She could still recognise her friends and family, no problem there. She reasoned that nothing could stay the same forever and things were in a constant state of movement and change. Her body was not the same one she had thirty or even ten years ago. To hell with it, she was fine and still able to drive, garden and enjoy her life. She always knew what change to expect in shops when she bought anything. She got into bed feeling quite cheerful.

Chapter 6

Sadie lived quite near Mavis, about two miles away. She had lived in her bungalow alone for over twenty years. Her husband had died suddenly at the age of fifty. She had always been a live wire, but after her husband died, something in her had also died. She had become quieter and more introverted, although at times the old Sadie would peep through and she would become the life and soul of the party once more. Now she was suffering from dementia and although not progressing too rapidly, it was obvious to her friends who knew her from old. She was still capable of coming out with some outrageous statements, to the delight of her friends.

After Sunday Mass, Mavis made a trip down to see her. There was no point in making a firm date to visit as she never remembered and was always surprised and delighted to see Mavis, even if she had only spoken to her hours before. Mavis brought her some freshly made soda bread and a jar of raspberry jam that she had made last summer.

She knocked on the front window as that was where Sadie always sat, looking out at the roadway and people had a habit of slowing down in their car and waving in at her. The local people were very good at keeping an eye on her and making sure that she was alright. Her daughter lived in Dublin and came down as often as she could.

'Well I never, it's M—M, it's you! How are you, love? I haven't seen you in ages, have I?'

'Yes, it's me, Mavis. You have been away for ten days, up in Dublin, with Mary, haven't you, Sadie?'

'That's right. I was up at that place for tests and things. I know I am forgetting things and Mary brings me there and they do tests.'

'Well, Sadie, I am also forgetting things these days, but what about it? So long as we can get out of bed in the morning and eat our breakfast, life is alright then, isn't it? I've brought you some of Rosemary's fresh soda bread, I know you like it'.

Mavis put on the kettle to make tea. 'And how is Mary?' she asked.

'Oh, I suppose she is fine. She's in Dublin you know. She is always busy.'

'When you were up in Dublin you stayed with her, didn't you?'

'Oh yes, that's right. We had a rare old time. We had lunch in a pub a few times, I liked that. I had a glass of Guinness too.'

'That's very good, they say it's an excellent tonic for you. I like it myself too. Are you going down to the Community Centre every day?'

'I do M-M-Mavis. It's very good and there is always music there. I so love the music and we sing all the songs and sometimes we dance too. Then there is a fellow who comes in and reads poetry and stuff and we often say it with him. It's stuff we learned in school years ago, but it all comes back.'

'Yes, I have heard it said that music is the one thing that we never forget. I try and play some every day and I'm sure it helps. How is Mary's little grandson keeping?'

'Sure, he is a darling child, and very affectionate. I love him to bits. That reminds me, Mavis, I saw your boy up in Dublin, what did you call him now? I have forgotten his name, but I've always remembered his face, so like, em, em, your husband, isn't he?'

'Indeed, Frank is the image of his father. Dennis never could see it, but everyone else could. But where did you see him in Dublin, Sadie?'

'Oh, he was driving one of them big trucks, massive things, like. He must have a great job up there. I waved at him and he saw me, but he didn't wave back. We were stopped beside him on the motorway, at those lights, whatever do you call them?' She rubbed her forehead and Mavis could see her struggling to remember.

'Do you mean those traffic lights, Sadie?'

'Yes, those exactly. He was stopped and we were stopped. I said to Mary, 'Look, that's-- em, my friend's son. What did you call him, Mavis?'

'Frank, his name is Frank. Are you sure it was him?'

'Oh, it was, I never forget a face.'

Mavis thought that this was highly unlikely and did not pursue the matter with her friend. She knew that she had deteriorated since she last saw her and felt sad and helpless.

At one o'clock, the carer that looked after Sadie arrived to make her lunch. She would stay until five, having left food ready for her dinner and then another carer would take over. She was middle aged lady and in lieu of payment she had accommodation there and kept an eye on the woman until she left for work in the morning.

Mavis left Sadie with a promise to come soon again and maybe go out for a drive. The woman said she would love that. Mavis made a note to remember this and try and come more often to visit her friend.

She arrived home and played the piano for an hour and then sat down in front of a blazing fire with the Sunday newspaper. It was nippy out today and she was glad of the fire. Rosemary would be in by dinnertime she thought. They had decided to just have fish and chips as they had their fill of meat for a couple of days. They were not sure whether Frank would be there for dinner or not. He had left after Mavis, for his day of golf. Anyway, it would be easy to put some frozen fish and chips into the oven if he appeared. She thought about Sadie and about her thinking that she had seen Frank. It was funny, but sad. She hoped that she would not go like that.

Rosemary appeared at seven and the two women ate dinner together. Rosemary had bought a bottle of wine and they were enjoying their time alone. Mavis regaled her daughter about her visit to Sadie. They laughed about Sadie's mention of Frank driving a lorry in Dublin. Rosemary remembered her as a very energetic and witty person, so sad to see her confused and mentally incoherent now. She had not known Mary as she was a good deal older than she was. Mary must be about fifty now she thought. They sat and watched some television and then Mavis went to bed.

Shortly afterwards, Frank arrived. He had eaten, he told Rosemary. She stayed watching the telly and Frank said offhandedly, 'You know, Romy, that Ma is quite worried about you'.

Rosemary turned towards him and said, 'Pardon'?

'You heard me alright sis, the poor woman is really worried that by staying here with her, you are going to lose your chance of meeting someone to settle down with.'

'That's rubbish Frank, and you know it. I get out and about and have plenty of friends to socialise with. I am not sitting here every night, you know.' She felt annoyed at this intrusion as she thought of it.

'Well, all I am saying is that she is worried. She told me that you are very naïve about life and living in the real world, and don't go telling her that I told you.

She told me in confidence. She would never suggest that you leave and find your own place.'

Rosemary was stunned about this revelation. She never once thought that her mother was anxious that she should leave here. Was it because that she worked nearby, and it was so convenient? No doubt if she worked further afield or in a different part of the country, then she would have had to find a place of her own. None of her friends lived at home. Susie was buying her own place, a small apartment on the outskirts of town. Aine shared a house with their mutual friend, Bernie. She was lost in thought and did not hear Frank's next remark. It was something about prices in Dublin.

She said, 'Frank I work here in County Tipperary. What good is an apartment in Dublin?'

'You surely don't want to stay here all your life? Dublin is so much fun and absolutely packed with action. Nothing happens here, Romy.'

Rosemary sighed and said, 'Frank, you might think the whole world revolves around Dublin and that's fine for you. I happen to like living here and seeing my friends daily. It's a friendly place and the pace of life is leisurely.'

'Spoken like a true middle-aged school marm,' he replied, witheringly.

'Well you don't appear that happy to me, or to Mum. Maybe you would be happier driving a big lorry around, like Sadie said she saw you doing.' She rose to leave and go to bed.

Frank laughed loudly and said, 'Sadie? That poor demented creature? Have a good look at her, Romy, that's Mum in the next year or two and you shortly after!' He continued to chuckle.

She ascended the stairs slowly. Where had her nice brother gone? When had he changed? Was it the posh private school that her father had sent him to? Mum had been against it and thought he would get just the same education at the local school. She said that he was bright, and Rosemary knew that was true. Mum said that bright children did very well no matter what school they went to. She had not wanted to leave school for a boarding school and was happy at the local girls' school. Maybe Frank was right. She was a home bird but did not see anything wrong with being one.

She stopped outside her mother's bedroom door and would have entered to say goodnight, until she recalled Frank telling her of her mother's comments about her naivety. She went on, up to the second floor to her own room, still feeling hurt. In her bedroom as she prepared for bed, she realised that she was crying again. How often she cried these days, she thought. Only since Frank came home; the only other time was when she and her mum talked about Dennis. They often had discussions about Sylvia. Rosemary loved hearing about her birth mother and Mavis had known her so well. She felt that she knew her, from all the conversations they had together. She never told Mavis that Frank had once accused her of causing her at her birth. The shock had stayed with her for years. When Mavis told her the real cause, mother to die eclampsia, she understood that she was not responsible at all, but the damage had been done. The guilty feelings she had acquired at his revelation, would always be there, when she thought about her mother.

Chapter 7

Monday morning started dark and dreary. It was lashing rain when Rosemary left for work. She told Mavis that she would make dinner when she came home but Mavis said not to bother, she would use her slowcooker, for a nice lamb stew. That way, she could have her choir here and not have to worry about it. It would be ready whenever they wanted it. Really these new gadgets were very handy and seemed to be getting better all the time. She had a slowcooker years ago, but unfortunately had smashed it. The new one was stainless steel.

As she went about her housework, she said a prayer that Frank would have a buyer today. They would both breathe easier when Frank was sorted. He had a kind of nervous energy about him that was unsettling for the two women. She sang as usual as she went about her work, thinking of the music for the choir and what music she would suggest next for James Regan. She opened the utility door to put some washing on and gasped in horror at the sight that met her; there was water covering the floor, ankle deep and her brush and mop were floating about, along with other things. The tap was running in the sink and had overflowed. She rushed into the room, shutting the kitchen door behind her, thankful that the water had been contained and had not come into the kitchen. She turned off the tap and pulled out the plug, then opening the back door, she took the brush and started pushing the water out, as fast as she could. It took her over an hour to clear the room of water and she was drenched in perspiration and her heart pounding, by the time she had finished. Opening all the windows in the utility and all the windows and French doors in the kitchen, she hoped the dry and breezy day would air the room and dry the floor out. There was linoleum here and she knew that it would have to be lifted to dry the floor underneath. She finally put on the kettle for a cup of coffee. She sat, recovering her breath and muttered aloud at her stupidity in leaving a tap running. That's what happens when you don't concentrate on what you are doing, she thought. She tried to think why she was running the water. It wasn't this morning, she knew. Must have been yesterday. She could not remember. Another mistake to record in her notebook, she thought, dismayed.

She thought, to hell with the housework! I'll go and play the piano and get my serenity back. She decided on a bit of Bach. His music demanded concentration and the mathematical precision helped her to put everything out of her mind. After an hour, she leant back and felt a lot better. She remembered the stew and went down to the kitchen to prepare tonight's dinner. It was cold with the wind blowing in. She shut the kitchen door and windows but left the utility ones open, shutting the utility door so that she could forget her stupidity for a while at least.

Norma called around three in the afternoon and they had coffee in the sitting room. They chatted about going away somewhere and Norma again mentioned Cape Clear. It sounded good, even if it was only for a couple of nights. It would be leisurely, and they would play bridge in the evenings. Norma had a couple of dates lined up and Mavis took a note of them and they said they would decide which one suited them all in a couple of weeks. It would be better to go in summer, when hopefully the weather would be settled, and the ferry crossing enjoyable.

At seven o'clock sharp, the choir practice began. Mavis enjoyed this so much and already had forgotten the traumatic start to her week. They were in the middle of that great hymn, 'Guide me O Thou great Redeemer', everyone really singing well and loudly, the basses and tenors perfectly balanced with the sopranos and altos, when the sitting room door opened, and Frank looked in. His face was dark and fierce-looking and the singing died away suddenly. Mavis looked up from the music to see what had happened and looked at Frank enquiringly.

'Yes, Frank?' She looked him without any smile and he immediately withdrew silently. The practice was quite spoiled as the momentum was gone, and the choir members felt as if they were intruding on the household, even though they knew that Mavis had welcomed them and wanted them there. It was an embarrassing moment; she tried to laugh it away and they sang a few more pieces although in a more subdued and quiet manner. They were all gone by eight o'clock.

Dinner was a quiet affair. Mavis was fuming inside, and Rosemary was quiet too. Frank though, was his usual outspoken self. 'Really Ma, have those people no homes to go to?'

Mavis put down her fork and looking directly at Frank, said, 'They are my visitors, invited here by me, into my house, and you had no business interrupting our choir practice.'

'Well, I must say, it's very unsettling to come home after a day's work and expecting a quiet meal to listen to that noise.'

Rosemary looked incredulously at her brother. 'Are you completely mad, Frank? The choir always comes here on a Monday night, and it is Mum's thing after all. Nobody dictates how you live your life. You have developed some bad manners along the way. You ought to be ashamed.'

Frank just laughed and shovelled more stew into his mouth.

Mavis asked him, 'Any sign of a sale then, Frank? You must be very eager to settle back into your own routine with nothing to annoy you.'

He looked at her then and said, 'I suppose you are dying to get rid of me, are you, so you both can retreat into your boringly middle class, mundane little lives?'

It was Rosemary who answered. 'Yes Frank, it will be a relief when you sell your apartment and find another home, we must be very dull company for you, used as you are to the high life.'

Dinner finally finished and both women retreated to their bedrooms. Mavis was totally exhausted after her mornings' work and emotionally drained after the tension at dinner. She felt that she was aging rapidly.

The rest of the week progressed normally. Frank did not come home for dinner for a few days and Mavis relaxed a bit. Total relaxation was impossible as they never knew whether he would suddenly appear; extra dinner always had to be made, just in case. She thought that she would go away for a few days when he next appeared, she just had to decide where. Even staying with Maureen was an option she considered.

Then on Thursday, there was a bit of good news. Frank rang his mother at lunch time and announced excitedly that he had sold the apartment for a good sum and he was over the moon. His mother's muted response caused a silence from his end. Then he humbly asked for her forgiveness for all the unpleasantness he had caused. This surprised her and she immediately replied that of course she forgave him and said that she had not realised that he was under such a strain.

'Yes, I suppose that I was under pressure. I don't want to be caught out, when house prices tumble. Now life is good again and I promise that I will leave you both in the peace you deserve. Sorry Ma, you deserve a better son.'

Rosemary was relieved that there was peace and forgiveness restored again. She could see her mother visibly become younger looking and her usual cheerful self. On Friday she came home and found Mavis in the garden, humming away as she weeded with a hoe. They had a cup of coffee together and then Rosemary went and collected her things for her first line dancing experience. Her mother said that she would just have an omelette for dinner as Rosemary was having a salad dinner with the three girls.

The line dancing was very strenuous, as the girls soon found out. Rosemary was sheeny with perspiration after twenty minutes. The music was loud and they all soon got into the rhythm of the movements. At the end they were divided into two groups and formed into two circles facing each other for a sort of Paul Jones dance. When the music stopped you had to dance with the person facing you, a set pattern of about four movements and then you reformed the circle and did same thing again.

Rosemary could not believe who she was facing when the music stopped. She had been concentrating so hard on learning the different routines, that she had been oblivious of anyone else there. There was James Regan opposite her, grinning his funny lopsided grin. They managed to perform the required movements and then moved on. Then the session ended, and Rosemary limped off the floor slowly. She met James again as they exited the door.

'It's a lot easier than that 'Golliwog's cakewalk',' he said.

Rosemary smiled at him and said, 'You can say that again!'

The four were glad to go into the pool and cool off. They swam for about forty-five minutes then got out and showered. The salad bar beckoned, and they once again enjoyed the fresh and delicious salads. They agreed to meet on Saturday night for drinks at the local pub. Rosemary was relieved that she had nothing planned for that night. She felt exhausted.

Frank was sitting chatting to his mother in the sitting room when Rosemary got home. He immediately got up and gave her a hug. She was more than surprised but did not show it.

'You will be delighted to hear that I am moving to an apartment over the weekend and have just come to collect my clothes. You have been great for putting up with me for the past few weeks. Wasn't easy, I know. I've brought you a few treats for having me here. You deserve a lot more, I know.' He smiled at the two women and said, 'I'm a very lucky man, to have such great women in my life.'

Shortly after this he collected his suitcase, hugged them both again, and they waved him off.

'Well,' mused Mavis, 'I don't know what to think. What happened to us all recently? Did we over-react or was he really as difficult as I thought?'

Rosemary could only shake her head. 'I think he was difficult and quite rude, at times, but he seems so sane and his old self again, I'm confused too Mum.'

Mavis opened a bottle of champagne that she had been saving for this moment and the two were soon giggling like schoolgirls and savouring the freedom which once again was theirs. After a couple of glasses, Mavis confessed that she had not been a very good mother to Frank, while he was here. Her daughter told her that she was an excellent mother, and that not many mothers would have put up with the moods and behaviour that he had displayed recently.

They both hoped that he would be settled into his new home very soon and that all the unpleasantness was a thing of the past and best forgotten.

On Saturday, Rosemary slept in and Mavis took the opportunity to go into town and see what sort of linoleum was available in the shops. She thought that she should choose a similar one as before. That way, it might not be noticed that she had replaced the original one. She arranged a date for the fitter to come and measure up, a morning when her daughter would be at work.

Rosemary was up and about when she returned and told her mother about the line dancing and how energetic it was. Mavis noticed that her daughter was in good spirits and thought that she had lost a bit of weight but did not mention that. She told Rosemary that she and her friends might go away for a couple of days after Easter and do some walking. She had the Easter ceremonies at the church and would have to be there for that period, but afterwards would suit her and her walking friends. She felt that she needed a small break. Rosemary agreed and thought it a good idea. She was going to France for a four-day break, during the Easter holidays with Susie, and looked forward to that. During the long summer holidays, she might go to Italy if her friends had decided in favour of it.

Later Susie called and Rosemary and she departed to have a night out in the town. She left her mother settled in front of the television and said that she would not be late.

'Never mind how late love, I will surely be in my bed by ten,' she replied.

At nine o'clock, the doorbell rang, and Mavis wondered who it could be. Rosemary had her own key. She walked out to the hall and looked through the glass panel in the hall door to the porch. There was James Regan standing there. She thought for a moment that he must have forgotten his music.

'Hello James, come in, are you well?'

'Hello Mavis, hope I am not disturbing you at this hour?'

'Not at all James, come into the sitting room.'

He advanced into the hall, looking up the stairs and into the front room as he made his way into the sitting room and sat down, still talking about the weather. Mavis wondered if he was just lonely and needed a chat. He refused the offer of a cup of tea. He wanted to talk about his music he said. He wondered whether he was too old to do piano examinations.

'No, not at all James, but why do you think it necessary?' Mavis was perplexed.

'Mavis, I need motivation and the discipline for this. I enjoy playing but I need a bigger challenge. You probably think I'm daft, but I have some time now to really put into it.'

Mavis was delighted. She also enjoyed the challenge of preparing pupils for exams, although it was years since she had entered anyone. She thought that James would be good enough in his playing, but there was more to it than playing pieces. Would he be up for the scales and technical work she asked?

James nodded his head and said, 'Absolutely, I know that I can do it.'

Mavis grinned and said that she would start at a level below his present one and begin work on the scales and arpeggios required. She went into the front room and returned to James with a couple of old exam books from previous years. They looked at the selection of pieces and James decided what he would start on. He left happily after another fifteen minutes.

Chapter 8

Life flowed smoothly like a river, and mother and daughter once again settled into the routine they had always enjoyed. Mavis brought Sadie out a couple of afternoons for drives in the country and she could see that Sadie loved it. They called to the Horse and Jockey on their return trips and had afternoon tea, which Sadie and Mavis both enjoyed. It is always the small things which give the most pleasure, Mavis thought. The leisurely afternoons spent like this were like a tonic to the women. For Mavis, the luxury of not having to do anything, was glorious. As for the tension caused by Frank in the house, it drifted away gradually, and she had no anxiety or worry now.

While Rosemary was away on a midterm break, Mavis had the linoleum in the utility replaced. It needed to be, as the water had got underneath and was starting to cause a damp smell. She did not say anything to Rosemary about the incident at the time.

The Monday night choir continued but they would have a break during the summer months. James continued with his piano lessons on Wednesdays and was enjoying the challenge of the new work.

Maureen rang at regular intervals and inquired each time if Mavis had seen a doctor yet.

'I would definitely see a doctor, if I were sick Maureen, wouldn't you? I have never felt better actually.'

Maureen again reminded her about the mistake she made in visiting her a couple of months ago. Mavis felt her patience wearing thin and told Maureen that unlike her, she had a lot of activities going on and plenty on her mind to keep her busy.

'Oh, don't go on the defensive Mavis. I am only worried about you, you know. In fact, there is another reason I am ringing you this time. My bathroom has been giving me trouble lately and I have decided to get a thorough job done on it. Everything is being replaced. I wondered whether I could come up to you for a few days and then I'll head up to Jenny for the remaining time it takes to finish.'

Mavis ran her fingers through her hair and said, 'Of course, Maureen, when are you arriving?' Inwardly she was dismayed and wondered how she would cope with a few days of Maureen's ranting.

'Well, I was wondering if I could come Monday morning? That's the day the men will start, and my neighbour will keep an eye on them. They will have a key to let themselves in each day.'

Mavis agreed to it all and when she told Rosemary, her daughter was horrified.

'How many days, Mum? What if she drives us to murder?'

The women knew that it would be a trying time. However, as it was just a few days, three at the most, they knew that they would cope. 'Pity she couldn't come on Friday and I would bring her line dancing,

,

that would shut her up for a few days,' Rosemary said wryly.

Monday dawned mild and sunny, and Maureen arrived at eleven o'clock. As Mavis brought her upstairs to the second bedroom on the first floor, next door to her own, Maureen looked around her critically. 'Looks like you could do with a spot of paint here too,' she remarked, as she entered the lovely bright bedroom, which was nicer than Mavis's, but smaller.

Mavis turned and said as she left the bedroom, 'I'll go and put on the kettle, Maureen.'

In the kitchen as she put out mugs and some biscuits, she told herself that she would not get upset about anything her sister-in-law said. I can manage for a few days, she kept telling herself.

Maureen entered the kitchen and began at once to prowl around, peering at everything. She opened the utility door and swept her eye around that. Eventually she sat at the island with Mavis and drank her tea.

'How is Rosemary,' she asked, 'Still living at home, I suppose?'

'Yes, she is kept busy with her schoolwork and organising different outings through the year for her pupils. She loves her work; she is fortunate.'

Maureen sniffed, 'Indeed, she is. To be able to live at home, at her age. Must be very convenient for her.

Bad training though if she ever gets a place of her own. Children can be spoiled so easily.'

'Do you think so, Maureen?'

'Oh, definitely! Although I had only one daughter myself, I can see the mistakes my friends made, glaring mistakes, I must say.'

'Probably good that you didn't have more, I dare say,' said Mavis taking a biscuit.

Maureen wanted to know what they would do that afternoon and what about lunch and dinner. Would Mavis like her to cook her famous casserole for dinner? Mavis thought about the heavy hand her sister- in- law had with salt and butter and shuddered inwardly and thought of poor Rosemary.

'Oh, not at all, Maureen. You are here for a rest! No work for you! On Monday night I have my choir here for practice and Rosemary always likes to cook dinner on Monday. As for lunch, I am bringing you to the new hotel here to a lovely salad bar, you will love it and it's so healthy.'

'Choir practice, here? Honestly Mavis! At your age you should not be doing that sort of thing.'

'But I like it, Maureen. In fact, I do nothing that does not please me or that I do not like. Life is too short to put up with unpleasant things, don't you think?'

Her sister-in-law had no answer for that. The two ladies went out for lunch and Mavis enjoyed hers as usual. Maureen wondered just how fresh the lettuce was and if it was washed sufficiently. She poked at everything suspiciously as if longing to find something to complain about.

While Maureen went to the bathroom, Mavis phoned her daughter and told her that there were chicken pieces marinating in the fridge for dinner and would she please cook, or else her aunt would and they knew all about her cooking, didn't they?

When Maureen emerged from the bathroom, Mavis suggested a trip to the garden centre just to see what was there.

Rosemary came home later and greeted her aunt, cautiously, preparing herself to answer a barrage of questions, both casual and personal. She was not disappointed. The questions began immediately, and Rosemary envied her mother up in the front room with her choir.

How was the job going; did she have many friends; any friends of the opposite sex; what were her plans for her future; was she looking at property with a view to moving to her own place?

Poor Rosemary patiently answered the questions as best she could, while concentrating on making the devilled chicken, and preparing some vegetables to go with the rice. She deliberately took long pauses in answering, hoping that Maureen would get bored. At one stage she asked her aunt if she would like to go up and see the news on the television.

'To be bombarded with that raucous cacophony! No thanks! I will never understand why your mother subjects herself to that.'

'What do you do with your time, Maureen? What are your hobbies?' Rosemary asked this in her sweetest voice, looking at her aunt with her head on one side.

'Well, I read a lot of course; intellectual material, naturally. We always need to improve our minds, don't you think? There is nothing but drivel on the television and newspapers have fallen in quality, sadly. Quality everywhere, in everything, is in decline.'

Dinner was lightened by Mavis recalling some funny incidents in her many choir practices over the years. Rosemary was the only one who found it funny and laughed with her mother as Maureen frowned over her dinner.

'Is this Irish chicken, Mavis?'

'I would expect so, Maureen, why?'

'Oh, I have heard recently that there is a lot of foreign chicken getting into the country, which is quite suspicious.' She made it sound like they were illegal immigrants.

'The agricultural department would surely be aware if that were the case, Maureen. We have never had any trouble with chicken. I buy it here in the local supermarkets or butchers. I get all my eggs from my farming friend and they are true 'free range' hens, roaming around her fields.'

'Hmm,' murmured Maureen, pushing her chicken to the side of her plate and eating her rice with relish.

'Now that rice, Maureen, is not grown here. Probably from India or such places and God knows where it's kept stored before it gets to us.' Rosemary nodded her head as she chewed her chicken.

Maureen looked at her rice with concern and stopped eating.

'That's why we wash it so thoroughly, isn't that right, Mum?' She turned to Mavis smiling and gave her a quick wink.

Dessert was homemade apple pie with fresh cream, and that was deemed acceptable by Maureen. However, she appeared to be taken aback when Rosemary started eating hers.

'Cream, Rosemary?' her aunt tut-tutted and shook her head. Rosemary took some more cream and piled it on her apple pie.

Chapter 9

Mavis felt exhausted in her sister-in-law's presence. She was continually having to watch herself and check things she did. She knew that Maureen's eyes were on her all the time, watching and waiting to pounce at the smallest mistake. She caught her loading her washing machine the following day and immediately stopped Mavis.

'No, no no, Mavis! You must separate your colours.' She bent and took all the clothes out again. She divided them into three piles.

'Dark colours together, all the underwear should be separate also, and the towels and tea cloths together. There you are now.'

Mavis turning to her in exasperation. 'So now I must do three separate washes, Maureen, must I? What will that do to the environment, not to mention my electricity bill? I do it all at thirty degrees unless there is something really dirty.'

She bent and pushed everything back into the machine and put in her detergent and set the machine. She glared at Maureen who had pulled away, shocked at this flouting of her expert advice.

Mavis put on her gardening shoes and told Maureen that she had weeding to do. She strode out and went up to her tunnel where she stood shaking with anger. She knew that this rage only raised her blood pressure, but she could not help it. Why did

Maureen always think that she knew best and make her out to be an idiot? She went outside and quickly weeded her raised bed outside the tunnel. After a short time, she felt calmer and was breathing normally.

Returning to her kitchen she discovered Maureen baking bread. She went into her front room and started playing the piano. That was the most calming thing that she could do and always worked well. Her sister-in-law appeared with a mug of coffee for her after thirty minutes.

'I have hung the washing out, Mavis. It should be dry by evening. It's not a bad day.'

'No, it's a lovely day out Maureen. What about a walk in the park? Do you feel up to that?'

'Well only if it suits you Mavis. I don't mind, one way or the other. What do you want to do?'

Mavis felt a twinge of guilt. Tomorrow Maureen would be going, and life would be simple again. 'Yes, let's have a walk around the park, it's a lovely place for a walk.'

They were dressed in comfortable shoes and light jackets and set off after lunch. The birds sang and sunlight filtered through the trees. People were walking their dogs and mothers were pushing babies in buggies. There were some old people sitting on benches and Mavis greeted them as they passed. For once, Maureen kept silent, and Mavis felt that it was a very pleasant way to spend part of the afternoon. It did not last for long, however. Halfway around the park, Maureen said, 'Now, I hope you don't mind me asking this, Mavis, but do you have good insurance cover?'

Mavis paused, 'Why do you ask, do you mean health insurance or house insurance?'

'Well both, come to think of it. It's just when I saw all those people in your house last night, I hoped that you had good cover. Imagine if one of them fell coming in or going out of your house.'

Mavis had to laugh at that. 'Really Mavis, they are not geriatric, you know.'

'Well, you can't be too careful, some people are just waiting for an opportunity to sue you and seeing as you have a big house, they might get ideas.'

'Honestly, Mavis, I don't know why you think like that. The choir members are all friends, all church members and not like that in the least.'

'Hmm, that's what a lot of people say, until something happens. You must just be careful and check on your insurance cover. You do have private health insurance, I presume?'

Mavis sighed, 'Yes, I have. Much good it does when the hospitals are overcrowded anyway.'

This was Maureen's cue. 'Indeed, you might be fortunate to get a trolley the way things are heading in this country. The health system is deplorable.'

She went off on a rant about the Department of Health and the obvious lack of intelligence therein. Mavis went into a reverie and shut out the strident voice of her sister-in-law. She came back to the present when Maureen stopped and was pointing her finger at something. Under the trees there was a plethora of plastic and glass drink bottles, empty crisp packets and general litter.

'That's what I mean, the brain-dead young people who do this! Who do they think is going to clear up the mess? I ask you, what sort of families do they come from? It all begins in the family, Mavis. Sometimes I think that men and women should have to get a licence to produce children, like you do for dogs.'

Some people were stopping to listen to the woman, some nodding their heads, some smiling. Mavis just felt embarrassed and said, 'Maybe if there were more litter bins provided, people would use them. The only bins I can see here, are already overflowing.'

That started another rant about the Council not doing their job in emptying the bins and the general lazy attitude of people who were employed in the Civil Service with pensionable jobs and who could not be sacked. She carried on like this until they reached home, and Mavis felt drained. She went into the sitting room and poured herself a whisky.

Maureen coming in after her looked aghast at her sister-in-law.

'It's only four o'clock Mavis! One should wait until dinnertime, I believe.'

'Oh, sit down, Maureen, have one yourself if you want to. I feel tired and bothered. I can't handle nonstop criticism of everything.'

Her sister-in-law stomped off and Mavis heard her rattling around in the kitchen. The telephone rang and Mavis got up wearily and reached for the phone. It was her niece Jenny. Before she could engage her in conversation, she asked could she speak with her mother? Mavis left down the phone and went and called to Maureen. She then took her topped up glass of whisky and went up the stairs to her bedroom. She took out her notebook and looked at it. Had she done anything daft today? No. That's good Mavis, she said to herself silently. Must contact Sadie before the weekend. She would take her for another spin somewhere and stop for afternoon tea again. Where had they gone the last time? She paused and tried to think. She could not remember. Looking back in her notebook she saw where it was and thought about a different place, she could bring her this time. Then she realised that Sadie probably would not remember anyway. That is the way I am going, she thought.

There was a knock on her bedroom door and Maureen entered. She went over to the window and sat down heavily on the window seat. Mavis could see that she was angry.

'I am so mad, Mavis. That was Jenny and she said that I cannot go to her tomorrow as she must leave tonight for a business trip to England. Honestly, could she not have organised all this beforehand? It is so inconsiderate! Now I will have to stay with you until the end of the week.'

Mavis thought that she too would like to leave on a business trip, or any trip at this moment.

Rosemary came home at six-thirty and brought a bunch of flowers for her mother and one for her aunt. She was happy and light-hearted as she sat down to the stew that her aunt had prepared.

'Well, Maureen, this time tomorrow you will be up in the 'big smoke', having a ball, no doubt.' She smiled around at the two women and took in the worn and strained look of her mother.

Maureen stopped ladling stew onto her niece's plate and grimaced. 'Not really, Rosemary. My daughter just rang me this afternoon to say she was off on a business trip. I'll be here until Friday or until the builders are finished their work.'

Rosemary's face fell as she looked at her mother. She did not know what to say and felt like crying, both for herself and for her poor mother who had visibly aged in the past two days.

'I hope all goes well Maureen, both for Jenny and the builders. When is Jenny due back?'

'Not until next week sometime, she does not have a clear idea of when exactly. That is what happens when you have an important executive job. You are at everyone's beck and call. I suppose that is why she is paid such an enormous salary.'

The two women murmured agreement.

After dinner, Rosemary thanked her aunt for making dinner and said that it was her turn tomorrow.

'Not at all, dear, it's the very least I can do while I'm here, and I am a big fan of simple, plain nutritious food, none of this spicy foreign food in my kitchen.'

Rosemary's face fell as she put the dishes in the dishwasher and felt pain and pity for her mother. Her mother had cast a desperate look at her as she and Maureen left the kitchen.

They spent the evening watching television in the small sitting room. When the news came on, Maureen got agitated as she usually did.

'Look at that! Drugs! Another haul! Worth a million, did you hear that? Now what I ask is, what do the guards do with all this stuff? Have you ever wondered, what do they do with it?'

The drugs had been caught in transit. A vehicle had been stopped on the motorway near the Naas exit. The driver was in custody and so seemingly was the haul of cocaine.

Maureen continued her tirade against drugs, dealers and users and the helplessness of the guards and the laws of the land. 'Every day it's the same. Raids on houses, drugs seized, gang warfare and people murdered in their beds.' She shook her head and clicked her teeth. 'And what do the authorities do with all this contraband, eh? That's what we need to be asking. She looked as though she would continue all night with her tirade.

Mavis suddenly had enough. Pleading tiredness, she took herself off to bed.

Chapter 10

Mavis slept badly even though she was tired. Her dreams were disjointed and disturbing. Rosemary had come in to say goodnight, shortly after she got into bed. They did not need to say anything. Disappointment and dismay showed on their faces. Rosemary kissed her mother tenderly and whispered, 'We are going to treat ourselves very soon, Mum, it won't be for long more.' She stroked her mother's face and tiptoed out of the room.

She felt a bit dazed when she awoke and looking at the clock realised that she had overslept. She got out of bed a bit too fast and felt dizzy. Steady old girl, she told herself and looked at Dennis's photo on her locker. You have got to help me through this, old boy, she told him. Make the time go quickly, there's a dear. She threw on some clothes and rooted around in the bottom of the wardrobe for her shoes. What did she say she must do today? Oh yes, James was coming this afternoon. Must remember that.

Relieved to find the kitchen empty, she made her tea and cut some bread. Her garden needed work, but she knew that she did not have the energy to do anything today. She sat on a stool at the island and surveyed the garden. She was blessed to have such space around her and thought ahead to the coming months when the carpet roses would be blooming magnificently. She had made a lot of gravel beds and the shrubs and roses looked stunning when they flowered, and it did not take much work or maintenance. Just a bit of pruning around the end of February. That had been done and now the new shoots were showing themselves proudly. There would be a lot of roses by the looks of the young buds already coming.

She wondered where Maureen was and almost immediately, she appeared around the side of the house.

'You were sleeping so soundly, I did not have the heart to wake you,' she said. I have been to the shops and have some nice bacon and cabbage for the dinner tonight.'

Mavis thought of her poor daughter's dislike of that dinner and decided that she would ring Rosemary to warn her. Maybe she could eat in town with a friend and avoid the upset stomach that cabbage always brought her.

'Oh look! You silly woman, you have two odd shoes on!' Maureen's shrill laughter grated on Mavis' sore head.

She looked down and sure enough, there was a navy canvas shoe on one foot and a red one, on the other foot. She felt a fool and annoyed with herself, for rushing her dressing.

'Oh no worries, Maureen. I have another identical pair upstairs in my wardrobe.'

Maureen looked at her frowning, not sure if her sister-in-law was serious or making fun of her.

'I think you should change them as you never know who might come to the door and what would they think if they saw that?'

Mavis looked at her sister-in-law and said in a strong voice, 'Maureen, I don't give a rat's arse what anybody thinks of me. What other people think, has never bothered me in the past and I can assure you, it won't bother me in the future. Are you controlled by what people think of you?'

Maureen tossed her head and said, 'I have never appeared in odd shoes, Mavis.'

James arrived at three o'clock. Mavis had been in the utility room ironing when the bell rang. Before she could get there, her sister-in-law had opened the door and surveyed the man on the doorstep. She looked at him blankly and asked, 'Can I help you? Are you selling something? I don't think we need anything today, thank you.'

James threw back his head and laughed. Maureen looked at him in amazement and was about to say something derogatory when Mavis came up behind her.

'Ah James, come on in. This is my sister-in-law, Maureen. Maureen, this is James, my pupil.'

Maureen continued to stare as he came past her into the hall. 'Pupil?'

Mavis ushered James into the front room closing the door firmly.

She apologised for her sister-in-law and they both laughed, and James said, 'We can choose our friends but nae our family, Mavis.'

Mavis nodded and told him that she was under strain and hoped he could entertain her for the hour and not expect too much from her.

'Will you not be wanting the "Gollywog's cakewalk" then, Mavis? I enjoyed that time we had to dance to it.'

They both laughed and tears started down Mavis' face when she recalled the mad gallop around the room and wondered what Maureen would have said, if she had witnessed it. She would probably be convinced that she was mad and do her best to have her locked up.

The hour went by and Mavis felt relaxed and easy again, listening to the music. James was getting to be quite a nice pianist. He had started a Field nocturne and was playing it so well that she felt like a young teacher again, full of passion for the music. He also did some scales and arpeggios and had obviously worked hard. She praised him and he blushed with pleasure. He asked if she had any recorded music of other Field nocturnes and she told him that she would search through her collection and maybe he would call by some evening and they could listen to some. She would be able to explain any technical difficulties in the ones he liked and would have an idea of what he would be able for. He thanked her for her time and her interest and told her how much he was enjoying the lessons.

They had a chat about bereavement and Mavis told him that music was the therapy that she would always recommend for healing. 'You don't even have to play an instrument,' she told him, 'just listening is enough to do the trick. It can release emotions and stress.'

As she said those words, she realised that her stress was gone, and she knew that she could face Maureen for a while longer.

She saw James out and he waved goodbye. She saw Maureen watching from the sitting room, where she was sitting with the door open. She had obviously been listening to James playing.

She looked at Mavis curiously and said, 'Why on earth is he learning to play the piano? Don't you think it a bit strange for a man of his age to be a pupil?'

Mavis shook her head at her. 'People of all ages learn different things, Maureen. He lost his wife a while ago and is trying to get over it. Music is a great therapy.'

'Hmm! I say, watch yourself Mavis. Men cannot be trusted, you know. You are a widow with a beautiful residence, and he is a widower. What is his profession?'

'I think he was an accountant. He had to give up his job to care for his wife; how he managed, I do not know. He now has a part time job, and he says it suits him perfectly. He says that he spent so long in an office without noticing nature or the different seasons, that he will never go back to that type of work again.'

'Hmm! It might suit him very much to move in with a charming widow who seems to be quite comfortable and well off financially.'

'No chance of that Maureen, I would never remarry. Dennis was the love of my life and nobody could ever match him at all. Besides, I am still in love with him.'

'Hmm,' was the only reply that Maureen could make to that.

Rosemary did not come home for dinner, having been forewarned and ate alone at the salad bar in the hotel. She was surprised to feel someone standing beside her and looked up from her book. It was James Regan.

'Hi Rosemary, mind if I join you?'

She closed her book and said, 'That would be nice, James.'

He put down his salad and sat down opposite her. 'I must say, this is a lovely place, isn't it? The salads are something else too.'

He was easy to talk to and an hour passed by very quickly. They discussed the line dancing and Rosemary asked about his progress with the piano. She had also learned piano as a child but had not been interested enough to keep it up. Frank had excelled at it and used to laugh at her efforts. In the end, it was easier to give it up completely, to save being criticised unmercifully.

James asked her about her job and interests. He was a good listener and she found herself chatting to him as if she had known him for years. After some time, she looked at her watch and said that she must go. He nodded and said he had enjoyed the chat. He would see her around.

She drove home, relaxed and relieved to have avoided Maureen's bacon and cabbage. She noticed another car by the side of the house as she drove in and wondered whose it was. She heard Frank's voice as soon as she entered and frowned. They were in the big front room and the fire was lighting. They all stopped talking as she entered.

'Frank has managed a night at home, Rosemary, isn't that wonderful,' her aunt gushed. 'I had hoped that I would meet my favourite nephew and here he is!'

'Is that your car outside Frank,' asked Rosemary, 'have you changed your sports car for a regular guy's car?'

Frank replied, 'oh it's only temporary Romy, I have ordered another one and it won't be here for a couple of weeks. Have you been out on a hot date?'

Mavis interrupted then and asked how his new apartment was going and had he settled in? Then Maureen asked why he had moved, and Frank told them about the forthcoming crash and how he had avoided it and had made a killing. His aunt clapped her hands in delight and told him that he was the clever one, so like his father with his shrewd business sense.

It was obvious to the two women, that Maureen idolised her nephew and they felt that maybe it was fortuitous that Frank had called. There would be no ranting and raving tonight, no criticism of anything, no unpleasant tension.

Then Maureen found a reason to tell them about Mavis's odd shoe episode that morning and Rosemary found it amusing but Frank looked quite serious and stared at Mavis worriedly. She laughed it off and was annoyed when she saw Maureen giving Frank a nod, as though she was saying, 'See? I told you.'

'Listen, you two! The day I come downstairs stark naked and say that I'm going to town, that is when you can become worried about my mental health.' She glared at Maureen.

'Well, I'm only saying. You must be more mindful of what you are doing Mavis. You would not want people to get the wrong ideas about you, would you?' Maureen looked at Frank for approval and was pleased when he nodded with her.

'Frankly my dear, I don't give a damn,' as Rhett Butler said in "Gone with the wind". Mavis defiantly got up and poured herself another whiskey.

Frank said, after a swift look at his aunt, 'Mum, you should go easy on the alcohol too, you know. It is said to affect the brain cells.'

Maureen nodded of course, and agreed, whole-heartedly. 'Frank, you are so right. We must be so careful of all substances that could, and do, affect our mental ability.'

Rosemary tossed her head and told them that lots of people lived to a ripe old age, both smoking and drinking. She hated it when people criticised her mother, whom she knew was in good health.

'Yes, that's true,' replied Maureen, 'but what is their quality of life like, one must ask? If you can no longer dress and take care of yourself, alcohol is a poor substitute, in my humble opinion.'

Frank nodded and said, 'Yes. Absolutely Maureen. Well put!'

Both aunt and nephew smiled at each other and Rosemary felt like being sick. She got up and bid them all a good night. Her mother left shortly after finishing her drink.

Chapter 11

Mavis lay in bed thinking and wished that she were starting the day instead of finishing it. Frank and Maureen were determined to think the 'odd shoe' business very strange. Maureen had again suggested that she should visit her doctor, just to get a check-up, nothing more. Frank of course, agreed with her and Rosemary said she thought that they were being ridiculous. She could see that her mother was upset, and these two people were belittling her and were too strong for her to argue with. They had both left the room for bed and left Maureen and Frank talking. No doubt about what they were discussing; Rosemary and Mavis knew exactly what it was they were talking about. Frank had found an ally in his aunt. Rosemary had gone into her mother's room and they had sat and chatted quietly for half an hour or more. She told her mother that they would have to be strong and try to laugh off the annoying innuendos coming from the two people downstairs. Mavis cried a little and said that she felt as if her life was coming off the rails recently. Her daughter hugged her and promised when their life was their own again, they would take a trip together somewhere. Mavis agreed.

As she reached her own room, she heard the door of her father's office closing on the first floor and wondered who was in there. She guessed that it would be Frank, but why would he be in there? She had forgotten to fill up her drink bottle with water and decided to go back down to the kitchen for some. Passing the sitting room, she saw that the television was off, and Maureen seemed to have gone to bed too. On her way back, she paused outside the office and listened. Frank was speaking on his phone to someone and then finished the call. There was silence for a few minutes. She heard the desk drawer being opened and closed. Curiosity got the better of her and she silently opened the door. Her brother was leaning down over the top of the desk, almost on top of it, she saw. Moving into the room to ask what on earth he was doing, he straightened up abruptly and wiped his nose. He saw her and asked what she was creeping about for?

'Are you doing what I suspect you are doing, Frank? Using cocaine?' She was shocked. She was truly horrified, and it showed on her face.

'Ah little sister, you are so innocent. It is the same as having a drink, you know, only better and after listening to my aunt all evening, it was necessary. If you lived in Dublin, you would realise that all the young trendy professionals use it. Don't worry, it's only rarely I need it.' He smiled at her and looked very relaxed. 'Please don't tell the mater, like a good girl.' He winked at her and got up to leave the room.

'No, I will not tell Mum. Don't you think that she has been through enough these days without

94

knowing the sort of son she really has? I can't believe you could be so stupid, for such a smart arse.'

She turned on her heel and walked back upstairs to her room. She sat on her bed and went over the scene in her mind. No way could she confide in her mother. Mavis would not be able to handle that news. Why was Frank back? The idea of him moving back in, even temporarily scared her. She now saw him as some sort of threat to them. Reluctantly she got into bed and tried to relax.

The next morning, Frank was first up, and in the kitchen when Rosemary came down to get her breakfast. He did not say anything so neither did she. She made her coffee and took it upstairs to the sitting room. He left before she had finished.

Mavis got up and felt as if she had not slept at all. Her body was stiff, and she had trouble getting out of bed. She took her blood pressure tablet with some water and immediately put them back in the drawer and took out the evening pill for cholesterol. She did not feel well and decided that she should go to the doctor and have a chat. John O'Dea was a dear friend and she had not been to him professionally for at least a year.

Maureen was having her breakfast and got up to make her sister-in-law a cup of tea. She seemed full of energy and agitated.

'Did you sleep well Maureen?' Mavis looked at her as she drank her tea. Maureen's face was rather flushed, and Mavis wondered if she was coming down with something and hoped not.

'To tell you the truth, Mavis, I hardly slept at all. I am so excited with what Frank has been advising me to do.'

Mavis looked at her enquiringly. 'What has he been advising you about, Maureen?'

'Well, he has told me all about the forecast of a property crash and advised me to sell while the prices are still high. The chances are, that I will be able to get a fantastic property once the bottom falls out of the market. It is the chance of a lifetime, he says, and he is going to help me invest in a suitable scheme that is fail-proof. I am so excited, Mavis.'

Mavis was alarmed. How was Frank now so knowledgeable about the property business? Just having a few rental properties was the small part of his business. The car dealership that his father left him was his main bread and butter. She suspected that he had used part of the trust fund that Dennis had set up years ago for his son. Hopefully, he had not used it all. Surely, he would be too shrewd to do that. Rosemary had not touched hers and it was a comfort to Mavis to know that it was still intact. Then she thought about Dennis briefly and was perturbed.

'Well, can't you say something? It's not often that you get free advice. The trouble with you Mavis, is that you are too tight fisted and suspicious.'

Mavis refused to rise to the insult. 'Let's say that I am cautious Maureen. I lived with a shrewd businessman for a long time and have learned a lot.'

'But you are sitting on a goldmine here. This house is worth an awful lot, Mavis, and then there is also the land. Remember, I grew up in this house with Dennis, it's been in the family for years and even though I love it dearly, I would not turn down an opportunity like this. As Frank says, you could build up to five houses on the land, without spoiling the landscape.'

Mavis smiled. Now it was five houses, before it had been two. Before long, it would be a proper housing estate! She turned to Maureen and smiled. 'Just be sure of what you are doing, Maureen. Don't jump into anything impulsively just because your nephew has told you things. After all, his information might be flawed. Nobody can predict exactly when property will crash.'

Maureen sighed and shook her head. 'My dear, don't come crying when this place has no value. I hope you have some good investments to get you through?'

Mavis said quietly. 'I live on my pension and don't need investments of any sort. My needs are little and at my age I have no desire for wealth of any kind.'

Maureen got up and brought her cup and plate to the kitchen sink. She turned to Mavis, beaming and said, 'You know what? I am leaving today and going back to Cork to see about putting my house on the market. 'Strike while the iron is hot', as they say. Jenny could be sitting on a goldmine too with her property in Dublin. I'll talk to her too.'

'Where will you stay, if the builders are still there?' asked Mavis, amazed at the change in Maureen.

'I'll ring up some old friends of mine who will welcome me, I'm sure. Might even interest them in the prospects ahead for people with good houses.'

Mavis decided that she was feeling very hungry and quickly put on bacon and egg as her transformed sister-in-law hurriedly packed her bag and left rapidly. She ate her breakfast slowly and relished the peace and quiet that had descended on her kitchen. When she had finished, she sent a text message to her daughter. It said simply, 'Alleluia, Maureen has left.'

She thought about her intention earlier to go and see John O'Dea, but as she was feeling so relieved now, she thought she would postpone it for a while longer. She hoped that Frank would not drop in anytime soon. She needed to get some tranquillity back into her life. She was disturbed when she thought of him and alarmed at the ideas that he had put into Maureen's head. What if he was wrong? She thought back to her own experience ten years ago and shuddered. Pray God, that history will not repeat itself, she thought.

The following weeks the two women had the house to themselves and all was peaceful and calm. There was no word from Maureen. The Easter season came, and the choir work kept Mavis occupied. Rosemary had gone away for a few days with her friend and Mavis and Norma had planned a trip to Cape Clear immediately after Easter with the other two walking friends. She was looking forward to it. James had called on a couple of occasions to discuss and listen to some music that she had suggested he try. Last night he had stayed behind after choir practice having asked if she would mind, as he wanted to discuss something with her. Supposing that it was related to music she was interested to chat with him. It proved a bit different to what she was expecting. He had appeared serious, even nervous, as he sat in the sitting room. She asked him if he would like a drink and he accepted a whisky.

'Mavis, what do you think of people marrying a second time? I mean, after having been married before?'

'Do you mean if you've been widowed? That sort of second marriage?'

'Oh yes, of course, after burying your first spouse.'

Mavis paused and sipped her drink. 'James, it depends on how you feel about the person involved. I mean, I was my husband's second wife. He had been married to my best friend and after she died, we eventually got married. I don't see anything wrong about it, James.'

James was swirling his drink about and looked uncertain. 'You don't think it's like a betrayal of the one you've loved,' he seemed earnest and sincere.

'Of course not, how could it be? Everyone is entitled to love, and happiness, and people are lucky I guess, if it comes around a second time.' She smiled at him uncertainly.

'What about age difference Mavis? How important is that in a marriage, do you think?' He stared at her face intently.

She suddenly remembered what Maureen had been warning her about and felt panic rising in her chest. She did not get a chance to answer that question as the telephone rang, and she escaped from the room to answer it. She was fifteen minutes on the line and when she returned to the room, James had gone. She sat down and said, 'Dennis I need your help here, old boy.

Later she took a stroll up to the paddocks, behind which, was a small wood. Every couple of years, Mavis had it thinned out and cut back a bit, otherwise it would be impossible to walk in. She loved the tranquillity and fresh woody smell. It was best early in the summer mornings when the sun was beginning to filter through the trees. She always came up here to feel closer to Dennis. He loved it here in Spring especially, when the blue bells and daffodils were in full bloom. Even at dusk like now, it was full of atmosphere. She always returned to the house much calmer and at peace with herself after a short stroll up here. Of course, it was full of crow's nests too or ravens as Dennis's father had insisted. The children had loved playing hide and seek here and spent many summers with their friends gadding about, putting up temporary tents and picnicking. They never came up now, she thought sadly. They have put away childish things, she thought, more is the pity. She wondered if any more children would ever come and play here.

Her father-in-law had a special relationship with the wood. Dennis spent his boyhood listening to stories about ravens, told endlessly by his father. Ravens were noted for their intelligence, innovativeness, playfulness and are fiercely protective parents. The stories told to Dennis, sometimes scared him and there are many myths attached to them in various countries. They were often associated with death, bad luck or such superstitions. As a result of these stories, Dennis had a great respect for them, like his father. They were mentioned a dozen times in the Bible, Dennis had told her. She sat deep in thought, remembering the many times she and Dennis had sat here, in their 'little wilderness' as they thought of it, discussing many things: their growing family, the business, their hopes and aspirations. It was the perfect place to think in peace. The wood was a world away. She thought fondly of Rosemary who had believed that leprechauns lived here. She had stopped coming here alone, when Frank told her that goblins and trolls also lived here, and often stole little girls. She loved it when her friends came to play, then they were always up in the wood.

This evening the sound of birds was absent, and the stillness of the place engulfed her, although in an agreeable manner. She sat and absorbed the sound of silence, which is so hard to find anywhere. She closed her eyes and m
entally made herself relax. She could almost feel Dennis sitting beside her. He had a habit of pushing her hair to one side when it was over her eyes. She tried to feel that movement of his. She smiled and then got to her feet. As she left the bench, she passed the two swings that Dennis had put up for the children so long ago. She saw them swinging slowly and recalled how the children had loved being pushed when they were young. She didn't question why they should be swinging when there was no wind.

Chapter 12

Mavis and the three women were on the ferry to Cape Clear. Una had driven Norma and herself to Breda's house which was in Blarney. Una left her car there and Breda drove the rest of the way to Baltimore. The sunshine was hot on their faces on the ferry and Norma kept applying sun cream liberally. Mavis did not care if she got a colour or not. She was enjoying the adventure and felt like a young girl again. They had spent the night in a hotel in Baltimore and enjoyed a good meal and then played the usual game of bridge, while imbibing a bottle or two of red wine. The village was once a fishing village and was situated in west Cork. Norma explained that the original name in the Irish language was Baile an ti mhoir, meaning town of the big house. Norma loved her native language and spoke it whenever possible. It was not Mavis's strongest subject, however. She would have loved to have been able to speak it, but the way it was taught when she was young, made it a subject she did not warm to. The ferryman explained that an English colony had been founded there in sixteen hundred and five, by an Englishman, Sir Thomas Crooke. He leased the land from the Irish clan leader, Fineen O'Driscoll. The town had been depopulated in sixteen thirty-one, when there was a pirate raid on the town by Algerian pirates. Nearly three hundred people had been taken, men, women and children and sold into slavery in Algiers and only two or three ever saw Ireland again. That meant that there was quite a lot of Irish DNA in Algiers, thought Mavis.

The other people on the ferry were all amazed at this history although the Irish among them had heard of the Sack of Baltimore often enough. After that, the Great Famine had struck, and the village suffered further losses.

The boat having landed, a Land Rover took them up the steep hill to visit the museum. There was also another nearby island called Sherkin where a young community seemingly were living, according to some people they spoke to. The museum was an enthralling place. It showed just how badly the island had been hit during the famine. Fishermen who could have survived starvation by fishing, sold their equipment in order to pay the landlord's rent, and in doing so, signed their death warrant. No wonder landlords were so hated in Ireland – a throw-back to the bad past.

The women wandered around reading all the literature that was on show. Mavis marvelled at how resilient humans are, to have been able to survive at all on such a remote and desolate spot. But the beauty of it was stunning. They walked back down the steep hill and had lunch at a waterside café. There were so many different nationalities visiting that Mavis almost forgot where she was. Then it was time to get another ferry out to see the Fastnet Rock and the most southerly point of the island of Ireland. The trip took about an hour. The lighthouse was awesome, and everybody was busy taking photos on their mobile phones. The ferryman steered around the lighthouse several times to the delight of his passengers. It seemed to be within touching distance and induced a feeling of respect and wonder. To see this marvel of engineering standing in the middle of the ocean, made all the passengers gaze at it, in silent reverence. Mavis sighed in pleasure. She felt hundreds of miles away from stress and family. She did not want to think that they only had another night in Baltimore before going back home.

Before taking the returning ferry, she and Norma went and explored a small graveyard on a nearby hillside. There were so many headstones with the name O'Driscoll! It seemed that they must have all been related and been very productive. They wondered what the island would be like in winter, when the seas were wild, and ferries could not operate.

'I would like to experience it, even just once,' Mavis confided.

'I imagine it would be so cold and inhospitable that you would go mad,' replied Norma, 'even today there is a strong wind and it's a lovely sunny day, imagine it with rain pouring down!'

'You would have no trouble drying your washing when it's not raining,' smiled Mavis.

'No, only trouble keeping it on the line. You'd probably have to run around picking it up from other people's gardens.' Norma nudged Mavis, 'We'd better go and queue for the ferry.'

The food that night was amazing. They all had the fish and were ravenous after the salty sea air. Later they visited a local pub and listened to traditional music, and Irish songs, sung by a few, obviously local characters with colourful personalities, before heading back to the hotel for a couple of hands of bridge and then turning in for the night.

Norma and Mavis shared one room and Una and Breda another. Norma had to hear the news before going to bed. She put on the television and sat on her bed, creaming her hands, watching it as Mavis had a hot shower.

When she came out, Norma said, 'Did you just hear that? A massive seizure of drugs has taken place in Dublin. The biggest yet, the guards say.'

Mavis towelling her hair, yawned and replied, 'Well that's good. Some people are going to be very sorry to lose their money.'

Norma agreed as she switched off the television. 'And maybe some young lives will be saved by it.'

They all slept well and woke refreshed. Mavis was sad to have to start the long journey back, but the three women had jobs to go to and it had been a lovely break. They agreed that they would have to do this sort of thing more regularly. It was a long drive back, but they stopped halfway and indulged in a homemade pizza at a little town.

When Mavis reached home, she was surprised to see the old car Frank had brought there a few weeks ago. She felt a sense of disappointment. She had looked forward to being alone with Rosemary and hearing all about her trip with her friend Susie. She had left for France before Mavis had left for Cape Clear. It seemed ages since she had her daughter to chat to and she missed that.

She entered the house and as usual called 'Hello, I'm home.'

Immediately Rosemary came tripping lightly down the stairs and engulfed her mother in a bear-hug. 'Great to have you back Mum,' she smiled at her mother tenderly. Mavis noticed the dark shadows under her daughter's eyes again and hoped Frank had behaved himself.

They went down to the kitchen and Rosemary put on the kettle. 'How was the trip, Mum, did you enjoy your little break? Anyone seasick?'

Mavis shook her head smiling, 'It was all wonderful Rosemary, we must go together sometime.' She turned serious then and asked quietly, 'How long has your brother been here?'

Rosemary grimaced and said, 'The day you left he arrived and has not left since. He was here when I arrived home that night'. She said all this softly as though not wanting to be overheard.

They heard footsteps coming down the stairs. Immediately, Rosemary lifted her voice and asked her mother if she felt hungry and could she make her something to keep her going until dinner? Mavis told her that she was alright for the present as they had stopped for pizza a couple of hours ago and it was so filling that she would not need dinner. Tea now though, would be welcome for sure.

Frank entered the kitchen and hugged his mother. 'Welcome home, traveller. Good time?'

'Oh, we had a lovely time. The weather was super, the trip to the island smooth and relaxing. We saw the island, learned its history and then went by another ferry to the Fastnet rock. You should go, sometime, it was a grand experience.'

Frank said that he was delighted she went and told her that she should do that more often, that she deserved a few breaks. He then announced that he must 'make tracks' as there was work to be done and he had enjoyed his break too. Mavis was surprised that he was leaving just as she got home but said nothing. She told him to drive carefully and come soon again, knowing that she was being hypocritical.

'Cheers, Romy, be a good girl and keep away from the boys,' he grinned at his sister as he went out of the kitchen. They heard his car roaring down the drive a minute later.

Mavis sipped her hot tea and looked at her daughter. 'How are things Rosemary, and has *he* been giving you grief?'

Rosemary looked at her mother. 'I don't understand him at all, Mum. I think there is something bugging him.'

She did not tell her mother the half of it. He had been so agitated when she arrived, and he could not keep still. He was wandering all over the house into the small hours. She was quite worried. When she had tried asking him what he was looking for, as he was in and out of all the rooms, her mother's, included, he became quite aggressive and rude. He scared her a bit. She had spent most of the past two days in her room – with the door locked! That was how unnerved she was. She was thankful that school was starting again on Monday.

Her mother asked about her trip to France and Rosemary recounted the trip with as many embellishments as she could. She did not want to start talking about her brother again. Mavis decided to have a very early night and asked if Rosemary was going out with her friends. Poor Rosemary had been nowhere since her mother left and decided that she would love a night out and went to ring her friends. Later she left for the local pub where she met Susie and Aine. After a couple of hours, she got over her traumatic time alone with Frank. She had already decided that she would not be alone in the house again with him, whatever happened. Mavis had a stabilising effect on him, and he was a different person when she was there.

As Mavis sat up in bed reading her library book, she thought about her friend Sadie and decided that she owed her a visit. She had not seen her since Easter Sunday, when a neighbour had brought her to the church for Mass. She reached for her notebook and wrote a memo to herself. She thought about what else she must do in the coming week and wrote a memo to clean her polytunnel and prepare the beds for planting out her seedling tomatoes which were not ready quite yet. They were in pots on a tray covered by a plastic dome, which sheltered them from frost. The courgettes need not be planted until the end of April, they took off so easily and took over if allowed. She told herself that two seeds would be more than enough this year, as they produced too many last year. Then she recalled that last year, she had decided two was enough and ended sowing two extra, 'just in case'.

She turned off the light and settled down to sleep, thankful to be in her own bed again. Sometime later, she woke up, feeling that something had woken her. She imagined that it must be Rosemary coming home and listened for her step on the stair. Then there was that sound again and she knew it was from outside, not inside the house. She wondered what Rosemary would be doing outside at the back of the house at this hour and looked at her watch. It was only eleven o'clock. A bit early for Rosemary to be back, surely? She decided to investigate and got out of bed. She did not bother putting on the light. Going to her window she gently drew back the curtain and looked out on the moonlit garden, thinking how beautiful if looked bathed in the soft white light. Nothing was stirring and she thought that she must be imagining things, when she saw the tunnel door opening with its funny high squeaking sound, and a figure emerged, closing the door behind him. At least she thought it was a male figure, it was difficult to tell. The head was covered in a type of hooded jacket that the young people all wear these days. He appeared to know his way about and came down the garden path confidently and passed under her window, going around the right side of the house. She quickly left her bedroom and went into the bedroom that was Frank's. She ran to the window and looked out onto the driveway. The receding figure was striding down the drive, head down and slightly hunched over. At the gate, he turned left and was lost to her vision. She stood for a few moments, wondering what he was doing in her tunnel at this time of night. Then realising that she was getting cold she retraced her steps to her own room.

,

The next morning, she lay in bed, luxuriating in the warmth and comfort of it, knowing that she was home again. Coming home was always good and it seemed that going away made you appreciate your own place more and indeed was *necessary*, to make you appreciate properly, just what you had left. Then she remembered the garden visitor and frowned. She would ask Rosemary if she could shed any light on the mystery. It was Saturday; a day that there was nothing that they *must* do, and both looked forward to it. Sunday was always busy for Mavis, the choir at church was both pleasurable but also a bit nerve-wracking. In recent years, she did not feel as confident and sometimes forgot which key she was supposed to be playing in. She tried to overcome this by making copious notes on her hymn sheets and keeping really focused; if her mind wandered, she was often caught out. She put on her dressing gown, another luxury, and the only day she waited until after breakfast to get dressed. Once in the kitchen she looked in the fridge and sure enough, Rosemary had bought bacon and sausages for the breakfast, another treat, as Sunday was busy and Mavis only got to eat at one, for brunch, which was nice too. When breakfast was just ready, her daughter wandered into the kitchen, also in her dressing gown and the two women sat down to enjoy this time that they loved together every week.

Chapter 13

As the women ate their breakfast, Mavis recounted what she had seen the night before in her back garden. Rosemary listened and frowned. Who would be in their garden at night? She did not doubt her mother's story, but she was perplexed. The idea that anyone would wander round a garden at eleven o'clock at night was strange, to say the least. Should she inform the guards, Mavis asked? Rosemary did not know and suggested they investigate what he may have been doing in the tunnel. The nearest house was Sadie's, two miles away.

After they had eaten, they wandered up to the tunnel, still in their dressing gowns and had a look inside. Mavis could not see anything out of place, no footprints in the raised beds nor anything moved. They returned to the house after a time, and both got dressed and went into town together to the local library. They were interested in local history and every month or so, there was a lecture in the library, given by a local historian. Today it was about the Quaker influence on the town in times past, which was considerable. They met a few people they knew. Mavis met someone she had not seen in ages and went for coffee afterwards with her. Rosemary went off to buy some bits and pieces she needed. They arranged to meet at three and drive home.

The day passed quietly and without incident. Mavis forgot all about the night visitor. She rang her friend Sadie and told her that she would see her soon. Rosemary was out again that Saturday night with her friends. They were travelling to Cork to attend a concert. The three ladies often went to concerts and although Mavis would have been welcome to accompany them, she was not that interested. Instead, she watched a couple of television programmes that she had recorded. At about nine o'clock the doorbell rang. She got up and went out and paused as usual to see who was outside. It was James Regan and she relaxed. The incident of last night was still vaguely on her mind.

She welcomed him in and again he apologised for disturbing her, asking anxiously if she had company or was alone. She told him that all was well, she was alone, and that Rosemary had gone to Cork. She brought him into the small sitting room, and they sat down. He had finished the grade four pieces that she had given him and would like to push on to the next grade if she agreed. They had a chat about that. Mavis pointed out that there was a choice in the pieces if he wished. She suggested that he take his time over the exam, he had a year and there was no hurry. He agreed that it would be better for him to take his time and if he felt he was not ready or in danger of failing, well, what about it? He could complete the syllabus and try again next year with different pieces; having the technical work all covered was the most important part. She gave him a few CDs to bring home. He was quite fluent with the modern and classical period, but the baroque period he found difficult.

She suggested they go into the front room and she would play a few pieces for him for this year's grade five and see the level required. He was eager to hear them. Mavis looked at the first two pieces which were from the baroque era and played one of them that she knew well. It was from the French Suites by J.S. Bach and was a Gavotte. He listened and made a few notes; then she played a Scarlatti sonata.

He held up his hand and said, 'Enough Mavis, I'll give the Bach a go, although it might be difficult for me, I'll give it my best.'

Mavis laughed, 'That's the spirit James.' She turned a few pages and started to play again.

It was the first movement of Beethoven's 'Moonlight' sonata, as most people commonly call. It. There was no movement or sound from James. She looked over at him when the music ended and asked what he thought?

She was alarmed to see James looking quite upset. 'It's really not that difficult, James. It's slow and controlled all the time.'

'It's not that, Mavis. I could not play that piece of music, I just couldn't.'

She rose and went over to where he was sitting on the sofa. She sat down beside him and gently asked, 'Why not?'

'That was Mary's favourite piece and very emotional for both of us. We would sit and listen to it and she always made me turn off the light and pull the curtains if there was a moon. She knew that she was dying at that stage. There was no more pretence between us.'

He looked at her miserably and his bottom lip was quivering, tears rolled down his face.

'Oh James, I am sorry. But what a lovely way to listen to that piece, it is so atmospheric, isn't it?' She patted his arm sympathetically. 'Music does that to people; it brings out emotions and passions that lie dormant. I understand completely, James. I cry regularly when I hear certain pieces of music. Did you ever hear Beethoven's Emperor piano concerto; or the overture to Wagner's Tannhauser? There are so many pieces of music that turn on my tears, I can't tell you.'

'But Mavis, what must you think of me, being so sentimental and tearful now, after the last meeting we had, and I was talking about marriage again.'

Mavis had all but forgotten the last meeting and now a cold sweat was breaking over her.

'Think no more of it, James. Bereavement and grief hit us at unexpected moments. We can't control these things, you know.'

'Yes, but what can you think of me, contemplating another marriage and crying after my poor wife?'

'You forget that I married a widower, and Dennis often cried about Sylvia, as did I, she was my dear friend. When Dennis cried, so did I, nothing strange about that at all, James.'

He looked at her curiously. 'Really? You and Dennis cried about his first wife? I find that rather moving.'

'Only because she was such a good friend of mine. Maybe it would have been different if I had not known her. Now, I think we both need a whiskey, James.'

Mavis did need one for sure, she hoped James would decline and go home, but no, he said that a drink was just what he needed. She poured them both a drink and went back to the sofa.

'Mavis, you know, I never drink at home. It is something I was warned about when Mary died. My brother told me to be very careful with alcohol because he had problems with the stuff early in his life. He terrified me! So, I only drink in company.'

Talk resumed about more general things, the weather, holidays, politics, religion. It was quite pleasant chatting like this, once the sensitive issue was finished with. He was such an interesting character and funny. Mavis laughed a lot during the rest of the visit. They had a couple more drinks and Mavis became quite high and giggly. It was a shock

,

when the door opened, and Rosemary arrived in. She looked a bit taken aback at the scene. Her mother was obviously a bit tiddly and James was in his stride regaling her mother with stories that had her roaring with laughter.

On seeing Rosemary, James looked at his watch and got up.

'Dear me, it's quite late. I am sorry Rosemary for keeping your mother up, please forgive me. She is a dear and wonderful woman, your mother. You are lucky to have her.'

As he made his way the door, he turned again to Mavis who had accompanied him out to the door. 'I still have not heard the answer to the question I asked the last time Mavis. I'll have to come back for that'.

He held out his hand and as she took it, he leaned over and kissed her cheek and again thanked her for all she had done for him. Then he was gone.

'Well, Mother! What's this then? I go out for the night and come home to find you entertaining a man, in your best room, and drinking whiskey. Pray tell me, what is going on?'

Giggling, Mavis told her daughter that her pupil had just come for advice about his piano playing. She hiccupped a couple of times and said she must go to bed. Rosemary stared after her mother ascending the stairs and wondered about life.

Chapter 14

The weeks rolled by, and Frank usually visited, twice a week. Mavis wondered how he could afford the time but did not question him. Maureen rang regularly and was smugly happy to state that she had sold her house in Cork and had got a great price for it. For the moment she was renting a small apartment and was biding her time as her nephew had advised her. She kept asking Mavis if she had come to a decision yet about selling, or had she applied for planning permission for her land to be developed. 'You must be prepared Mavis, don't put these things on the long finger or you will regret it,' she admonished her sister-in-law.

Mavis did not have to say much as Maureen spoke non-stop and barely listened to her anyway. She had been to see Sadie yesterday and found her friend a bit more lucid and talkative. They went to Thurles for a spin and to see Mavis's old school and called into the hotel there, where Sadie had friends. They had a cup of tea before returning the way they came. It was about four o'clock and Mavis asked Sadie is she would like to go and have a proper afternoon tea with all the trimmings. Sadie was very keen to do that. Parking at the Horse and Jockey, she said, 'Oh, this looks very nice, Mavis, I haven't been here before, have I?'

Mavis answered her, 'Well Sadie, if you were, you will probably remember it when we go inside.' She did not want to tell the woman that they had been there quite recently.

They both enjoyed their little sandwiches and cream cakes and felt quite replete after it all. 'I don't think I will need my dinner tonight, Mavis, there would be nowhere for it to go, I'm stuffed.'

Mavis agreed and said that it was a great place for the afternoon tea. When Mavis drove to the house, she helped Sadie out and walked her to the door. Her key was always under the flowerpot on her doorstep, so she opened the door for her. As there was no sign of her helper, Mavis stayed on, until the woman who shared the house with her, and helped care for her came home from work. She could have left but she felt responsible for her until there was someone else there. Sadie was quite happy in her armchair in front of the television.

Driving into her own house later, she saw Frank's car by the side of the house. He never stayed for long these days and she was touched that he visited so much. He was on his mobile when she entered, and she heard part of the conversation; 'I tell you it's impossible, everything is shipshape at my end of the business anyway.'

As soon as he saw his mother, he put the mobile away and smiled at her. 'Hi Ma, how is it going for you? I've been all over the country since I saw you last and I'm quite exhausted.'

'Are you hungry Frank? Would you like me to make you something now?'

'That would be good, I would love one of your spicy omelettes, if that would not be too much trouble.'

Mavis went to the fridge and got her ingredients together. Frank left the kitchen and she heard him again on the phone up in the hall before he went into the front room and closed the door.

Rosemary appeared then at six fifteen and she made another omelette for her. It was a favourite with the children when they were growing up. The two ate their dinner and Mavis had a glass of wine. She was too full after her delicious tea. They chatted amiably enough, and Mavis mentioned Maureen's phone call about the fantastic price she got for her house. Frank nodded and said, 'She is a wise old bird, that Maureen. No flies on her!'

Rosemary told them that she was going out later and asked Frank what time he was leaving?

'I intend to stay the night, as it would be late to be getting back to Dublin and I've had a full day's work already. You don't mind Ma?'

Mavis shook her head, without saying anything, what could she say anyway? So far, all was well, no tension or unpleasantness.

Mavis and Frank watched the television until ten o'clock and then she turned and said that she had to go to bed. She was also tired. Frank turned and smiled at her and told her to sleep well and that he would go early in the morning.

James came the following afternoon, and they spent an hour going over some new pieces and some scales. As he packed up to go, he asked Mavis had she considered her answer to his earlier question.

She hummed and hawed a bit but knew he was waiting and would not be satisfied until she answered him. She was standing by the piano and he was still sitting on the stool. She frowned and asked him exactly what the question was again? Of course, she knew! She was just procrastinating. He stood up beside her and said softly, 'Age, Mavis, how important is it, do you think? I mean the difference in age between a husband and wife.'

She moved over to the door and stood as though deep in thought. 'I suppose it is quite important in many ways. It never seems to matter how old a man is though, does it? He always manages to get a woman, doesn't he?' She laughed and said, 'Humans are humans and emotions and passions don't change much over the years, there will always be human love.'

James sighed and said, 'I hope you are right, Mavis you have given me hope, you lovely lady.'

Then it was the peck on the cheek again and he was gone. As she looked after his car disappearing down the drive she wondered if she had given him too much hope. Should she just come out and say that any relationship with her was impossible, she was not interested; that she still was in love with Dennis. She sighed as she closed the door.

The evenings were stretching at last, and she felt she must do something in the garden to keep her mind off other things. It was too early to start dinner. She put on her gardening shoes and headed up to the tunnel. There was something that she should have done weeks ago, she had only remembered it last night; fertilise the shrubs. She sang as she worked and rooted about for the potato fertiliser she knew was up there somewhere. Eventually she found it under a flowerpot and decided to mix it with her special 'seaweed magic', as she called it. She emptied the entire bag into the outside water trough and mixed it up with the handle of a gardening fork. She worked steadily until dusk, emptying watering cans of the liquid all around the base of her plants. She would have to get more fertiliser to complete the job. Then she hurried down to start dinner. She had lost track of the time. Poor Rosemary would be starving.

Her daughter was in the kitchen ready to serve up the spaghetti Bolognese that she had made and laughed at her mother's shocked face. 'You were so happy up there, Mum, I could hear you singing as you worked. I wish everyone could be as happy as you when you work.'

The two women had a glass of red wine with their pasta and Mavis realised that, yes, she was totally happy once she was working. Then she thought of James and wondered whether she should mention her fears to Rosemary. She decided that it would not be fair to burden her daughter with her problems and kept silent. That evening she watched one episode of a good thriller that had recently started on Netflix. Some evenings she could watch through three or four such episodes, but not tonight. Rosemary was busy working in the office and she stuck her head around the door to say goodnight.

She opened the top window as she usually did and pulled the curtains. She loved fresh air coming into the room and was convinced that it was healthy and kept colds and 'flu away. Then she opened her notebook and ticked off the jobs she had made a note of, the night before. This way, she felt she was keeping her brain active. She made a fresh note to buy more potato manure, as it was called. She took her cholesterol pill and put them back in her drawer, taking out her morning blood pressure one at the same time. Then it was time for a few pages of her 'calming book'. She never got beyond two or three. She woke at some stage still clutching the book and put it on her locker. Then she heard the noise that she had heard some time back. Was it the tunnel door squeaking? She got out of bed but could see nothing, there was no moon, and the place was pitch black. Oh bother, she thought, who cares anyway? She crept back into bed and slept so soundly that she had forgotten the incident by the following morning.

Rosemary was still enjoying line dancing with the three friends and it had grown into a routine now that she would have missed if she had stopped. The salad bar had grown a lot in popularity and now it appeared to be busy all around the clock. They were joined there most Fridays by a few of the men who did line dancing, James among them. They were a very lively bunch, a bit loud at times as the laughter was always nonstop. There was a walking-club, that Aine and Susie wanted to join. It had been functioning for some years and was very popular. A group of walkers met every Sunday morning at eleven and walked until about mid-afternoon, usually ending up in some pub where they had something to eat after their hike. They asked Rosemary what she thought, would she be up for it? Bernie was the only one not interested as she had other commitments on Sunday. Rosemary thought about it for a few minutes and said that she would give it a go. Aine was delighted and Susie too. After all, if it was too strenuous, she would not have to do it again if she did not want to.

The following Wednesday, Frank arrived once more and spent the night. He never offered an explanation as to why it was necessary. He seemed in good form and did not annoy Rosemary in any way. In fact, he complimented her on looking well and thought that she had lost weight and that it suited her. She was flabbergasted but kept quiet. Mavis noticed the improved atmosphere and was very relieved. Maybe they had imagined it all, being too used to their own company. As usual, throughout the evening, Frank's phone kept pinging away and he would smile and shrug his shoulders and left the room, mouthing 'Business', to the two ladies.

The fourth time it happened his face looked a lot different when he returned to the room. He looked darkly around him and after a few minutes, told them he was going to bed. Rosemary wondered if he was still using what she had caught him taking before. She did not think that he would be so foolish; maybe some of those high-fliers took it to wind down like their fathers would have taken a drink. Still, she knew, it was wrong, it was a bad business.

Frank had gone before both Rosemary and Mavis had breakfast. Mavis realised that she and Rosemary would have to adjust to having him there on a temporary basis for however long. Still, Mavis worried about his business. It had been a thriving business when Dennis died and left it to him, and he had added to it, she knew. Things had been really vibrant then, now she wondered; he had sold his luxury apartment and he was driving, what she termed, an 'old banger'. He had also borrowed that five thousand and not repaid it to date. She spent the morning cleaning the house and going over all these things in her mind.

Again, when James left, after his lesson, Mavis went up to continue spreading fertiliser on her many shrubs in the garden. Having rainwater was very convenient and eco-friendly too. She had put more potato manure into the other water trough and would be finished that job by the weekend, then she found some more fertiliser that she had missed before and poured that in as well. Her garden would not be suffering this year for want of feeding. Marie had offered her more chicken manure, but she said that she had enough for now. She would start planting out lettuce and salad stuff soon. First, she would have to start cleaning the tunnel with soapy water. She was relaxed today as James had passed no comments on marriage or age differences between men and women and she was relieved somewhat. Perhaps he was getting over it, she thought. It could have been just a stage he was going through with grief and everything. As usual, she sang as she worked.

Rosemary came for dinner and they enjoyed a quiet evening watching television. Rosemary told her mother about the walking club and wondered she would mind being alone most of Sunday?

'Have you ever known me to be lonely, my love? I like my own company now and then and am never bored, as you know. With the good weather coming there is so much to do in the garden, the days won't be long enough.'

'Mum, I really think that you should get a bit of help. I'm not much help in the garden, as you well know, but I think you need a bit of help, even once a month would help, wouldn't it? Will I ask around?'

Mavis thought about it and then admitted that she could do with a bit of help, especially the bit of digging. It wasn't much that needed digging, just the bed for the potatoes, but her back was not what it had been in the past. Dennis used to say that she was 'a horse of a woman', and they would both laugh at the description. Later they recalled this saying when he was dying and poor Dennis had whispered, 'Yes, a horse of a woman who I would bet my life on.' Now, reminiscing on this scene, tears came to her eyes. Not so much a horse now, my dearest Dennis, more like a lame donkey.

Chapter 15

May arrived and with it some lovely weather. The garden was beginning to show a lot of growth and the wisteria and clematis looked very healthy. Mavis loved her garden and knew that July saw it at its best. She thought she would host a barbeque sometime before August for her friends. She liked to entertain but had slowed down a lot since Dennis died. Rosemary was off to Italy sometime in July with a few of her friends and some teachers from her school. They were going south this year and wanted to see Bari and Puglia in particular.

One day Mavis had a phone call from Jenny in Dublin. She had not seen her for a couple of weeks when the girl had called in to break her journey to Cork to visit Maureen. She was a very sensible and practical girl, no airs and graces, unlike her mother. Mavis often wondered how Maureen had come to have such an ordinary child as Jenny, who was around the same age as Frank. She had met Jenny's father often and had always liked him. She wondered whether Maureen missed him and if she had ever tried to win him back.

Today, Jenny was a bit agitated. She was worried about her mother. It seemed that Maureen had suggested she move in with her daughter until she could find a 'suitable' house in Dublin. She said that she would like a change of scenery and was worried that all the suitable houses would go very quickly once the crash came. Jenny was appalled at the idea of her mother moving in with her. She had got used to her independence and anyway, she did not get on terribly well with Maureen. What should she do?

Mavis was alarmed too. What on earth was Maureen thinking of? She would not know many people up in Dublin after spending her life in Cork, would she? Jenny asked if it were possible to see Mavis or if she could come up for a day or two and they could discuss it?

Mavis did some quick thinking and told Jenny she would ring back in an hour or two and she was not to worry about things. Rosemary had told her last week that she had next Friday off and as it would make a nice long weekend, she was considering a trip with her friends.

When Mavis rang her at lunchtime and explained Jenny's predicament, she suggested that she drive her mother up to Dublin and they could see Jenny and maybe see a show at the same time. Delighted, Mavis told Jenny that they would both be up in a week's time.

Later she walked down to Sadie's house as the day was so fine and warm. It was a lovely walk along the quiet road. Ravenswood boundary reached quite a distance along the road, the stone wall bordering it and the trees behind it tall and dense, which was why her father-in-law had named the property as he did.

There were trees on the opposite side too, bordering neighbouring land. In winter it could be a bit dark and spooky, walking along this road, and she had never allowed the children walk alone when they were young. Today the sunlight filtered through the trees and cast shadows on the road, and it was lovely. Mavis hummed as she strode along. She had brought the usual soda bread and some ginger biscuits that she had made this morning.

Sadie was sitting outside in her front garden and enjoying the sunshine. Her carer made tea when Mavis arrived. Sadie said that she loved this time of the year. She seemed to be fine and not too vacant. Her carer was Margaret O'Neill today, a local woman from the nearby village further down the road. She asked Mavis had she heard about the O'Brian boy, Bill? When Mavis professed her ignorance, she was told all about it. His mother was Margaret's sister who sometimes cared for Sadie. Margaret shook her head and sighed. Bill was a tear-away and always a handful. Her sister had her hands full, from the time he was ten years old. He had gone off again, not for the first time, but he had never stayed away more than three days; he was missing for a week now and she was worried sick.

Mavis, sipping her tea, asked if the mother had contacted the guards yet?

'Sure, they only laugh at her! In the past, when it had started, she always rang the guards and then he would turn up, so this time, obviously, they told her to go home, and he would turn up as usual. Now it's just over a week and poor Brigid is beside herself.'

Sadie said, 'He's probably slipped down a hole in the bog.' The two women turned to look at her. She nodded her head and repeated, 'The bog'.

Margaret said, 'There is no bog near here, pet. You're thinking of county Laois, where you grew up, aren't you?'

Sadie nodded. The women smiled at each other and understood that poor Sadie was trying to keep up with the news. They changed the subject and talked about Sadie's garden which was small but beautifully kept.

Mavis asked her who kept the garden and did all the work? Sadie replied that it was Patsy, her husband and that he was always working in the garden. Did they not meet him a few minutes ago? Margaret hid a smile as she brought the used cups and plates into the house.

Mavis did not mind Sadie's slips. For all anybody knew, she might see her husband around the garden. It could be his spirit, couldn't it? She had no trouble accepting such a belief but would never say it aloud knowing what others would make of it. 'Mad Mavis!' The mind is such a complicated thing, not one human being can fully comprehend it, she thought.

As she walked back home, she thought about Maureen and wondered how they could advise

Jenny. Then she had a terrible thought; what if Jenny said no, and then Maureen decided she wanted to move into Ravenswood? She knew that Maureen loved the place where she had grown up and felt that she resented Mavis for living there now. I must be strong, she thought. No pity and no yielding! Her sanity would not stand being in Maureen's company day and night, nor would Rosemary's, she knew. At dinner, Rosemary expressed those same fears to her mother, but wondered why Maureen was contemplating such a move at this stage of her life.

'If you suggested such a change, Mum, she would say you should see a doctor and would be convinced you had lost your marbles.'

Mavis laughed and agreed. 'What would be her reaction, if I suggest the same to her, do you think?'

'Oh, hers would be a brilliant idea, whereas yours would be pure madness.'

The next day was Wednesday and Mavis cut the lawn at the back of the house. She had a ride-on lawnmower, so it was not a big chore. She had arranged for an acquaintance of Susie's mother, to come a couple of times a month to do the heavy work. He had been once already, and Mavis was very pleased with him. He did exactly what she asked him to do and was very neat and tidy. After a light lunch she had a nap and set her alarm for two thirty although she would never sleep longer than thirty minutes. James would arrive at three.

James was progressing with some grade five level pieces and seemed happy enough with them. Mavis knew that he would have no trouble passing an exam at that level and was happy to see his confidence growing. At four o'clock, she looked at her watch and he put his music away in his folder.

'Now Mavis,' James said, 'I want to ask you once again, if you have thought about my concern from a while back?'

Oh no, thought Mavis. Not again. She smiled at James and asked if he would like a cup of tea. He followed her dutifully down to the kitchen and sat at the table looking out onto the garden, as she put on the kettle and put out cups and some biscuits. She must take the bull by the horns, once and for all, she decided. Dennis, give me strength and diplomacy, she prayed.

Having poured the tea, she sat down and took a sip, then she began, 'James, don't think that I am not flattered by your attention, but my situation is unchangeable. I am still in love with my husband and could never love another man like that.' There, she had said it out loud, it was all now in the open.

James had been drinking his tea, and he suddenly choked, and tea came down his nose. Mavis sprang up to get a paper napkin for him. When he finally stopped coughing and spluttering, he looked at her with a shocked expression on his face and wiped his nose. Then he looked at her again and his face dissolved into a huge smile, then he began to laugh. Mavis looked at him perplexed.

'Mavis, dearest Mavis, I'm sorry. You've got hold of the wrong end of the stick. I was trying to find out your thoughts on age difference in marriage, because I am very fond of your daughter, Rosemary. I have seen quite a lot of her lately between line dancing and the walking club and we get along very well, even if there is an age difference.' He looked up at Mavis, his eyes twinkling and moist from the laughing and choking.

Mavis could only feel relief. 'Oh James! How wonderful! I was so worried by your questions and jumped to the wrong conclusion of course.' She started to laugh and then the two of them were laughing uproariously.

The kitchen door opened, and Frank entered. He did not look pleased when he saw his mother laughing with a strange man in the kitchen. Mavis waved to a seat and asked Frank if he would like tea. She was still smiling broadly as she poured a cup.

'I'm afraid I am too busy for tea,' Frank stated, and staring at James, walked back out of the kitchen. They heard his heavy tread on the stairs.

'Sorry Mavis, I think your son might also have the wrong idea,' he chuckled, as he got to his feet and picked up his file.

At that Mavis got into another fit of laughing and still laughing, escorted James into the hall where they waved goodbye, unable to speak.

Mavis went into her sitting room and poured herself a whiskey. She toasted Dennis and thought to herself, thank God, that's sorted. Now I can relax again. Then she considered what he had said and was doubly thankful. Could it be that Rosemary had found a man? If he were her choice, she would be very happy for her, she knew he was a good and sound man.

Then she remembered Frank's appearance. What was he doing, acting like he owned the place and not even mannerly enough to say hello? She felt peeved by his attitude. Maybe it was time to take the bull by the horns with him too? This seemed to be the day!

Mavis had dinner ready at seven o'clock. Rosemary had come in at six thirty and was in good spirits. She immediately told her mother that if necessary, she would talk to Maureen and let her know that she could not move in with them.

'I've been thinking of this, day and night since you told me. We are going to be united in this, my mother. No shilly-shallying, no beating about the bush, we are going to give it to her straight, if it comes to it.' She thumped the kitchen table with her fist to emphasise her point.

Mavis looked at her daughter lovingly and smiled. She would not tell her daughter about the interesting afternoon she had passed. In time she would learn about it and no doubt, it would go down in the family archives to be passed from generation to generation.

She told Rosemary that Frank was upstairs, and would she call him for dinner. Rosemary was surprised that her mother had not mentioned it when she came in. She had not seen the car in the drive. She rose and went to the hall and called him. There was no reply, so she went up the stairs and knocked on his bedroom door. He opened it violently and stood glaring at her. His eyes looked slightly out of focus and she was a bit scared.

'Dinner is ready, Frank, if you want some.' She turned and went back down the stairs, wondering what was up with her brother.

Several minutes later he appeared in the kitchen. He seemed calmer and thanked Mavis for dinner and apologised for coming without any notice. The women tried to keep up a normal conversation about generalities to cover his silence. He did not eat much dinner. Finally, Mavis asked him if everything was alright? He grunted and said something about business being difficult and people being difficult. His sister asked him if they could help in any way. She was concerned about the way he looked.

'

'Yes, you can sell this bloody place and give me my share of my inheritance,' he said quietly, pushing back his chair and left the room, noisily.

'Frank is in trouble, Rosemary. I think it must be some financial difficulty if he wants me to sell the house. What on earth has happened to his business interests? Your father left them in a healthy state, I know that for sure. What are we going to do?' She put her elbows on the table and held her head in her hands.

Rosemary sighed and told her mother that they would not accede to his demands. He was like a spoilt little boy, she said. Time to keep firm and not tolerate any of his nonsense.

'Oh, you are so strong, Rosemary, so like your father. If we knew what the problem was, we might be able to suggest something, but we don't.'

The two women sat up in the sitting room after the dinner and silently watched the news. They kept it low and were half afraid that Frank would reappear to unsettle them and make more demands. They both went to bed by ten o'clock and both locked their doors. The day had been so funny at first, hilarious in fact, and then this dark shadow had come down and covered them both. There was an air of menace about the house now, Mavis felt. Something had changed and she was afraid.

Chapter 16

Mavis and Rosemary had breakfast together and listened to hear if Frank was up and about. There was no sound. Rosemary kissed her mother goodbye and went off to her work. As she drove out, she looked towards the side of the house and sure enough, there was Frank's car. She had not seen it last night when she came home. She hoped that her mother would be alright. She would call her the first chance she had.

Mavis washed the breakfast dishes and last night's dinner dishes. Then she went into the utility to do some ironing. She was calm and rested even though she had not slept well. Thoughts kept going around and around in her head. She had gone through the children's early days, seeing them in all their different stages. Could she have done more for them? Did she favour one over the other? What would Dennis think of the present situation? As she ironed, she mulled over the past and tried to find out where Frank had changed, if he had changed.

Hearing him in the kitchen, she stopped ironing and pulled out the plug. That would wait.

Stepping into the kitchen she greeted her son and asked if he would like breakfast? He looked awful; pale with bloodshot eyes and his hair was uncombed, which was unusual; Frank liked to look smart, no matter what time of day or night it was.

'No Mum, I do not feel like eating at all. I must have a bug or something.' He laughed dryly. 'I never refuse food, as you know, Ma, so I must be sick.'

Immediately Mavis felt sorry for her boy. 'Why don't you go back to bed, Frank. You might be cooking up something. Would you think of going to the doctor?'

'No, I'll recover, I'm sure. The thought of food makes me feel nauseous right now. I'll just have a cup of coffee.'

Mavis went and put on the kettle. Frank looked out the window and ran his hands through his hair a couple of times.

'I suppose you are disgusted with me for saying what I said last night. You would be right to feel that. I've been a bit of a fool recently but that is all past now. No more foolery, Mum, it will all work out.' He turned and smiled at her and her heart melted.

'I'm glad you see that Frank. Selling Ravenswood is not really an option for me, you know. You just sort yourself out Frank and all will be well. Rosemary and I are going to see Jenny, who is worried about her mother. Maureen has plans to move in with her and you can imagine her distress at that.'

She smiled at her son, but he frowned and said, 'Maureen is an idiot and not so bright.'

Mavis was shocked by this but said nothing. She recalled Maureen's excitement regarding Frank's advice and wondered what on earth was going on.

'Do you have to go into work today, could you not take a day off sick?' She did not know what to say to his previous comment.

'No, I must go and carry on. Business as usual as they say, Ma. Don't fret about me. I'll be fine, don't you worry. There are a lot of viruses about these days. I'll survive.'

Mavis went into town for her weekly shopping after saying goodbye to her son. He was in the sitting room when she left, watching the news. He told her that he would be probably gone by the time she got back and would see her soon. She kissed him goodbye.

She did her shopping and then bumped into a friend from the choir, Helen. They had a cup of coffee and Mavis was brought up to date with all the latest news and gossip. Her daughter Norah was a nurse in England and had been home recently for the wedding of one of her nursing friends there. It had been a lovely wedding, Helen said, and the bride looked beautiful. She took out her phone and showed her some photos of the bride and her daughter, Norah.

'Who did she marry, is he English?' Mavis asked as she studied the photos.

'No, he is a local from the same village, Moineir, just outside Clonmel,' Helen replied. 'He's a doctor and working in London. You might have heard of his father; he owns the Moineir Stud farm there. The aunt owns a lovely hotel there, very grand it is. That's where the reception was held, and a lot of the guests stayed there that night. Norah enjoyed herself very much. It took a few days to recover and then she went back to England.'

Clonmel was in South Tipperary and it was a long enough drive from Ravenswood. Mavis did not go that far very often. She wondered whether the drive would be too long for Sadie. She would like to see that hotel. They discussed the new hair salon just opened in the main street and Helen thought the young girl, who owned it, was quite an expert. Mavis thought about her own hair and realised that it was months since she had been to a hairdresser.

'I might try it, look at me! My hair is too long and a mess. I wonder if she would be busy now?'

'Why don't you drop in and see? You don't need an appointment; there are two of them there and as it's nearly lunch time, you might be lucky'.

Mavis and Helen left the café and parted company at the library. Mavis crossed over to the other side of the street and found the salon, which was close by. There was one other person having her hair blow-dried, and Mavis was seen immediately. She chatted to the girl who did her hair and learned about where she was from. The hour passed and Mavis came out delighted with her new look. She had not intended to have a colour put in but was gently persuaded to by the girl. It was not a dramatic change, but it certainly took years off her. She wondered if anyone would notice. She marvelled at how a visit to the hairdressers could make you feel good. She promised herself that she would do it more often. It took her a few minutes to remember where she had parked her car. Then she remembered her shopping and thought with dismay about her frozen food. Would it be alright or thoroughly defrosted in her boot?

She checked her shopping bag as soon as she reached her car, and the frozen stuff did not seem to be too soft. It should be alright if I put it straight into the freezer, she thought. She was suddenly tired and thought a nap would be good.

When Rosemary came home, Mavis was just coming downstairs from her bedroom.

'Wow, Mum, you look very glamorous. Let's have a proper look.' Rosemary took in her mother's new hairdo and was very impressed.

'It's lovely Mum, very subtle, I love the highlights. Very professional it is, who is the hairdresser?'

Mavis told her about the new salon as they went down to the kitchen.

'Oh-oh, Mum, I smell burning!'

Mavis quickly went to the oven and took out the casserole that she had put in before going for a nap. 'No, it's just perfect, Rose, look.'

Mavis wrinkled up her nose and said, 'I smell burning Mum.' She went into the utility room and her mother heard a wail. 'Oh no, my silk blouse.'

Puzzled, she stood at the door and looked in. She saw Rosemary holding up her Italian silk blouse. The mark of the iron had burned right through it and looking at her ironing board, she saw it was burned right through to the wood. She looked at her daughter in disbelief.

'Mum, I told you before not to iron my things. I can do that myself.'

Mavis could see that Rosemary was very annoyed and was blaming her.

'Rosemary, I don't know what happened. I'm sure I pulled out the plug when I went to get Frank's breakfast. I don't think I went back in to finish my ironing.' She was puzzled and tried to remember. Did she go back and resume ironing? She could not remember.

Rosemary put the ruined blouse in the waste bin outside the door. Her mother was mortified and felt that she should remember ironing such a delicate item, in fact, she knew that she would not attempt it. But then, what had happened?

'I will replace it Rosemary, I just don't know how that happened.'

Rosemary looked at her and saw her distress. 'Oh Mum, never mind. I got it in a sale.'

She did not tell her mother that it was pure silk and had been reduced from two hundred euros to ninety, which was an expensive item on a teacher's salary. She was now worried. Her mother had gone out shopping and left the iron on. Could it have caused a fire?

Mavis was also thinking the same thing and was annoyed at herself for not checking all the electricals before going out. She always pulled out the television plug or made sure the switches were all turned off. She looked at the iron and saw that it too, was ruined. The fabric had stuck to the iron and she knew there would be no way of cleaning that off. She would have to buy a new one and get a new cover for the ironing board.

The women ate their dinner in silence. Afterwards they went upstairs to watch television. Rosemary told her mother that they should leave early, about nine thirty and be on the motorway when most of the morning rush was over. Mavis agreed.

'I'll go and have a bath now and wash my hair. Then I'll be ready to go as soon as we have breakfast,' she said. She got up and left the room. Mavis turned the station on to hear the national news. As soon as the presenter came on, Mavis had a strange feeling. She used to get this strange feeling sometimes, as a child, a déjà vu experience. She knew exactly what the newsreader was going to say before she said it, and felt a chill going down her spine. Her hands were lifted to her mouth as the presenter announced that the missing sixteen-year-old boy's body had been found. It was Bill O'Brian and he had been discovered in the Midlands, in the bog. He had been beaten and then shot. The guards suspected a gangland murder.

These were now such a common occurrence unfortunately and were usually forgotten in a week or so. Because of the likelihood of drugs being the cause, people were more inclined to push this news to the back of their minds, almost making drug deaths acceptable in a strange way. It would be different if it were what people termed, a 'normal' murder, a wife or husband being murdered or a random shooting like what happened in the States. That would be spoken about for longer and remain in people's minds.

Chapter 17

Mavis was quiet as they drove along the motorway. She was thinking of the boy's mother and wondered how a young lad from Greenways could have been in trouble with gangs, at that age. Rosemary said it was the times they were living in. Drugs were everywhere and were destroying communities and families. She knew her mother was very innocent about modern life and told her a few home truths about life nowadays, both in the country and city. Her mother could not believe that a small rural village like theirs, could even know about drugs, never mind take them. She felt sickened about it all. Then she suddenly remembered what Sadie had said that day and felt something like an electric shock go through her. She told Rosemary about the conversation she had with Sadie and Margaret O'Neill, but her daughter thought that her mother must have misheard.

'No Rosemary, she mentioned the bog, twice I think, it's really uncanny.'

They continued in silence. The traffic was very light, and they were on the outskirts of Dublin in no time. Rosemary then realised that all the roadworks had finished and that was why they had reached there so quickly.

'We might be too early, after all that,' she told her mother.' We needn't have left so early. Jenny said one o'clock, didn't she?'

Mavis sat up straighter and looked around her. 'Look where we are, Rosemary. If we are early why don't we go and say hello to Frank and see how the garage is doing?'

They were about a mile from where the garage that Dennis had built up so successfully, was located. They continued to the next exit and Rosemary turned right. A few minutes later they were in the parking area of the posh looking garage. The display rooms were all lit up with the latest electric cars on show. It looked like a prosperous business.

The two women entered the reception area, looking around appreciatively. A tall beautiful blonde young lady glided over to them and smiled a ravishing smile and asked how she could help. She did not have an Irish accent and they guessed she came from some European country. The name badge on her blouse spelled Sonja.

Mavis smiled and asked if they could see the 'boss'. Sonja beamed at them and said apologetically, 'So sorry madam, Paul...Mr. Kavanagh 'as gone to meeting this morning, will be back after de lunch.'

Mavis was so shocked she could say nothing to this. Rosemary immediately asked if Frank was about that morning. Sonja flashed her shiny smile at them again and shrugged her shoulders slightly.

'Oh Frank, he ees driving de van today. Maybe in Waterford, maybe Cork, I am not so sure, but usually he ees returned 'eer at seex o'clock. I can geeve a message to heem, yes?'

Rosemary said, 'Yes, please. Tell him that his mother and sister called by.'

Then the two women were walking back to the car. Mavis felt that she was dreaming and hoped to wake up soon.

Mavis turned to Rosemary, her eyes brimming with tears. 'He has sold the dealership to that Paul Kavanagh, Rosemary, why on earth would he do that?'

'Later Mum, we'll talk about this later. Try to just concentrate on Jenny until we get home, alright?' Rosemary was stunned too and tried to keep her head from turning somersaults.

Jenny arrived at her house just as the two women arrived on her heels. After kisses and greetings, they went into the kitchen. Jenny unloaded her shopping on the worktop and lots of interesting dishes soon appeared.

'I have not had time to cook a proper meal, ladies, I apologise. Work is demanding these days. We have a very convenient delicatessen down the road and their food is always freshly prepared and delicious.'

Mavis had a look and exclaimed, 'Oh lovely. I just adore these tapas-like dishes, so does Rosemary.'

'Yummy, Jenny. We will enjoy this I promise. I wish we had a proper delicatessen in Greenways. The

supermarket is alright but is not a patch on this.'
Rosemary helped Jenny put out plates.

Jenny opened a bottle of white wine that she had in the fridge and they all had a glass as they sat down to eat. They talked generalities first, not wanting to get straight into the difficult subject that was on their minds. Later in the sitting room, Mavis had another glass of wine as she was not driving. Rosemary and Jenny had a coffee and the talk slid around to Jenny's mother.

Jenny leaned forward and told the ladies that living with Maureen would be a nightmare and as she worked from home, there would be little or no escaping her. Rosemary asked if she could not go on an extended trip overseas.

'What then, Rose? She will have settled into life here after a few weeks and would not mind my going away at all. I've thought of everything and I feel like I am losing my mind.'

'Pity that Robbie is still not about,' said Mavis. 'If he were still here, she would not dream of wanting to move in.'

Robbie had been in a relationship with Jenny for about three years. They had broken up and he had left fourteen months ago. Maureen had loathed him and thought that her daughter was much superior to him. She was over the moon when they broke up.

'Why does she want to move in, Jenny? I thought she was renting until she found a good house in a

,

good area.' Rosemary was puzzled by her aunt's motives.

Jenny explained that her mother hated where she was renting and could not bear the people who were renting alongside her. She was getting impatient for the crash to happen and was still looking at houses, but the prices were too high still. Her old house had already gone up in price and she was livid about that. She took everything so personally. Jenny said that she would need psychiatric care if her mother came into her house.

It was Mavis who had a brainwave. 'Jenny, you must tell her that you have a lodger staying; a man from Hungary or Poland or wherever, and that as the third bedroom is your office, that would only leave the sofa in here.'

'But why would I have a lodger, Mavis?'

'To help pay the mortgage, girl, why else?' Mavis nodded her head at Jenny. 'She doesn't need to know you don't need help with the mortgage, does she? Tell her that Robbie's going, left you with the total mortgage to pay.'

Rosemary thought it was a brilliant idea. 'Yes Jenny, that's it exactly. I think it would work out very well.'

Mavis was getting excited now as well. She leaned forward in her chair. 'Do you have any of Rob's old clothing left here?'

Jenny looked at her aunt in surprise. 'Why on earth would I?'

Mavis grinned and wagged her finger, 'What would Maureen say if she saw men's underpants and socks hanging on the bathroom radiator?'

Rosemary roared laughing and Jenny joined in when she imagined the face of her mother looking at these items.

Mavis continued, 'You must go out to Dunne's stores and get a few pairs of socks and underpants and a couple of large string vests and drape them over the rads. Also, go into the charity shops and get a few pairs of tatty trainers, smelly, if possible, and put some downstairs inside the front door and some in your spare bedroom. You must make it look as if you really do have someone living here.'

'But what do I do when she sees that he is not actually here?'

Mavis grew impatient. 'For the love of Moses, girl, play it by ear. He's gone off to Hungary for a few days or else he's working night shifts somewhere. Use your imagination.'

Rosemary was amazed at her mother's imagination. She smiled and said to her cousin, 'Jenny, I think this is the best idea I've ever heard. If she does want to stay a night, offer her the lodger's bed but suggest she should change the sheets first as he is not as clean as you would wish.'

'No,' Mavis said firmly. You could not offer her the lodger's bed. It wouldn't be right. After all, he has paid for his accommodation and will be back soon.'

They all roared laughing and Jenny was uplifted. She knew that her mother would not come into the house if she knew that there was a lodger there. It was up to her to make it look realistic. She would go to the charity shops tomorrow and get a pile of old clothes and strew them about the spare bedroom. Then Jenny got serious and asked if they had thought about what they would do if her mother wanted to move in with them? This silenced the two women. They could not use the same excuse, and there were plenty of spare rooms in their house.

Mavis said that they would cross that bridge when they came to it. She was happy for Jenny that the problem might be solved. 'If she doesn't fall for that, Jenny, you may well have to go out and look for a large, menacing-looking Eastern European. Try the gym that you go to, you might have to bribe someone but make sure that they don't think you are offering something that you're not!' She grinned at her niece.

The girls roared laughing and thought Mavis was a scream. The afternoon ended on a much lighter note and after cup of tea and slice of walnut coffee cake, mother and daughter left. Their mood grew sombre as they drove down the motorway towards home. They had changed their minds about going to a cinema or anywhere else in Dublin; what they had learned earlier that day had ruined any ideas of going out for enjoyment.

As they entered the house, the phone was ringing. Rosemary lifted it and said 'Hello.' Immediately her face changed and lit up with a smile. Mavis looking at her knew that her daughter was in love and she felt a fleeting happiness for her until she remembered her son Frank.

'Mum, would you mind terribly if I left you for a while. I must go and see someone in town. I won't be late though.' She looked at her mother anxiously, knowing that Frank was very much on her mother's mind.

'Something tells me that this someone, is someone very important to you, Rosemary,' her mother smiled and winked her eye at her.

Rosemary blushed, 'I don't want to say anything just yet, I wouldn't want to get your hopes up you know, it may just fizzle out in a short time.'

'Oh, I wouldn't say that love, I think this man is persistent.' She tapped her nose and winked again.

Rosemary wondered how her mother had guessed that. 'When I come home, we will discuss Frank. In the meantime, try and relax and don't worry too much. There might be a simple explanation.'

Chapter 18

Rosemary met James in the pub in the town square. It was small and intimate, and she and the girls sometimes went there. It was early in the evening, so the place was quite empty. Later, it would be busy and bustling and noisy with the sound of young people enjoying themselves.

She felt very much at home with James now. They had been on a lot of walks with the walking club and over the weeks had found themselves walking together more and more. They talked about many things and both had common enough interests and opinions on life. James spoke to her about his deceased wife, and she was a good listener. He always felt better after talking with Rosemary. He asked her whether her mother ever mentioned him and when she shook her head, he smiled.

'When I think about the day we met,' he smiled and shook his head.

Rosemary laughed. 'She will take the credit no doubt, for introducing us.'

'I think you should tell her soon who the mystery man is,' he suggested, sipping his drink.

Rosemary then told him that her mother had rather a lot on her mind right now, but as soon as they had straightened a few things out, she would tell her. He looked at her serious face and asked, 'Anything I can help with Rose?'

She shook her head and sighed. 'It's just a bit of family business and I would rather not discuss it now; hopefully it will soon be resolved. If it doesn't, I will gladly unburden myself.'

'Just remember, I am here and live nearby, so if I can help at all, don't hesitate, please, my love. You have done a lot of listening to me and I am extremely grateful.'

Mavis sat in her sitting room with the television on. She could not take in what was on the screen as her mind kept replaying the scenario in the showroom this morning. Why could Frank not have told her that he sold the business to Paul Kavanagh? Why was it necessary? The place had been debt free when he got it; he had spent a good deal of his trust fund in buying that fancy apartment and flashy car. It seemed to all, that he was doing very well. He certainly looked like a successful businessman. She nibbled her lip as her mind wandered all over the place.

Her mobile pinged and she fished it out of her bag and answered it. It was Margaret O'Neill, Sadie's carer. She had wondered if Mavis had heard the news. Poor woman! She just wanted to talk about the tragedy and needed a listener. Mavis listened and did not need to say very much. His poor mother was devastated about the news and did not believe that her son could be mixed up in any funny business, although she did admit that he had been a difficult child. At the end of the conversation when Margaret was all talked out, she mentioned Sadie. How strange it was that she had mentioned the word 'bog'. Did Mavis recall that, she asked?

'Indeed, I did, Margaret. It hit me this morning driving to Dublin. It was very strange that.'

As she finished the call and put her mobile on the table beside her, she heard the key in the front door and took it for granted that Rosemary was home. When it was Frank who entered the room, she was taken aback.

He came straight in and sat down beside her on the sofa. She looked at him without speaking. He certainly looked a lot better tonight, she thought. He took a deep breath and began, 'I hear you called at the garage today. I'm sorry I was out. I hope Sonja did not give you the wrong impression, her English is hopeless, but Paul can't resist a pretty face!'

Mavis put up her hand to stop him. 'Frank, just tell me; have you sold the place to that friend of yours, Paul?'

Frank shook his head and said, 'Mum, it's complicated; we are in a partnership together. We needed to amalgamate, to pool our resources for a big investment. We are both in this together and I trust Paul and he trusts me. When we come out of this investment, we will both be very wealthy and then the partnership will be dissolved. You have no need to worry Ma, no need at all.' He leaned back and smiled at her. She immediately felt a certain relief and a weight was lifted from her shoulders.

'Well, it would have been nice if you could have confided in us. We got an awful shock when we learned that Paul is the 'boss'.'

'Mum that is for appearances only and we're holding our cards close to our chests and don't want too many people to know about this. Will you trust me?'

What could she say? Part of her was relieved but there were still a lot of questions that she would have liked to ask. Now was not the time. She was tired after the travelling up and down and the lively afternoon spent with Jenny. She nodded her head and said what was foremost in her mind; 'Please be careful Frank, that's all I ask, be careful and keep within the law.'

He stayed for a cup of tea and then left. He was gone by the time Rosemary arrived home at eleven. Mavis still sat silently watching the television screen. This time her mind was preoccupied with Bill O'Brian and his poor mother. She would go down to the village and have a quiet word with her tomorrow and then call into Sadie.

Rosemary was amazed that Frank had come down to explain to his mother and thought that it was a good sign.

Mavis spent some time repeating his explanation about the partnership, which they did not pretend to understand and were a bit dubious about it all, but both women went to bed a little easier in their minds.

Next day, Mavis told Rosemary of her plan to visit Brigid O'Neill to offer her condolences on the death of young Billy. Rosemary was meeting with her walking friends and heading to south Tipperary, to a small village called Kilcash, and there was a group of them planning to climb the local mountain there, Slievenamon. Most of them had done it before, but not Rosemary or James, Aine or Susie. They would have lunch locally and would be home later in the afternoon.

The day was sunny and a perfect May day. Mavis decided to walk to the village, which was about three miles away. She could do with the exercise. She passed Sadie's house and knew that she would call there on her return journey. She realised that Brigid might not be at home or that there might be many neighbours in with the bereaved woman. She strode on regardless. She tried to put herself in Brigid's position; how would she feel? Stunned and heart broken, she imagined.

When she reached the village, she could see Brigid's house clearly. There were a couple of cars outside the house. Going up to the door, she was about to ring the bell when the door opened, and a couple of neighbours came out. Mavis knew them and nodded to them. One of the women put her hand on Mavis' arm and whispered, 'God love her, you just don't know what to say, do you?'

Mavis went into the room, led by Margaret, to where her sister Brigid was sitting. There were just the three of them. She embraced Brigid warmly and held the crying woman. Someone brought in a tray with tea and biscuits, and they all sat drinking and chatting quietly. Brigid explained that she knew Billy was a troubled lad but did not understand the extent of his troubles.

'I just thought it was a bit of divilment, you know? I don't think there was badness in him, only divilment. It was only lately that he changed, and I began to suspect he was taking stuff, you know, drugs, although where he got them, I don't know.' She shook her head and dried her eyes, which were so red and puffy from all the tears the poor mother had shed.

The door opened and a strange man entered. As the women started to rise, he lifted his hand and told them to stay as they were. He introduced himself as a Detective Inspector Savage, Aidan Savage, and he was from Clonmel, although Mavis could hear a Kerry accent. He apologised for intruding and offered his sympathy to Brigid and her sister Margaret. Mavis was introduced to him. She asked if he would like her to leave and he said not at all.

He came from Clonmel to ask a few questions and hoped that they did not mind the intrusion at this time. He was investigating drug dealers in the area and Bill's name had come up in their questioning of a suspected drug addict, and former dealer. He reassured Brigid, that Bill himself, was not under investigation for criminal activity, but they had to probe the information that they had got. From the confession they had got from their Clonmel suspect, they understood that Bill was a very minor player in the activities of a very superior gang in Dublin. He was what was called, a 'gofor'. Looking at the blank faces of the women, he explained that a 'gofor' is someone who collects or picks up packages of drugs for delivery, he might or might not deliver to buyers, and might or might not collect money for the same. He was a small cog in a big wheel. He looked at them to see if they understood what he was saying.

'Does that mean he was using the stuff too? Could that happen?' Brigid asked her question fearfully, her hands clenched in her lap.

'He could well have been using too, sometimes it happens, then problems arise when it comes to payment. He might not have been using, did you think that he was, Brigid?'

'I started to suspect he was using something; his mood changed a few months ago and he became quite aggressive and moody, whereas before that he was a lazy, laid-back sort of lad. But he started giving me a bit of cheek, you know, he had a bit of an attitude. That was not always there, only in the last few months, I'd say.' She sniffed and wiped her eyes.

'Did you notice any different routine to his day, or did he mention any particular friends, can you remember, Brigid?'

'Well, I seem to recall him leaving the house at night, late, after he was supposed to be in bed. If I asked him in the morning, he would say he got a mobile message from a friend who was stuck for a lift. He had a motorbike, you see. That happened a few times. But he could have been out more often than that; I often heard the front door opening, sometimes at dawn, as though he was returning from being out. Those times he did not use his motorbike. It's noisy so I would have heard it, you see?'

'Did you ever hear a car arriving for him or dropping him?'

'Not those nights no, so he must have gone somewhere local, within walking distance.'

The detective nodded. 'Did he mention any names of friends, at all?'

'No, he had a few friends in the village, but he also had friends in Clonmel; friends who went there after they left school. He didn't finish his schooling, but he kept in touch with his friends.' The mother started crying again. 'Maybe I was too soft with him, maybe I should have insisted that he finished school.'

Mavis put her arm around the woman on the sofa beside her. 'We do all we can, Brigid, we all do that. In the end our children make up their own minds'

Margaret agreed with Mavis and said, 'You were a great mother, Brigid, and we all know that you did not have an easy time of it too, you did your very best, girl.'

The detective asked Brigid if he could see Bill's room, or would she object to that? The mother said that it was fine with her, she would not mind. Margaret said that she would take the man up to see Bill's bedroom.

Mavis told Brigid that she would leave as she could hear more people arrive in the hall. She told the mother that she was always available to talk to, or if she wished to visit her anytime, just say when. They embraced again and Mavis left.

She walked slowly back up the hill towards home. She felt sad and distressed for the family she had just left. She did not feel like visiting Sadie but thought that she should. As she neared the house, she saw that Sadie was sitting in her front garden, enjoying the sun. There was no way that she could pass now, without calling in.

'Hello Sadie, how are you? It's Mavis here, I've just been down to see Brigid.'

Sadie looked up and smiled. She had a vacant look on her face. 'I'm going to Dublin next week, you know, to see Mary.'

'Well, that's lovely Sadie. Will you stay a few days there? It'll be a nice break for you.'

'Oh, I'd never do that. Mary is at school there and I could not stay there. No, I'll come back home after the visit.'

Mavis could see that this was not a good day for Sadie. 'Who is with you today, Sadie,' she asked?

Sadie frowned and scratched her cheek. 'I'm not sure. They keep changing a lot. Some of the people sure, I don't know at all.'

Mavis knew that this was not true and knew that Sadie could not remember who was caring for her at this moment. Just then her regular carer emerged with a tray with two cups of tea on it.

'Hello Mavis, lovely to see you.'

Mavis said loudly, 'Oh, it's you Lily, nice to see you too. Isn't the weather gorgeous?'

'Have you been down to see poor Brigid? The poor woman! I don't know how she'll get over this tragedy. To lose your only child is cruel, isn't it?'

Sadie moved her head and looked at Mavis. 'Where did she lose the child? Nobody loses children, not these days.'

Lilly and Mavis looked at each other and said nothing.

Mavis walked home after the visit feeling a little depressed. She knew Sadie was deteriorating and wondered how long she would last. As she reached her place, she thought she would go and sit in her wood for a while and have a chat with Dennis. Sometimes life gets too much and it's hard to remain interested in everything. One gets tired.

She had a light lunch from the produce growing in her garden and tunnel. She looked at the news, there was no further mention of Billy's murder. But what was one, among so many murders that were now a daily happening in her country? As a young child, she had never heard of a murder in Ireland, only in England. People would talk about it for months. Nowadays, it was forgotten in a week, there were so many such happenings.

She sat on the bench in her wood and closed her eyes and meditated calmly. When she returned to the house an hour later, she felt more relaxed and at peace.

The rest of the evening she spent playing the piano; it always restored her mind and lifted her out of herself. She quite forgot all about the problems and injustices in the world for a short time. She could almost hear Dennis saying in his quiet way, "we cannot control anything very much Vera, certainly not all the problems that exist." She smiled as she closed the piano. That is exactly what he was likely to say. There were times when he felt very close to her, and that brought a warm reassuring feeling and confidence. She. wondered whether other bereaved people felt the same sort of consolations.

The next morning, she was wakened by a strange noise. She lay still in her bed, listening and trying to work out what the sound was. It sounded like a tapping on her window. She sat up in bed puzzled. There is was again, tap-tap-tap. Gently she eased herself out of bed and moved towards the window. She just held the curtain aside and came face to face with a big raven, sitting on the windowsill. The bird saw her but didn't move. Human eye met bird eye and neither blinked. After about two minutes the raven flew off in the direction of the wood.

Mavis was quite pleased. She felt no fear of it being an omen or bad luck or anything like that. She was not superstitious. She sang as she made her bed and tidied her room. She would have breakfast and then shower before going to church.

Chapter 19

The following weeks went by quickly. In early June, the choir took their summer break and there would be no more rehearsals, either in church or in Mavis's house. She left James decide if he wanted a break, but he did not want the summer to pass without a lesson. They agreed to check beforehand and if either were busy then the lesson would be cancelled.

Frank made a few impromptu visits and seemed in good spirits. Nothing was mentioned again about the previous conversations regarding the partnership. Mavis was busy in the polytunnel and in the garden. The work was beginning to pile up and she was grateful for the help of the local handyman, John-Joe, who came twice a month. He made a difference to her workload and she had more energy to do things that she enjoyed in the garden.

Rosemary was happy in her work and in her social life. She told her mother that she was seeing James Regan and looked at her for approval. Mavis smiled broadly and said that she was thrilled as he was a lovely person and very trustworthy. Rosemary was content.

'Just don't expect any big news anytime soon. I don't want to rush things Mum. I need to be sure that I can make that commitment, I know that James can.'

Mavis told her daughter that she was a sensible girl and always so sincere, that James would be very understanding. 'I don't understand how some people can rush into marriage without proper consideration,' she confided. 'It is for life after all, isn't it?'

'It is for me Mum. I want to have a happy marriage like you and Dad. That's what I call a true marriage'.

Mavis was working in her tunnel and singing as usual. All her vegetables were growing well even though it was early in the season. There were two beds that she had not yet tackled. They would be for the tomatoes as they were now big enough to plant out in a couple of days. She was nursing them still in their incubators at night and in the tunnel during the day. Today she decided to remove the newspapers and cardboard covers from the beds and dig them over. The chicken manure would be well rotted, and she would give them a good watering to prepare them. She was halfway through her task when her fork caught on something where the cardboard had been. Curious, she bent down to see what was on her fork. It was a bag of some sort, plastic by the look of it. She had to pull the bag off the prongs of the fork. Sitting down on the bed she took the bag and looked at it. It was full of something and she could not remember putting it there. She took off her gloves and opened the bag. She eyes nearly popped out when she found that there was a fat roll of money inside. What on earth? She took out the roll of money, and saw they were all fifty-euro notes, held together by an elastic band. She tried to imagine how much money was there and guessed hundreds if not more.

Hurriedly she left the tunnel and went down to the kitchen. She put on the kettle and stood looking at the money. She counted it as she had her coffee, and it was over two thousand euros. Where did it come from and whose was it? She was stumped for an answer. She could hardly wait for Rosemary to return to tell her about it and ask what she should do.

Rosemary was excited as the school year was ending and the trip to Italy was looming ahead rapidly. She had lots to do and shopping for her holiday. The other three girls were also high with excitement.

 When she came into the kitchen that evening, she was confronted by her mother with a pile of money in front of her. Sitting down she heard about the find in her mother's tunnel and was as puzzled as Mavis, as to who put it there and why?

They ate their dinner and talked about all the possibilities they could think of. Suddenly they both stopped eating at the same time.

'The night prowler,' they both exclaimed.

After that they were convinced that whoever had been prowling around the garden must have put it there, but why? Why did he not come back for it? Rosemary thought that they should notify the guards as it was so suspicious and there was no way that they could keep it. Mavis agreed and rang the local station after they finished their dinner.

They had a visit around eight o'clock and ushered the young guard in. They had to fill in a form, stating where the money was found, and the guard counted it out in front of them and the amount was agreed. He also felt that it was from ill-gotten goods, but if it were not claimed in a certain time, it would probably revert to them. The two women laughed, and Rosemary said that it would be very welcome for her Italian holiday.

'What an exciting day you have had, Mum. Keep digging, you might find more.'

Mavis was shocked by the suggestion. She had stopped digging when she had snagged the bag and had not continued. Maybe there *was* more there! She told her daughter that she would do a thorough search tomorrow and who knows what she might find.

The next morning as soon as she had her breakfast, Mavis went up to the tunnel and continued digging in the unplanted beds. After thirty minutes she unearthed another plastic bag, under the manure. She continued digging until both beds were thoroughly dug over and all the manure well covered. She did not find any more. Again, she counted the money, and it was just under two thousand euros. Smiling to herself she had her coffee, before getting into her car and driving to the local police station. She presented herself at the desk and told her story.

'Ah, yes! The lady who is digging up money.' The middle-aged man at the desk smiled at her and produced the same form as before. 'Sure, if you keep doing this, everyone will think there is a fortune to be made gardening.'

Mavis laughed and agreed. 'I never made any money before with my vegetables, now it looks like I've hit a gold mine.' She stopped smiling. She suddenly thought about the beds with vegetables now growing well, her onions and garlic, spinach and lettuce. She hoped she would not have to dig them up. Well, if they ask, I will refuse. They will just have to wait until harvest time.

She left the police station feeling a bit deflated. Could the police insist that she dig up the rest of her tunnel? Surely not. Nobody at the station had asked her any questions at all, so she did not get a chance to mention the 'night prowler', if someone came to ask questions, she could then offer her theories about the money being in her tunnel.

Back in her kitchen, she made herself a large salad and some potato salad from last night's leftovers. She went upstairs for a nap and entered her news in her notebook. She was tired from the digging and the excitement and dropped off to sleep. Her rest was interrupted about ten minutes later by the telephone. As she fumbled her way to the writing table under the window, she felt like she had slept hours, though she knew by the clock that it was only minutes. Before she could say Hello, her sister-in-law's strident voice, assaulted her ears.

'Mavis, I must see you as soon as possible. Life here in this apartment is becoming unbearable in the extreme. There are some very strange people living here, if you must know and I think I am losing my mind. I will see you on Friday, mid-afternoon, if that's alright. We need to talk.'

Mavis tried to think about the coming weekend, was there anything planned? She could not think properly. Her brain was still too relaxed. What could she say to put Maureen off?

'Well, alright Maureen, if you want to call by. I can't think right now if Rosemary has anything planned, but you are welcome to call anyway.'

'Right, I must dash now. I have so much to tell you. Until Friday then, Mavis. Cheers.'

And that was that! Mavis was left holding the phone and looking at it. What on earth would Rosemary say? Was Rosemary going to be here? Oh, she hoped so. She went back and took her notebook and sat looking at the dates. Rosemary was going to Italy Friday week, well that was alright then. She would not have to put up with Maureen on her own.

James rang at two forty-five and asked if she was free for a lesson or if she was too busy? She was going to put him off but then realised she would be sitting and fretting about Maureen's visit. Better to sit and listen to James playing the piano, she thought wryly.

James was in great form as usual, although Mavis had learned enough about him to know that his easy affable ways, sometimes hid his grief. But he was improving both in his playing and his attitude, she knew that.

She spent the hour listening to him and offered some technical advice when it was needed. He was playing John Field Nocturnes very well and it relaxed her, just listening. She almost forgot about Maureen at the end of the hour. When he finished and they discussed further music, she offered him a cup of tea and he accepted. As they sat in the kitchen, they laughed at the last time they had done this. He told Mavis that he and Rosemary were seeing a lot of each other and asked if she had been told? Smiling, Mavis nodded, and said she hoped that it would all be a 'happy ever after' story. He nodded too but cautioned her not to jump to any conclusion, as it was still very much up in the air. They were getting to know each other more and more.

Mavis said, 'As the song goes, "Que sera, sera", but I do have hope for the two of you, I really do.'

Rosemary was disappointed to hear that Maureen was coming on Friday. They knew that they would have to spend some time between tonight and tomorrow night discussing how to manage her, and what excuses they could make against her moving in for however short a time. Mavis told her daughter about her further find and of her visit to the police station. Rosemary was amazed.

'How much more is up there, Ma? You will have to bring in an excavator and raze the whole place.'

'That's exactly the thought that occurred to me at the station. Suppose it is stolen property, could they insist that I dig up the whole tunnel? I'm nearly sorry I involved the law at all.'

Rosemary laughed and thought they wouldn't. 'And to think that you and Dad used to preach to us, that money doesn't grow on trees! Little did he know that it grows underground, here at Ravenswood!'

Chapter 20

True to her word, Maureen arrived on Friday afternoon at four o'clock. Mavis busied herself, making afternoon tea. She had baked scones and a sponge cake that morning. Her daughter arrived just as she was pouring tea. They were out on the patio under the pergola. The day was sunny and warm and the roses just in bloom, although not all of them. The wisteria was just waiting to burst into flower as was the purple clematis. On a normal day, Mavis would sit here, thankful to be alive and enjoying her garden. Today her thoughts were gloomy and anxious.

As soon as Rosemary joined them, Maureen exclaimed. 'Oh, Rosemary, what a blessing you are to your mother!' The two women looked at her in surprise, which was Maureen's cue.

'You will never guess! My only daughter cannot give her own mother a bed for a short period. She has taken in a lodger, an Eastern European lodger. I don't know what to think. She says it is to help with the mortgage, if you don't mind.'

Rosemary interrupted her. 'Maureen, you have no idea how expensive it is to live in Dublin and have a mortgage to pay. I would not be able to afford it on my teacher's salary.'

Maureen impatiently waved her hand. 'But Jenny has a very important job, executive status, of course

175

she should be able to afford a mortgage, even if that Robbie fellow has absconded.'

Mavis shook her head and murmured that maybe Robbie should have stayed and pulled his weight. At this, Maureen bristled and said, 'Rubbish, he was never good enough for my daughter, good riddance, I say.'

Rosemary decided to be cheeky. 'Could you not have stayed in the box room, Maureen?'

'Box room indeed, as if that would even make a decent bedroom. No, that is her office and full of equipment and computers and stuff. I was offered the sofa, if you don't mind, as if I was nobody of any consequence. And, you will never guess! When I visited the bathroom, the place was full of his awful underwear. Can you imagine it? His bedroom was a shambles, clothes all over the place and I can tell you, the place smelled as if he never opened a window.'

The two women could hardly keep a straight face and Mavis began to cough and had to run into the kitchen for a glass of water. Rosemary got up and busied herself adding more hot water to the teapot. Poor Maureen was in a state and looked as though she had buried her best friend.

An hour later, she had exhausted herself; ranting and raving about the ingratitude of children, after she had sacrificed herself, to give her everything. Self-pity threatened to engulf her, and Mavis could see what was coming. She would play on their pity and milk it for all it was worth. She immediately told her what a wonderful mother she was and surely, she understood poor Jenny's dilemma. She must have felt awful at having to deny her mother accommodation at this time.

'What about renting a small place in Dublin, Maureen? You could find an apartment near Jenny, could you not? With the house in Cork sold, you should be able to find somewhere reasonable.' Mavis was trying desperately to steer Maureen's thoughts away from Greenways and Ravenswood in particular.

Maureen looked at her in horror. 'I am already paying quite a lot for the apartment in Cork. Prices are high there as well, you know.'

Rosemary excused herself and said she must get ready for her line dancing and swim afterwards. Mavis asked if she would be here for dinner and was relieved when Rosemary said that she would.

Maureen asked if she was serious about line dancing. Rosemary assured her that it was very much in vogue just now, all her friends were doing it. She assured her aunt that it was more fun than the gym.

'You need to be careful Rosemary, you are no spring chicken, you know. You wouldn't want to get too scrawny. Men don't like scrawny women, you know.'

Rosemary replied without missing a beat. 'Ah, my man loves me regardless, Auntie Maureen.' She knew that Maureen hated to be called Auntie.

As Rosemary hurried into the house, Maureen turned to Mavis and asked in a shocked voice if she had heard correctly?

Mavis said casually, 'Oh yes. Rosemary has had a romance in her life for quite some time now.'

She stood up and started to collect the tea things and put them on the tray. She left her sister-in-law silenced and went to put on the lamb tagine she had prepared earlier. She ducked into the utility room and poured a small whiskey and gulped it down. That was something she had prepared for earlier, too. A small bottle of whiskey in the cleaning cupboard behind the detergent and a small glass. She smiled to herself. She felt like a naughty child showing defiance to her elders. Hope she doesn't stay for too long or I'll be an alcoholic, she thought.

Maureen came into the kitchen and asked if she was in her usual room, she thought she might have a shower before dinner. Mavis had no choice but to agree. There had been no discussion about how long she would take up residence at Ravenswood and Mavis felt nervous.

When Rosemary returned, they had a gin and tonic before sitting down to dinner. Maureen asked what the dish was and said that she was not really into spices and all that foreign stuff. Mavis calmly said, 'Well, that's a pity Maureen, we love spicy food and cannot eat bland food more than twice a week.'

'I consider my health my wealth, Mavis, and Irish people are not used to this sort of food at all. Potatoes and plain meat and root vegetables were always the mainstay of the Irish and look how strong we always were.'

Rosemary said, 'We have come a long way since the Famine, Maureen. All the different nationalities that have migrated here have brought a wealth of interesting foods too. Spices as well as herbs, are in fact, medicinal. It's been scientifically proven.'

Maureen was not convinced. 'I hope you don't expect me to eat this sort of food every day, Mavis. My digestion is too delicate for it.'

Mavis replied, 'Oh no, Maureen, while you are here, I suggest that you cook your own food, and we will eat as we always eat. That would be the best solution, don't you think?'

Maureen looked at her sister-in-law askance but did not offer a reply.

Rosemary looked at her mother, 'What a good idea Mum. That way, everyone is pleased.'

The mother and daughter had already discussed this problem and thought of the solution.

Maureen could not keep silent a moment longer. 'Well, I certainly didn't expect to have to cook my own meals, when I came. In my days living here, visitors were not expected to do that.'

Rosemary smiled at her aunt and replied, 'But Auntie, you are not really a visitor, are you? You are family and that's different.'

The trio sat watching television later that night and Mavis turned to Maureen during an ad break and asked her how long she would be staying at Ravenswood. She had been building up courage to do this all day and finally did it. Maureen said that she really didn't know, it would depend on how the property market was doing, and whether she had houses to view in Cork or Dublin. Mavis was dismayed. It was all up in the air. She could be there for weeks.

At ten thirty Rosemary and Mavis got up to go to bed. Maureen asked them if they always went to bed so early. Mavis told her that they both had very full days and early to bed was the way they functioned best. They left a disgruntled woman sitting alone, watching the television.

Mavis was up at eight and went to water the vegetables in the tunnel. Her handyman was coming later to trim the laurel hedge and weed a few of the beds. Even though they were gravel beds, weeds still came up wherever they could, showing the power of nature over man's feeble attempts to control them. She was happy in her own company and loved this quiet time. The sun was warm even at this early hour and the only sounds were the birds. Mavis was perfectly happy. She refused to contemplate the days ahead with her difficult sister-in-law. She probably would not stay long, now that she had to look after herself, she might decide that Cork was not so bad.

Rosemary joined her about nine o'clock, with a cup of tea for her mother and one for herself. They sat on the old bench outside the tunnel and enjoyed the peace. They had both slept well and were determined not to let the unwelcome visitor spoil their interior peace. Rosemary was meeting the girls in town to do shopping for Italy. Tonight, she was meeting James and they were dining out. Suddenly she turned to her mother and said, 'Come too, Mum. You can say it was planned some time ago, James would be delighted if you came.'

Mavis was doubtful. 'Would it not be bad mannered, to leave her?'

'No of course, it wouldn't. What sort of manners has she got? Arriving and planning to stay, without asking you if she could or what you think of it?'

Rosemary was right. Maybe some shock treatment was needed in Maureen's case. The child in Mavis said it was right. 'Yes, I will come, and I just hope James won't be offended.'

Her daughter clapped her hands and laughed. 'That's my Mum, time to stand firm.'

Maureen came down to the kitchen at eleven and was disgusted not to find a cooked breakfast waiting

'

for her. As Mavis came into the house just then, Maureen asked, 'No cooked breakfast then Mavis? Dennis always liked his cooked breakfast, didn't he?'

Mavis replied calmly, 'We have a cooked breakfast on Saturday in winter but in summer we have it on Sunday. Rosemary likes to do the cooking. If I start with a fry in summer, I cannot do any gardening. Brunch is better then. Have a look in the fridge, there is yogurt and plenty of fruit; healthier, don't you think?'

Maureen looked very doubtful and aggrieved as she put some toast in the toaster and searched the fridge for something to put on it. Mavis put Marmite on the worktop and a selection of jams and marmalade.

'May I ask what we are having for dinner tonight, Mavis, not leftover tagine, I hope?'

'Oh! that reminds me, Maureen, I have to go out tonight, so I thought we would go to town and get you what you might like to eat tonight? I am sorry, it was arranged some time ago.'

'Right,' said Maureen, tight-lipped.

'I'll drive you in, as I need to go to the library.'

Dinner that night was most enjoyable. They went to the new Japanese restaurant in the city. It was popular with all age groups and was humming with activity. They had a drink at the bar while waiting for their table and James kept them laughing with funny stories about his childhood.

Rosemary then told James about Maureen taking up residence without any politeness or asking if she could. Mavis and Rosemary had James laughing out loud when then relayed the story of the lodger staying with Jenny and Maureen's face when she saw the underwear in the bathroom.

It was eleven o'clock by the time they returned to a dark house. Maureen had obviously gone to bed early.

Rosemary whispered to her mother that they should dine out more often while their unwelcome guest remained in residence.

,

Chapter 21

Monday morning was damp and miserable and there would be no gardening today for Mavis. She was happy with the work that John-Joe did on Saturday and the clipped hedge looked good. Mavis contemplated cleaning some inside windows to pass the time and before she would allow herself to play the piano. Maureen was sitting reading the weekend papers and appeared to be quiet and content.

At eleven thirty, there was a phone call from the police station in the town. Mavis was surprised and listened to what they requested. A few minutes later, she told Maureen that she had to go into town unexpectedly and would return shortly. The rain was lashing down at this time and Maureen had no desire to go out with her.

As she drove, she wondered what the guards wanted. It was too soon to return the money to her surely, they would not have had much time to look for the owner. She parked the car and went to the desk and said who she was. Immediately she was escorted into an office, the door of which was marked Superintendent.

The Superintendent thanked her for coming in so promptly, as he shook her hand and introduced himself as John. She was offered a chair and then the door opened, and another man came in. This man she knew but could not remember his name.

She frowned in concentration until he came over and shook her hand.

'Aidan Savage, Mavis, you remember we met at the O'Neill house.'

'Oh yes! I remember you now. That was a sad day.'

'Indeed, it was. Now you must be wondering why we've asked you to come in?'

Mavis nodded, feeling a little nervous, although why she should feel like that, she could not understand.

It was good that she was sitting, as his story unfolded. She listened, shocked at the revelations that were coming out of his mouth. He told her that the money which she had dug up, had young Bill O'Neill's fingerprints and others, and Bill's DNA all over both rolls of money. Also, there was heavy contamination on the money, involving cocaine. They wanted to come and see where exactly the money was found and examine the area for any remaining forensic evidence.

She was then asked if she could think of any reason why the money would be buried on her property? She looked at them blankly and shook her head. They asked if they could come up today or would that inconvenience her? Again, she shook her head. She was unable to think at all. Bill's murder had something to do with the money in her tunnel. It was unbelievable. When she stood up to leave, she remembered the night prowler. Turning to the two detectives she said, 'Months ago, you know, I heard something one night and saw a figure emerging from my tunnel. He walked down the drive and onto the road. I thought it odd at the time, but nothing was stolen. Then another night I heard the door of the tunnel again, as the hinge squeaks a bit, but this time I didn't pay any attention. I was not going to go out and investigate in the middle of the night, was I?'

The two men looked at each other. 'You are sure you saw a figure? Could you describe the figure or was it dark?'

Mavis thought for a while. 'I think there was a moon, though I can't be sure. I felt that it was a male figure, in a dark jacket with a hood, the sort all these boys wear nowadays. He was in no hurry but was sort of hunched over going down the drive, as though maybe carrying something heavy, but I can't be sure now, it was ages ago.'

The men were very grateful for the information, Mavis felt relieved that she had remembered that, and she was glad to be able to do something to help them. Nobody had been apprehended for the murder yet and the village people were still in shock about it.

When they reached Ravenswood, Mavis went in and put on the kettle. Maureen's eyes widened when she saw the police car in the drive.

'What on earth have you done now?' she asked, making Mavis feel as though she had been caught shoplifting. Mavis muttered under her breath and went out into the garden where the two men were now heading up to the tunnel. Maureen made to follow, with her umbrella until Mavis turned around and told her to stay and make tea for the men. Maureen paused at the note of authority in her voice and did what she was told. She was one hundred percent certain that Mavis had broken the law somehow and was in dire trouble.

The men were in the tunnel looking about when Mavis went in and joined them. She showed them where she had found the money and said that the other beds had plants growing in them and had been untouched by the intruder, she was sure. The other two beds, she explained had been covered with newspaper and pieces of cardboard to keep down the weeks until she needed them.

'I know exactly what you mean, Mavis. My wife loves growing vegetables, and we have a small plot, and she covers the beds the same way, until they are needed', Aidan offered.

Mavis was grateful for that information as she thought she might come across as a bit of an eccentric.

'Now Mavis,' said the senior of the two men, 'would it upset you awfully if we requested that we dig up these same two beds, and scan the soil for any further signs of drugs for forensics?'

Mavis face dropped. Her courgettes were just beginning to fruit and her tomatoes beginning to flower. Detective Savage saw her pain and suggested that she could lift the tomatoes and carefully put them in big pots until they got the 'all clear' and possibly too, the courgettes. She looked at the tomatoes and thought that it would be possible to do that without damaging them. She smiled at the men and told them to go ahead and do what they had to. She would repot everything that she could.

'After all,' she said, 'getting to the bottom of poor Bill's death is more important than a few vegetables.'

They nodded their agreement and retraced their steps. They declined tea and said that they would let her know when to expect the forensic team, who were coming from Dublin. The rain had stopped as they got into their car and departed. Mavis went straight up to the tunnel and repotted her tomatoes and gently dug around the courgette plants and carefully lifted and put them in the largest pots she had. She did not hear Maureen come in and she made Mavis jump when she came up behind her and touched her on the shoulder.

'What on earth are you doing now, you crazy woman? Are the guards coming back for you or what? Why were they up here, Mavis? I bet you've been growing cannabis!'

Mavis sighed and said, 'I have done nothing wrong, Maureen, I just happened to dig up some money here a while ago and we thought the guards should have it. It was probably stolen.'

Maureen looked at her incredulously. 'You just happened to dig up some money? Here, in your tunnel?'

Mavis knew that she was not believed but didn't care at that moment. She picked some radishes that were in the same bed as the tomatoes. She may as well eat them now, they would not transplant, she thought.

'So, Mavis, how much money did you dig up or were they gold coins, you found, perhaps?' She laughed at the idea.

'No Maureen, not gold coins, there was over two thousand euros in the first bag and just under two thousand in the second bag.' She straightened up and left the tunnel, leaving Maureen staring at her with her mouth open.

'Now I've heard it all,' she muttered to herself.

Later that evening, Maureen took Rosemary aside after dinner and whispered, 'I must speak with you, later in my room.'

The girl had no idea what her aunt could wish to say privately and hoped it was nothing to do with her moving in on a more permanent basis. It did not seem to bother Maureen that she now usually made her own dinner. They would have to think of something else to make her wish to move back to Cork.

Her mother was preoccupied, Rosemary could see that, and they could not talk freely as Maureen followed them everywhere and listened to any comment that Mavis made.

Later at eleven o'clock, Rosemary learned all about the visit from the guards and Maureen's firm belief that Mavis had broken the law in some way.

'If she thinks for a moment that I believe that story of hers, about digging up money, she is mistaken. I did not come down in the last shower.'

'But it's true, I was there and helped her count the money.'

'Did you actually see her dig it up though?'

Rosemary shook her head, 'It was all on the table when I got home, and Mum was shocked. I suggested that she should dig a bit more the next day and see if she could find anymore, but that was more in a joke, you understand? I believed my Mum.'

'And she did find more, did she?' Maureen smiled at her niece sarcastically.

'She did actually, another plastic bag. She counted the money and decided to go to the guards. It was obviously stolen.'

'Did you see your mother unearth this second bag of money, or was it just there, when you arrived home?'

'No, I was not there when she found it, I was at work. But we are both convinced that it was stolen, because some months before, Mum saw a prowler coming out of the tunnel in the middle of the night. She heard him again some nights later.'

'She informed the police, did she?'

Rosemary shook her head, 'Well there was nothing moved or stolen as far as we could tell, Maureen, so why would we bother the guards? What could they do when there was nothing stolen?'

'Hmm! I have my own theories about all this unearthed money; it's too suspicious by far, Rosemary. Something is not right, it smells 'off', if you ask me.

Maureen was ready to launch into what those theories were, but Rosemary was tired and told her that she had told her all she knew and was now going to bed. She had work in the morning and as it was the last week of school, there was a lot of preparation for the new school year ahead.

Maureen was peeved to be cut off mid-stream but there was nothing she could do. She sat and thought about it while inwardly fuming. Then she had an idea. She looked up a number on her mobile phone and rang it. As soon as Frank picked up, she announced that she thought he should come down as soon as possible as something was very wrong at Ravenswood.

He sounded both annoyed and angry at getting a phone call from his aunt and tried to explain how busy his life was at present. He would come down as soon as he was free.

Maureen would have none of it.

'Frank, it concerns your inheritance, I think Mavis has finally crossed the last frontier as regards her sanity. Lord knows what will happen if you don't intervene while there is still time. This is terribly serious, I mean it.'

Frank was alarmed at the word, inheritance, enough to tell his aunt that he would be down on Saturday next as he hoped he would be free. Maureen felt relief and satisfaction for once. She would get to the bottom of all this. The children would thank her when they realised how she had saved their inheritance. She then retired to bed, satisfied.

Chapter 22

Rosemary was excited at the prospects of going on holidays. It was the build-up to holidays, that was so thrilling; the packing, getting to the airport, the sudden panic of whether she had her passport or flight tickets, the childish excitement of her three friends. It all added to the good feeling of getting away, off on a big adventure. Her only regret was leaving her mother with Maureen over the weekend. They were certain that Maureen was bored out of her mind. She spent the day on her laptop, looking at properties for sale in Cork and Dublin.

On Friday, she had her last line dancing for a couple of weeks. She met James at the salad bar, after a quick swim. They chatted animatedly and James asked her if she would come away with him, for a weekend or a couple of days before school began in September. She was delighted and agreed. September was months away yet and she knew that she would like to spend time alone with James, away from the usual local scenes and mutual friends. She asked him to choose somewhere to go and keep it as a surprise.

She left James to go and do her last-minute packing and checking her list. As she left her bedroom, bringing down her suitcase to the hall, to have everything ready for the early start in the morning, her mobile rang. It was Susie, in a bit of a state. Her dog, Charlie, was supposed to be looked after by a friend until she returned from Italy. Now the friend could not oblige, she had to travel to visit a sick relative. Her own mother was also away. Susie was beside herself with panic. It was too late to organise a kennel, they had to be on the road for the airport at seven.

Rosemary thought quickly and told Susie to hold for a minute. She made her way to the sitting room where her mother was and made her request. Mavis did not hesitate for a moment.

'Of course, I'll take the dog. That's not a problem. Tell her to bring the dog when she calls for you in the morning.' Mavis liked dogs and there had been dogs at Ravenswood when the children were small.

Susie was thrilled that her problem was sorted so quickly and so grateful. The dog was old and was no trouble at all.

The next morning Mavis and Rosemary got up at six o'clock and had breakfast together. There was no movement from Maureen's room and Rosemary was glad. When Susie arrived at six thirty, Charlie was introduced to Mavis and all his food and bedding brought in. Rosemary suggested that he could sleep in the utility room. The old Labrador padded around gently exploring his new residence. Mavis opened the kitchen door, and he went eagerly out into the garden to size things up. The girls left after much hugging and Mavis exhorting them to be careful in their travels and enjoy themselves. Rosemary promised that she would text or email when they arrived in Bari.

When they had disappeared down the driveway, Mavis suddenly thought that she would enjoy having a dog to look after. She went out to the garden and the dog followed her up to the tunnel. She had both doors open these warm days. She looked sadly at the tomatoes in their pots. They seemed to be still alive, and she watered them with the seaweed mix from the troughs. The courgettes looked a bit wilted. She sighed and thought it would be the first year she did not have courgettes.

At noon, two men arrived from Dublin as they had pre-warned Mavis. They took a lot of equipment out of the car and brought it up to the tunnel and then dressed themselves in white protective suits. Maureen stood watching them from a distance.

Mavis had gone out earlier with the dog on a lead. She would have a nice long walk and not think about what was happening in her tunnel. She did not believe they would find any more money. How could they think there were drugs there as well? Just because traces had been found on the money, she thought. But the money was well insulated from the soil, so she did not expect them to be long at their job. She took a side road after Sadie's house, instead of going down through the village. The road was narrow and always quiet, and Charlie padded along, pausing to smell the wall and posts along the way. He had taken to her straight away and Mavis marvelled at the friendliness and trust of animals. She began to think about getting another dog for company. She would consult Rosemary when she returned.

On the way back, she went into Sadie's and found her sitting in the garden in her usual place. She was pleased to see a visitor, although Mavis felt she did not recognise her and introduced herself as she always did.

'Hello Sadie, Mavis here, this time with a dog. This is Charlie, Sadie. I am looking after him for one of Rosemary's pals. They all went off to Italy this morning on holidays.'

Sadie put out her hand to pat Charlie who stood before her panting and with his tongue out.

'Hello, you lovely dog,' said Sadie stroking him. 'I think you are thirsty boy, aren't you?' She looked at Mavis, 'He needs a drink of water.'

Mavis went and got a bowl from the kitchen where the carer, Lily, was washing up. Sadie was right, Charlie gulped down the water and licked the bowl. Mavis had not realised the dog was thirsty, but Sadie had. Lily came out and asked Mavis if she would like a cup of tea. Mavis would have loved one, but looking at her watch, saw that it was after one. Time for lunch, she thought. She was also sure the forensic people would have left and maybe she could replant her tomatoes. She told Lily that she had better go home and explained to Sadie that her sister-in-law, Maureen was staying with her for a few days.

'I remember her, that Maureen. She was a right bossy-boots, so she was. Is she still like that?'

Mavis was surprised that Sadie could still describe exactly how Maureen was.

'Yes, Sadie, you could say that she has not changed much over the years.'

'People like that never change. She gave her brother a hard time of it, didn't she?'

Mavis did not know what to say to that. She had not been aware of Dennis being bossed around by her.

'Yes, and she gave his wife a hard time too,' Sadie continued frowning. 'I suppose she always wanted to continue living there and couldn't, with a family coming along.'

Mavis knew nothing about this, even though Sylvia and she were close. 'Ah well, I suppose when she got married, she had to move away, Sadie.'

Sadie snorted and said, 'She only married to spite her husband's mother, who hated her and didn't want her son to marry her, sure, she never loved the poor lad, we all knew that.'

Again, Mavis was astounded at Sadie's memory, how did she remember all that? As she walked home with Charlie, she mused on the vagaries of dementia.

,

Maureen tried to get as close as she could to see what the men were doing. They had closed the doors of the tunnel which was annoying. They seemed to be sifting through soil and were taking samples in plastic bags. She would have liked to question them, but they did not seem to want to engage with her. After an hour hovering around the tunnel, she left in disgust and went back to study the housing market on her laptop.

Mavis was disappointed to find her tunnel still occupied when she walked back from Sadie's. Charlie seemed tired out after the long walk and immediately plopped down on the patio and slept. She ate lunch with Maureen who moaned about people who took over your space with no explanations of what they were doing. Deep in her heart she did not believe her sister-in-law's story of digging up money. Why were the police taking this seriously, and wasting taxpayer's money?

She wondered when her nephew would arrive and hoped he was not going to pull out of their meeting. There were other matters she wished to find out from him, regarding the housing market, which to her, did not seem to be in danger of diving to rock bottom, as he had said. She regretted selling her house so readily. If she had waited a bit longer, she could have been a few thousand richer. The more she brooded on the matter, the madder she became and felt short changed.

At three o'clock, Frank arrived in the old car which now seemed to be his main transport. Maureen wondered how he could have settled for that, after the swish car he previously had. She was relieved and happy to see him. He came into the house with a frown on his face. He wanted to know whose car was there, besides the two women's and Maureen's. Maureen beckoned him into the sitting room and put her finger on her lips. Mavis was in the kitchen and the two came down and sat down to coffee which Mavis had made as soon as she saw the car arriving.

Frank then caught sight of the two men emerging from the tunnel, still in their white suits. He got agitated and asked Mavis, what on earth had she been up to? Mavis sighed and starting at the beginning, told Frank about digging up the money in the tunnel. He was visibly agitated then. 'Why, in the name of all that's holy, did you involve the police in this?'

Mavis looked at him and asked, 'Surely that's obvious? It was not mine. I didn't put it there. Besides, the police have found Billy O'Brian's fingerprints and DNA on the money and traces of cocaine.'

Maureen was startled by this revelation. 'You never mentioned that to me, Mavis. How could this be connected to that lad who was found murdered? You are not making sense.'

'I'm not making any sense of it either, it's what the guards told me, and those two up there are from forensics, that's all I know. It looks like they are finished now, thank heaven.'

They all looked up at the tunnel. The men were now moving towards some flower beds and taking samples again, at least, that is what it looked like. They were moving further down the garden and checking under shrubs and roses alike and inserting some sort of probes into the soil.

'For the love of God, do they have nothing better to do?' fumed Maureen, 'What could they be looking for in the rose beds?'

Frank made no comment. He rose from the table and went out to the garden, nearly tripping over Charlie, as he did not see the dog. He strode up the garden and the women could see him gesticulating to the men and waving his hands about. One of the men stood listening to him and obviously he made a comment to Frank and bent down again. Frank turned on his heel and strode back down the garden path again, his face dark with anger.

'The absolute cheek of them! No explanations given, even though they know this is my home. I told them that I would be taking the matter further and they would be hearing from me'.

He was so irate that Mavis was curious. It was not such an intrusion surely if there was a connection to a murder victim. As she looked at her son, she saw something else besides anger, was it fear?

Later that night after a silent dinner. Maureen again broached the matter of money being found in the tunnel. Mavis sighed. She was sick and tired of the whole business and wanted a bit of peace and quiet now.

'Are you sure that you didn't put the money there Mavis? You know, some people like to squirrel away a bit of cash for security and sometimes they forget where they put it. I have heard of some old people who don't trust banks and they hide small amounts, here and there in their houses.'

Mavis looked at her as witheringly as she could. 'The two amounts were not exactly 'small amounts' in my estimation, Maureen. I would never keep that much money anywhere in the house, or in my tunnel, come to that.'

Frank asked quietly how much money was involved and when told the amount he visibly paled.

Maureen fearing that the subject was slipping away from her grasp, then turned her attention to Frank and asked him when he thought the bottom was going to fall out of the market.

'How on earth do you expect me to predict that Maureen, what am I now, a soothsayer or something?'

Maureen was quite still for a moment. She was in shock. This was a different nephew to the one who was so exuberant about the property market months ago.

'But I sold my house already, Frank and now it's gone up quite a bit in price, not down, like you told me.' Maureen's voice was quivering slightly and now Mavis felt sorry for the woman.

'Well, I didn't tell you to go and do that, you can't blame me. The market is going to drop, that's all I can tell you. That's all I was told, and I've sold my apartment, but it has not gone up in price. It's still the same. It's a waiting game, Maureen. Like all investments, you don't go into it unless you can take a hit.' Frank did not look at his aunt, in fact, he seemed preoccupied with other things.

Maureen paled and went very silent, which was a first for her. What did Frank mean, to take a hit? She could not afford to take a hit. She had invested her money with him, having been told it was a fail-proof investment. She felt rather nauseous and left the room and went upstairs to her room.

Chapter 23

Frank had already left when Mavis got up the next morning. Could he not have said goodbye to his mother, she asked herself sadly? Where are her beautiful boy gone? She felt bereft, especially as Rosemary was gone on holidays and there was nobody to talk to about her life. She could never talk openly to Maureen, there was only coldness there, not closeness. How she would love to be able to chat with Dennis. She would go to church later, there was no choir until September. She decided to take Charlie for a stroll up to the wood.

Charlie was quite at home and slept in the kitchen not the utility. His bed was under the window and he was awake and looking out the window when she entered the kitchen. He went outside with enthusiasm as she had her cup of tea. She would cook the 'full Irish' breakfast when she had her walk and hoped that Maureen might be getting lonely for Cork. She walked up the path to the tunnel first and looked inside. She was relieved to see that it was only two beds that had been dug up. Not too much damage, she thought. I will replant my tomatoes later and they should be fine. The onions and garlic she had lifted early in June were now dried out she thought. She could now store them.

She led the way to the wood and then the dog took off, scampering ahead and investigating every strange smell he found. She could hear the ravens, rooks or crows, whatever they were, making an almighty commotion. It was a discordant sound, but one she had gradually grown used to. She was soon sitting on the bench she had shared so often with Dennis, the sunlight dappling the floor around her and a slight breeze shimmering the leaves. Charlie had disappeared but she was not worried. He would find his way back.

She sat and closed her eyes and breathed deeply, in and out, in and out. It was calming and she certainly needed calming. Suddenly the image of the night prowler returned, and she knew in her heart that it had been Billy O'Brian who had been in her tunnel. Why? Her mind had no answer to that, but she felt unhinged that her property, and Billy, might be connected. She opened her eyes and they seemed unfocused, as though she had left her reading glasses on and was looking into the distance. Then that 'feeling' came, that strangeness that came occasionally. She looked around her and did not recognise where she was. The wood was gone. It was all open; the area looked so different without trees. Then she saw houses coming gradually into focus, lots of them. Where was she? She looked around in alarm and stood up, panic rising in her chest. Then the image receded, and the trees were back again, and all was the same as it had been before. She stood uncertainly and looked around her.

Was she really here in the wood, or was she dreaming in bed? No, she was here beside the bench and there was Charlie, wagging his tail and looking up at her. Turning, she led the way back to the house, feeling a bit perturbed and disoriented.

Maureen was in the kitchen grilling the bacon and sausages when she returned. 'Goodness, you were out early, weren't you? I suppose having a dog to care for, makes for a bit more work, eh?'

'Yes, you have to walk dogs certainly, but I need exercise anyway, so it's good.' Mavis washed her hands at the sink and put out a bowl of water for the dog on the patio. She felt she should comment on the previous evening's revelations.

'Maureen, I am sorry that you sold your house too early, maybe, but surely with what you got for it, you will find something suitable soon. You mustn't worry about things.'

Maureen turned to her sister-in-law and replied bitterly, 'Yes no doubt I would find something suitable with the money I got for my house, but the trouble is, I invested all of it with your son.'

Mavis looked at her in horror. 'What exactly did you invest your money in, Maureen?'

'How do I know what the investment is? Frank told me it was fail-proof and what fools he thought his mother and sister were, for not doing the same thing.'

Mavis sat at the table. 'So, you are telling me you don't know what you invested in? But you surely have some paperwork or documents specifying what the investment is and what the return should be?'

Maureen pursed her lips together and said, 'No, I have nothing, I trusted Frank implicitly.'

Mavis ran her fingers through her hair distractedly. 'I cannot believe you are that naïve Maureen. Nobody invests without documented proof and with an accredited broker.'

'Well, he's your son and my nephew, and I trusted him. I still do. I'm sure it will all be fine. It just takes time, and I didn't realise that. He should have told me it would take time and advised me not to sell the house. He was darn quick to take my money though.'

Breakfast was a silent meal and Mavis had trouble taking this news in. What had Frank invested in and was Maureen's money safe? What if it wasn't? This did not bear thinking about.

'Is he still in bed?' Maureen asked. 'Possibly we can have another chat and I can find out what exactly the investment is in.'

Mavis looked at Maureen, 'He was gone when I got up. I didn't hear him go, but it must have been early. You must find out as soon as possible about your money, Maureen. You need to know where it is invested in case you find a house soon. You need to be able to access your money. Why on earth did you not bank it?'

'Because as I told you already, Frank had a fantastic investment all lined up, are you stupid or what?'

Mavis did not reply as to who was stupid but got up and dressed herself and went to church. No point in asking Maureen if she wanted to come. She didn't believe in 'that sort of thing' and thought 'religion was for peasants'. Mavis often wondered where you would find peasants in this day, and age?

At church she prayed as she never prayed before; that Maureen would go back to her apartment; that her money would be returned to her, intact; that Frank would be sorted out and would not be involved in bad investments. At the end of Mass, she stayed in her seat with her eyes closed trying to still the chaos in her mind.

She felt a hand on her shoulder and looked up. There was her old friend John O'Dea. She smiled up at the kind old face gazing down at her. She got up and hugged the man who was part of her life with Dennis.

'How are you my friend,' he enquired.

There was something in John O'Dea that brought forth anything that might be bothering you and she immediately said, 'Oh John, not in a good place, I think.'

He took her arm and said, 'Come on, let's go baby, as Marlon Brando would say. We're off for a coffee, no ifs or buts.'

They went to the new hotel where the salad bar was and found a little table for two in the lounge, which was quiet at this time on a Sunday morning. There, Mavis spilled all her worries out, unconnected as they seemed. John did nothing but listen, nodding occasionally. They each had two coffees and still she had not come to the end of her story. Maureen was her biggest concern and her investment. She also told him about their trip to Dublin and finding the strange arrangement with the dealership and the 'partnership' with Paul Kavanagh.

'Am I worrying over nothing John, or do you think that Frank is in trouble?'

John hesitated for a moment. 'I think you have reason to be worried about Frank. He may be in financial difficulty for all we know. The partnership sounds like a strange set-up, and you say it is to be annulled once this deal is through?'

She nodded her head, 'That's what he says.'

'If he is bankrupt, Mavis, that is not your problem. He is a grown man and must make his own decisions, and he has, by the sound of it. As for your sister-in-law, I can only say, what a stupid and greedy woman, and you are not responsible for any of it. Try and step back from all this Mavis. You are what age? Seventy?'

She nodded and laughed. 'They think I am going senile too, John. I look at them and wonder where common sense has gone.'

'Who thinks you are going senile, Mavis?'

'Well, I've done a couple of stupid things recently and Maureen thinks I should see a doctor and I think Frank agrees with her. Rosemary doesn't think it, I'm sure.'

She told John about the trip to Dublin instead of Cork and they laughed about it. Then she told him about the tap left on and the flooded utility room. He stopped her there and asked her if she knew how many people did that sort of thing? Hundreds, he said, and they were not all even fifty. She agreed with that and said it was the sort of mishap many people had, their minds being on other things.

'That's it, Mavis, their minds are on other things. It's the one problem we all have these days. There are so many things on our minds that it requires a special effort to live in the present and watch what we are doing.'

She left John in a better frame of mind. She felt quietly joyous and uplifted. She would live in the present and watch everything she did. She would keep her diary more up to date and would concentrate on whatever job it was she was doing. She felt invigorated.

Rosemary had texted her twice since she left, and she was relaxed about her being away. She would not worry her daughter, about the latest development with Maureen and Frank. She drove home on a high and suggested that Maureen and herself treat

,

themselves to lunch at the gardening centre, which did an excellent Sunday lunch. Maureen agreed without complaint.

Chapter 24

The detective was back to Ravenswood twice during the week; once with the forensic men and the second time alone. The one called Aidan Savage, came into the kitchen and spoke with Mavis. He accepted a cup of tea and they went outside and sat down on a bench. He explained the dilemma they now found themselves in. Mavis looked at him curiously and waited. It seemed that drugs had been found both in the tunnel and around the grounds, in the rose beds and under shrubs. The men were puzzled by the findings. There were even strong traces of drugs in the water troughs. He looked at Mavis with his raised eyebrows. As he stirred his tea, he mused out loud; 'I mean, why would anyone in the drug business spread the drugs around the garden? A bit of a waste of money, don't you think?'

Mavis nodded in agreement. 'Absolutely! Madness! The only thing I spread around my garden is fertiliser.' She stopped and put down her teacup. 'Do you know something, I spread fertiliser not so long ago, before summer. Some of it was stored in the tunnel…. I think.' She searched her memory of the stuff she had spread. It had to be fertiliser, what else would she spread?

The detective looked at Mavis and saw a worried looking elderly woman. 'Is there any way you could have confused the fertiliser with something else Mavis?'

She looked at him worriedly, 'Aidan, I don't know. The stuff I found under a pot was what I believed was potato manure and I emptied it into one of my troughs, with my seaweed water. What would the drugs have looked like?'

'Well, generally, powder, depending on what type of drug it was. The lab reports say the main drug was cocaine. That's a white powder.'

Mavis paled and felt her breathing become rapid. 'I could have used it by mistake, Aidan, will it kill all my plants?'

He laughed and confessed he did not know. 'Might put them into fast-grow mode Mavis, you might have a bumper rose crop.' He finished his tea and stood up. 'We need to find out how the drugs got into your tunnel Mavis, that is the big mystery.'

Mavis nodded. 'What about the night prowler. You know, I feel in my heart that the intruder was poor Billy O'Brian, I don't know why, since I have never met him.'

Aidan took out his notebook and said, 'Mavis, I need to have the names of all the people that have been in your house recently.'

Mavis sighed. 'Well I have the choir every Monday night for an hour but that stopped in June, for the summer break, I will write you out a list of their names; then there is James Egan, a mature pupil who comes on Wednesday afternoon, he's from the town; my sister-in-law, Maureen has been here quite a lot but she is sixty six and not into drink or drugs, although both might improve her outlook on life; John-Joe who does occasional gardening; and the other three are myself, Frank, my son and Rosemary my daughter who is a teacher in Greenways. That's the lot, Aidan.'

He returned his notebook to his pocket. 'Your son Frank, what exactly does he do for a living?'

Mavis swallowed and told him about the garage and car dealership left to him by Dennis.

On her return to the house, Maureen who had been watching from her bedroom window, wanted to know all about the tunnel business and asked if any more money had been found? When Mavis reported about all the evidence of drugs being found in the garden and tunnel, the woman was flabbergasted.

'You mean you were busy spreading drugs around your garden and digging up money too? Mavis, I mean for a seventy-year-old, you lead a hectic life. You really do need to see a doctor if you're doing that sort of thing.' She looked disapprovingly at her sister-in-law.

'On the other hand, Maureen, most people hearing that, will think I need locking up, wouldn't you say? Except for the money part, they might envy me that.'

When Frank returned unexpectedly that afternoon, Maureen could hardly wait to tell him what his mother had been up to. She did so in the kitchen. Mavis had brought Charlie for a long walk. She needed to clear her head and get away from Maureen. On her walk her mobile pinged and it was a text from Jenny, wondering how her mother was and if Mavis was coping alright. The girl felt very guilty about the way things had turned out. Mavis stopped in the park and found a bench to sit on. She rang Jenny and explained about the 'hectic life' she was leading. Jenny listened without interrupting. When Mavis paused for breath, she said that she would tell her mother to come up and stay.

'What about the lodger, what will you do with him?' Mavis wanted to know.

'He'll have gone home for a holiday and the room is vacant for a couple of weeks. It's the least I can do, you have suffered enough Mavis. I will tidy up the 'Eastern European's' clothes and the place will be shipshape again. You should have seen her face when she came out of the bathroom Mavis. It was a brilliant idea and I love you for it. It's given me a huge breathing space and now you need one.'

Mavis did not object for once. She did need a break. There was too much going on. She wished Rosemary were there, but she was not due for another week. She hoped that Maureen would take Jenny up on her offer and leave her house, she desperately needed silence about her to think. When she reached home, she was disappointed to see

Frank's old banger parked around the side of the house. When she went down to the kitchen, she could see from his face that his aunt had given all the latest news.

'Hello Mum, I hear that you have been having exciting times here in this neck of the woods.' He looked white and pinched looking and though his voice was quiet, she knew that meant he was very angry.

'If you have already been told all about it, then there is no need for me to add anything, is there, Frank?' Mavis walked over and filled up the kettle for a cup of tea. Maureen sat silently at the table, watching her. She willed herself to stay calm and cool.

'What are you doing home in the middle of the week so early. Is work that slack?'

She stood at the worktop looking at the two, her arms folded. She looked out the window and saw Charlie at the door, his tail wagging. She poured him a bowl of water and brought it out to the patio. She went back in and poured herself a cup of tea. The two were drinking theirs and she didn't offer them a top up.

Frank had not answered her question about work. He asked if the guards had finished their job there or if they were going to come and dig up the entire garden? Mavis could not answer that.

She shrugged her shoulders and said, 'I don't know Frank, but you do realise that they are investigating the murder of young Billy O'Brian and his prints were found on the rolls of money. He deserves justice, don't you think?'

'Hmm, he was nothing but a common little drug dealer and criminal and probably deserves what he got. They are all attached to criminal gangs, monsters, all of them.' Maureen finished her tea and got up to put her cup in the sink. She turned and looked at Frank and nodded her head sharply.

Frank coughed and started speaking. 'I was wondering Mother, where are the deeds to this house.' He smiled slightly and spread his hands. 'I'm just worried that you have them in a safe place and might forget where they are,' again he laughed lightly.

Mavis looked at him and then at Maureen. 'You have no need to worry Frank. I would never keep them in the house. They are in a safe place.'

Frank persisted, 'But if anything were to happen to you, how would we know where to find them, Mum. These are important matters especially when you get on in years.'

Mavis washed her cup and dried her hands on the towel. 'Have you not heard of solicitors, Frank? They are the ones who look after one's affairs, usually. Don't you have a solicitor for all your business Frank; the deeds for the garage, your various properties etcetera?' She left the kitchen and went upstairs to her bedroom. She locked the door, took off her shoes and lay down on her bed. The breeze wafting in from her open window caressed her face and she closed her eyes and dozed.

When she woke an hour later, she could hear the telephone ringing but stayed where she was. It rang out after a while. She wondered why neither Maureen nor Frank answered it. She lay still and savoured the peacefulness of her bedroom. After another hour relaxing, she got up and went down to see about food for the dinner. She put a chicken in the oven and went out to pick some fresh vegetables. Frank's car was still there but Maureen's was gone. She dug up some of her potatoes and picked some salad stuff from her tunnel. The tomatoes would not be ready for weeks after their traumatic handling.

She was disappointed when she saw Maureen's car come up the drive and park beside Frank's. She then remembered Jenny's chat in the park, on her mobile. Had she rung her mother yet, she wondered? Frank and Maureen came in together and Maureen went upstairs. Frank came into the kitchen and put two bottles of wine on the worktop.

'There you are, Mum. I hope I did not upset you earlier talking about the deeds to the house, did I?'

Of course, he did, but Mavis was not going to let him see that.

217

'Not a bit of it, Frank, why should I be upset? I suppose it was curiosity. All children are curious. And you must not worry your head about me. They are safe and sound. I have made out an Enduring Power of Attorney you know? Just in case anything should happen to incapacitate me.'

He turned eagerly to her, 'Well thought of Mum, that's very sensible. Who is to be the executor, a family member I expect?'

'Yes Frank, I have made Rosemary my executor. She knows me and lives with me, so all is well. If I become feeble-minded and unable to make decisions, Rosemary will do so on my behalf. So, you mustn't worry about me, son.'

She looked at her son and did not see relief on his face. His frown told her that it was unexpected news and not at all welcome.

'Well Ma, I am the eldest, surely it should be me?'

'No Frank, you live a distance away and as I said, Rosemary knows me best, as a woman.'

During dinner, which was a trifle strained, Maureen offered the news that her daughter needed her in Dublin for a couple of weeks and that she would be leaving in the morning. Mavis asked about the lodger, whether he was no longer there or was she going to use the sofa? Maureen replied that he was abroad and that she was going to use the time to talk to her daughter about having strange men staying in the house. She would make her see sense. In fact, she just might give up the lease on the apartment, which after all, was quite expensive and stay in Dublin until her investment materialised. She looked at her nephew while saying this.

Frank turned to his aunt and told her that she might have to wait a while longer.

'How much longer, exactly, Frank. I am finding things difficult enough now. I can't wait any longer.' She looked expectantly at him.

Frank gave his nervous cough again and Mavis wondered what else was about to happen. She had a feeling that there was something happening here that had already been rehearsed.

'Mother, I was wondering. Could you possibly give Maureen the money she's invested and when the deal is done you will have the money back with interest?'

Mavis paused eating and put her fork down. So, this was the plan, was it?

'Such a lovely idea, Frank.' She sighed, 'It's out of the question, I'm afraid.' She continued eating.

The two exchanged looks. Maureen chimed in sweetly, 'It won't be for long Mavis, Frank says it should all be finalised in a few months at most.'

'Oh, so you know how long it's going to take? I thought you were just asking Frank when it was, as though you did not know?'

'

Frank poured more wine for them all. 'It's really not a big problem, Mum. You are assured of a great return, although Maureen here will not be getting any interest, only the capital she invested. You'll be the winner Mum.' He smiled at his mother and lifted his glass to her.

'I don't think either of you understand. I cannot lend you money that I don't have. I simply do not have that sort of money.' She sipped her wine and then continued eating.

The two people sitting at the table with her, looked at her in disbelief.

'You must have savings and investments, Mum. You don't spend much. You must have something you can cash in.'

Mavis smiled at them apologetically. 'Nope, no investments, no savings. There is only this house and property.'

Chapter 25

The atmosphere was frigid after her announcement. Maureen continued to stare at her, and Frank quickly drank two glasses wine. After some time had passed, Maureen put down her fork and cleared her throat.

'That's all very well Mavis, but Frank is your son and it's your duty to help him out here. He is the eldest and if Dennis were here, he would be more than willing to help me out. I am his sister, and he would never see me out of pocket. You won't be out of pocket either, when the investment matures. I'm the one that will be out of pocket, the amazing interest promised will be sadly lacking. I can only hope to be able to buy a house similar, to the one I sold.'

Mavis paused as she sipped her wine. 'How do you propose I help him out? I've told you there is no cash left.'

Frank turned to his mother, 'We are asset rich Mum, you could easily sell one of the fields above.'

'You forget that there is only one access to those fields, the driveway to the house.'

Maureen piped in, 'You can always apply for permission to make another roadway up.'

'How long would that take, do you think, Maureen?' Mavis asked her.

'You could always borrow money on the strength of the house and land, Mavis, don't be so dim.'

Maureen shook her head at her sister-in-law's lack of knowledge.

'Well, I do not want to go down that path yet, Maureen. I did not invest in any shady deals.'

Frank blustered, 'Not shady Mum, a supergreat opportunity for the daring.'

'I don't think your aunt would be so daring now, would you, Maureen?'

Maureen tossed her head and repeated her demand. 'You are his mother, and you have a responsibility and an obligation; I want my money now.'

Frank again interjected, 'I am sure that you could raise a small loan with the house or even just the land as collateral.'

'A small loan? How will I repay the small loan? Out of my pension? Anyway, we are not talking of a small loan here, are we. What did you invest with Frank, Maureen?'

Maureen said shortly, 'I invested the five hundred thousand from the house and one hundred thousand in savings. And got some friends to do the same.'

Mavis looked in horror at Frank. 'What on earth is this investment in, Frank, a gold mine?'

Frank, for once looked uncomfortable. 'I know you don't really understand, but my friend Paul has a lot of important and influential connections and they simply cannot be wrong. Just because the crash has not come exactly six months as predicted, means nothing. It is coming, believe me.'

'Mavis, it is your son we are talking about. He is your responsibility. You brought him up, after all, insisting on that expensive private education.

Mavis looked at her with her mouth open. 'Really, Maureen? I think it was more your father and brother's idea.'

Frank swallowed his wine and stood up. He was angry with both the women.

'Shut up, both of you. I am not stupid, and I am entitled to one third of this house and property, don't forget that. I know my rights; I have already seen a solicitor about my rights. So, I can insist that you sell Ma, and divide up the loot between the three of us.' He was very red in the face and ran his hands through his hair distractedly. 'I didn't want to get nasty and demand my due, but you have been obstructive Mum and now I am putting my foot down.'

Mavis sipped her wine, deep in thought.

Maureen smiled up at Frank, 'You are right Frank, you do have rights to the house and the property. Well done on getting in touch with a solicitor.' She smiled triumphantly at Mavis. 'You don't have a choice, Mavis dear. You will have to put the whole estate on the market and no delays please.'

'I don't think so, Maureen.' Mavis shook her head.

Maureen turned to her nephew in exasperation. 'Frank, at the end of the day, she is not even your real mother, just a stepmother, a nobody. She should have no rights at all. She did not inherit this place. It was in the Joyce family for more than a hundred years, I'm sure.'

Frank swallowed and nodded his head in agreement with Maureen. 'I know that, she was Dad's second wife.'

'Which solicitor have you seen, Frank? Was it your father's old solicitor?' Mavis asked.

'It was indeed. They have looked after the Joyce affairs for a very long time. The son is now head of the company.'

'While you were there, did you ask about the deeds of the house, Frank?'

'Actually, I did, he told me they don't have them, and we need to have them for the solicitor to view.'

Mavis leaned her elbows on the table. 'You better sit down, Frank. I have a story to tell you that I never intended to tell you, but you may as well know now.'

Mavis took a deep breath and started. She had the attention now of the aunt and nephew. She explained how her dear departed husband had always been impetuous and daring but always managed to land on his feet. All his investments and ventures had paid off and his friends had also benefited. However, six months before he died, his latest gamble fell flat and he lost an awful lot of money, millions, so did his friends. He was in shock because he believed that he had the Midas touch and could not lose. Imagine her shock when she discovered that he had not only gambled his properties, savings and any investments he had, but had also put Ravenswood up as collateral, not the dealership, which he had earmarked for Frank, but their house and land.

Frank and Maureen looked aghast as the story spun out. Maureen had her hands up to her mouth. Frank looked quite sick.

Mavis continued after another deep breath. Dennis had been mortified and disbelieving at first, but after a few days had confessed his folly. He didn't expect Mavis to be able to forgive him, but of course she did. She had always believed in him although she did worry about his impetuosity in rushing headlong into investments without prior investigation. She had told him not to worry. Her father had left her money, that had been left to him by his father. That was the way money was handled in her family; not used or squandered but kept safe for another generation. She had told Dennis what she planned to do, and he could not very well stop her, as they would soon have nowhere to live. She went to her own solicitor and explained the mess and between the jigs and the reels, she was able to purchase Ravenswood with her own money. The deeds were now in her own name, with her own solicitor.

There was silence from the listening pair. Maureen shook her head.

'I don't believe it, for a moment. My brother would never have done that.'

Mavis sighed deeply. 'I would say that the shock contributed to his death a few months later. He knew it was bad enough losing everything himself, he could not forgive himself for leading his good friends down into the abyss too. That's what killed him.'

Frank put his head in his hands and Maureen went up to the sitting room in a huff. Frank got up and opened another bottle of wine. He stayed at the table, drinking. He looked at his mother in horror. Before she left the kitchen, she brought in Charlie. Then she stood in front of Frank.

'I am truly sorry Frank, that I have no money. You and Rosemary have both been left money in the trust fund, generously provided by your father and grandfather, you also got your father's business, so you have been well cared for, my boy. You both had a good and expensive education and now it's all up to you. This house is all I have, and I am not selling it until I must, so please understand that. Your aunt has been a bit impetuous, but as you say, the investment will happen sooner or later, isn't that right?' She left him then and went upstairs.

Mavis did not sleep for hours, going over the evening's conversation again and again. The hurt she felt when Maureen referred to her as being only the stepmother and Frank agreeing. They were her children as surely as if she had given birth to them.

She had known them from the time they were born. She knew also that she would forgive Frank, children caused hurt and anguish but had to be forgiven; that was what parents did. She fell asleep at last and overslept. It was after nine when she awoke.

Yawning, she went downstairs and opened the kitchen door. She was met with billowing smoke and an acrid smell. She rushed in to find an electric plate on and a saucepan sticking to the plate and burnt to a cinder. She turned off the cooker with a shaking hand and rushed to open all the windows and doors in both the kitchen and utility room. She was coughing and gasping for breath and went outside to breathe. What on earth had happened? After a while she went back into the kitchen and with a teacloth tried to grasp the remains of the handle on the pot. It disintegrated of course and she saw that the electric plate would have to be replaced if that were possible. Otherwise, it meant a new cooker.

Then she remembered Charlie. She looked over at where the dog slept, he was still, as though asleep. She walked over and discovered that Charlie was dead. She stooped down and felt the dog, his beautiful body was totally still. She stayed in that position, looking at him in sorrow. When had death visited him; was he in distress? He looked at peace. She straightened up and sat at the island, still looking at him. What would she tell Susie?

The kitchen door opened, and Maureen came in. 'What on earth is that smell?' She went to cooker and looked at the ruined plate. 'Holy God, what happened here?' She stepped back and looked at Mavis sitting at the island in silence. 'What have you done, Mavis?'

Mavis looked at her sister-in-law and said, 'Nothing. The plate was left on.'

Maureen looked around and said, 'Well there is no damage, except this awful smell, no doubt we are lucky not to have been burnt in our beds.'

Mavis did not reply. Her thoughts were wholly on the dead dog.

Frank then appeared and looked a bit hung over. 'What is the awful smell? Someone burnt the breakfast?'

Maureen was exasperated, 'How did the hot plate get left on?'

Mavis said, 'I have no idea. The saucepan had left over potatoes in it. I was keeping them to make potato salad. I'm sure I switched off the cooker.'

Frank said, 'Mum, everyone makes mistakes, you know. It could happen to anyone.'

'Lord, it was lucky we were not all killed in our beds,' Maureen said in a most disapproving voice. Then seeing the immobile Charlie, she asked, 'What's wrong with the dog?'

'He's dead, that's what's wrong.' Mavis said bitterly.

She left the kitchen and went back upstairs to her room. She sat on her bed and wept for the friendly and happy dog, who had given meaning to her life since Rosemary had gone on holiday. Why had this happened? She sat and thought. She had made the dinner; she knew that she never left the cooker on once she had finished cooking. There was Frank, saying everyone made mistakes. What did he mean? She knew well enough; he blamed her. She wept again.

Later when she came downstairs, Maureen was bringing her suitcase out to her car, chatting to Frank. She heard Maureen say, 'This house is not safe anymore with Mavis.'

Frank carried the case out for his aunt and was murmuring platitudes. She could not hear what he was saying. She went out to the front door and watched her sister-in-law bring the last bags of clothing out. Maureen caught sight of her and said something further to her nephew. She waved and got into her car and was soon on her way. No apologies for having imposed on Mavis and no thanks for her hospitality.

Mavis watched as she drove out of view and returned to the kitchen. Frank joined her shortly. He patted his mother on the shoulder and said, 'Don't fret, Mum, I'll bury the dog, it was quite old anyway, wasn't it?'

'He was. A lovely healthy dog that I was caring for. He should not have died.'

Frank smiled at his mother. 'Mum, it wasn't your fault, these things happen, you know.'

'No Frank, these 'things' do not and should not happen. I know that I did not leave the plate on. Why would I?'

'It's the easiest thing in the world to do, Mum. Forget it now, will you?'

'No, I won't forget it. You make me feel as if I am not completely sane and compos mentis and I know that I have not reached that stage yet.'

Frank buried Charlie under an old apple tree up in the first paddock, watched by a weeping Mavis. Then he left for Dublin leaving his mother sitting in the kitchen, subdued, silent and sorrowful.

Chapter 26

Over the coming days, Mavis worried about how she would tell Susie about Charlie. Every time she went over the past week in her mind, she felt bitter and angry. How could Maureen talk like that about her, telling Frank that she had no rights and was just an outsider, after being the boy's mother since he was four years old? She was disappointed in Frank's response too; he did not stand up for her or contradict his aunt. What was happening to her family? She had not wanted to divulge Dennis's indiscretion but felt it was necessary that they understood it was now her house, bought out of her funds. She felt quite ill and decided it was time to see her doctor as Maureen had kept telling her. She rang John O'Dea and made an appointment for that afternoon.

Her appetite was gone, and she just had a cup of tea for lunch. Even playing the piano proved impossible for her. She drove slowly to town to John's surgery; driving made her nervous now and she wondered if she was still capable.

John welcomed her and brought her into the kitchen, next to the office. He made a pot of tea and put out biscuits on a plate while chattering away. He noticed her lack of response and looked at the woman he had met at the church not so long ago. Something had changed. She had a vacant look in her eyes. He realised that she probably had not heard a word of what he had been chatting about. He pulled his chair closer to hers and put the tea and biscuits in front of her. 'Tell me all, Mavis. What is troubling you, my dear woman?'

'I don't know where to begin John,' she admitted.

'Take your time. I'm finished for the day,' he said sipping his tea.

The silence continued for quite a time, then Mavis began to speak.

She related the most recent events, the traumatic recounting of Dennis's losses to Frank and Maureen, and her buying the property; the smoking hot plate which caused the death of the dog she was caring for; the money she had unearthed and the drugs which were spread around the garden and which she probably spread and her certainty that the murdered boy was somehow involved and may have been the night prowler.

After she had told her story, John did not reply immediately. He got up and made fresh tea and brought it to the table.

'Were there any other accidents in the house?' he asked.

Mavis shook her head. Then she remembered the ruined silk blouse and the iron left on, which she could not remember doing. 'That's the trouble, John, I just don't remember doing these things. I could have burnt down the house twice and I already told you about tap left on, which overflowed in the utility room.' She dabbed at her eyes with a tissue.

John leant over and patted her hand. 'There is a lot of unhappiness and insecurity hovering around you at the moment----not your unhappiness and insecurity, I have to say. Other people's unease and worries. Maureen is a very domineering personality and has gone in over her head with this investment or whatever she has trusted her money to; Frank may also be in over his head.'

Mavis nodded her head. 'Something is definitely not right with him, John.'

'Have you lent him money, Mavis?'

She nodded. 'Yes, five thousand, a few months ago which he said was just until the end of the month. So far, he has not repaid it.'

'Have you checked your bank statements regularly and spoken to your accountant?'

'Well I do not have much apart from my pension, although that is subject to tax too as there is a small pension from the time I worked in England.'

John scratched his chin and said, 'I think you should see your accountant and see how things are and what exactly your liabilities are and check out your account at the bank and the savings account you have.'

'John, my needs are limited, and I do not spend much money at all, but I will do that.'

'Right, that's sorted. Now come into my office and let me take your blood pressure and I'll take bloods too and drop them into the hospital on the way home to make sure your cholesterol is normal. Have you had your eyesight tested in the past two years?'

'I had that done last year for my driving licence renewal.'

John weighed Mavis then and checked with her past records. He sat her down and asked her a few more questions and asked her to spell a few words backwards. She laughed as she did it.

John looked up from his notes and said, 'Mavis, I think you are in great condition for your age, and I cannot detect any signs of dementia at all. I think all your problems are being exacerbated by two people in your life. I hope you will have some peace from them soon and don't be worrying about young Billy. He is not your problem and was just an unfortunate young fellow caught up in the ugly world of drugs and money.'

John told her that he would ring with the results of the blood tests. Then he spoke quite seriously to her. 'Mavis, you need to be more mindful of everything you do. Watch what you do, and if necessary, make a note of it. It helps if you make a note of all you must do in the day and at the end of the day and tick everything you have done, even if it is only trivial things. I would like to see you in two weeks for a follow-up.'

The same week, Mavis rang her accountant and made an appointment to see him. She contacted the bank for the past year's statements. She was looking forward so much to seeing Rosemary again but terrified about how she would explain about Charlie.

James came for a lesson, having checked beforehand if she was available. Mavis was pleased to see him and be entertained for an hour. He was looking forward to seeing her daughter again, he told her. He had missed her. Line dancing was over until September, but he was walking weekly with the club. He was doing some part time accountant work for a couple of businesses and he said it was enough to keep him going.

Mavis was still fretting about the money and drugs that were found on her premises. She rang the number Detective Savage had given her, to ask if there had been any further developments. He told her they had no further news and she should not worry about the affair. After her meeting with the accountant, she was worried, however. Lorcan found some irregularities in her account; some cheques had been cashed, for amounts totalling fifteen thousand. That had almost cleared out her current account. Her accountant wanted her to seek help from a solicitor but Mavis, suspecting her son, could not do that. She would sort it out herself, she told him.

Jenny rang one afternoon, and Mavis could tell the girl was stressed. Her mother wanted to move in with her and give up the lease on the apartment. She did not know what to do. Mavis, herself stressed, could offer no help. She asked Jenny if she knew any foreigners at the gym or any place she frequented. That was the only solution she thought. Maureen would not tolerate being in the same house as a lodger, she knew that. She did not think that her sister-in-law would have the nerve to come back to Ravenswood.

Jenny did in fact, know a very nice Polish man and said that she would think about it and see if it could be organised. She was desperate enough to try anything. Mavis told her to bring out the clothes again and maybe the trick would work again. She also told her niece that there had been a nasty altercation between herself and Frank and her mother. She felt that Maureen would have no choice but to return to Cork.

'Go for it, Jenny. Your sanity is at stake, I should know, my dear.'

Jenny laughed at her aunt and told her that she felt better after speaking with her.' I will let you know how I get on, Mavis.'

Sadie was due a visit and Mavis called to see her the day after she saw her accountant. Today she was very lucid and knew Mavis straight away. They had a decent conversation for once. Margaret O'Neill was with her and Mavis asked the woman how her sister was coping and had she had any more news about young Billy? Margaret shook her head and just said the guards believed there was a vicious Dublin gang involved. Other young fellows from a few small villages around had all been involved at one time or another. The enticement included designer clothing and motorbikes, all of which poor Billy had acquired.

'Life is very difficult for single mothers now, isn't it? It was never like that in my day. Well, it *was* difficult, of course it was. It's never easy being a single parent.' Sadie knew exactly what was being discussed. 'Those drugs make everyone's life a misery, and they seem to be everywhere, don't they? It must be awful being a mother these days.'

Mavis agreed. She did not tell them about how her property had been the place where drugs had been or about the money which she had dug up. She did not want that spread around the village. If it got out, there was nothing she could do about it, but it would not be her doing. She did not think the guards would talk about it either.

She suddenly felt more energetic as she remembered that Rosemary would be back on Saturday. She told the two women how she missed her daughter and would be delighted to see her again. She told them where Rosemary had been, and Margaret spoke about her trip to Italy a good few years ago.

Sadie suddenly spoke up, 'Oh Bari is where St. Nicholas's bones are buried, you know, Santa Clause; in the cathedral there.'

Margaret and Mavis looked at her in surprise. They did not know that. Without doubt, when Sadie was lucid, she was very lucid.

Mavis took her leave of them and said she would see her next week. An outing for afternoon tea was overdue, she said.

'Oh lovely! I do so love doing that, Mavis. Maybe we'll go to the em, em, yes, the Horse and Jockey again. That would be smashing.'

Chapter 27

When Rosemary rang to say they had landed, Mavis quickly told her about Charlie and asked her to break the news to Susie. She did not want the girl to get the awful shock when she arrived. She had a couple of hours in the car and would absorb it over the journey. Rosemary sympathised and asked about how it happened. Mavis said she would explain when she got home.

When they arrived, Mavis had lunch ready for them. She hugged Susie and apologised profusely. She was quite weepy about the whole matter. She explained what happened and she could see that Rosemary was shocked. Susie put her arms around Mavis and told her that she was not to blame. Poor Charlie was quite old, and it would not have been a painful death, it also saved her making a difficult decision in the near future. Mavis brought her up to the old orchard and showed her where he was buried.

After Susie left, Rosemary questioned her mother further and was obviously worried about the accident. She wondered why Maureen had left and Mavis admitted that it was probably the accident that decided her.

'Are you sure it was an accident Mum? Not just trying to get rid of Maureen, were you?'

'No Rosemary. I cannot remember leaving on the hot plate, why would I, when we ate dinner here in the kitchen? Anyway, I always turn off the cooker when I'm finished.' She began to cry softly. 'Oh Rosemary, it's been a horrendous time, I am so glad that you are back.'

Rosemary was horrified to see her mother cry. She had never witnessed that before. She insisted that Mavis tell her everything that had happened while she was away. She listened intently as her mother described the forensic people finding drugs all over the garden and her own belief that the night prowler had been Billy. She then explained all about Maureen being anxious about her investment in Frank's scheme, whatever it was and then the awful events of the night came out about their harassment of her into selling land to cover her money and Frank's agreement with his aunt. Then she had to relay the worst part of it all; Dennis and his lost investments and her having to buy Ravenswood, to let them both know there was no money available to pay off Maureen.

Rosemary's eyes widened as each sentence came out, hardly able to believe her ears.

'Poor Mumsie, how bloody awful, to have to endure all that at your age. I would have come back home if I'd had an inkling.'

'I am only telling you now, Rosemary, so that you are up to date with the drama that's been unfolding.

A visit to the accountant has shown me that cheques have been drawn on my account that I didn't sign. I am going to have to confront Frank. Now I know for certain he's in trouble.'

The doorbell rang and Rosemary went. Mavis could hear James in the hall and was delighted that he had called. She wiped her eyes and put on the kettle. After a while, they both entered the kitchen and Mavis greeted her pupil with a big smile.

They sat and had tea and cake. Rosemary asked her mother is she would mind if she went out for a while with James.

'Of course not.' She smiled. 'It's been a long time since you had a good chat, so off you go. I need an early night as I have not been sleeping too well.'

On Sunday the two women went to church together and later had dinner at the garden centre. Rosemary was too tired to go walking, she said. Next week she would start again. Now she just wanted time to spend with her mother.

On their arrival home, they were both dismayed to see Frank's car parked at the side of the house. They looked at each other and Rosemary squeezed her mother's arm.

'We'll play it cool Mum. We're not taking any cheek or harassment.'

Frank was in the kitchen frying bacon and greeted them quietly. He looked unkempt and was in an old track bottoms and top which didn't match.

'Well ladies, have you dined? Good time abroad Rosemary?' He grinned at his sister.

Rosemary answered, 'Yes, we've eaten, and I had a lovely time in Italy. Nice to get home though.'

'What did your friend think of her dog's sudden death? Did you tell them, Ma?'

'Yes, I did, Frank. Susie took it very well.'

'It's just lucky we were not all burnt in our beds that night, Romy. You had better be very alert from now on.'

'I'm sure it was just an accident; they happen to a lot of people.' Rosemary glared at her brother.

'Hmm, that's not what aunt Maureen thinks, is it, Ma?'

Mavis sighed and said, 'No, Maureen thinks I've lost my marbles. But I have seen the doctor and he said that he finds no signs of dementia. My accountant does find that some things are missing though, like fifteen thousand.' She stared at her son and could not believe that he did not even flinch.

'Now Mother, when you start losing things like money and then start digging up the same, you need to ask yourself, what's happening, don't you?' He put his bacon on a plate and brought it over to the island. He buttered bread and poured himself tea and started eating, behaving as if he did not have a care in the world.

Rosemary and Mavis stared at him as if he were from another planet.

Later as they sat watching television, he joined them and only left every time his phone pinged. Mavis went up to bed at nine thirty. She was mentally fatigued these days. Rosemary said goodnight to her mother and said she would see her in the morning. She was texting her friends and James, on her phone and was not watching the television. Frank stood up and switched it off. He sat down again and turned to his sister.

'Romy, we have to talk, it's really important to get Mother's issues dealt with. I have been very worried about her.'

Rosemary put down her phone and said, 'I don't know what you are worried about Frank, she is fine and if the doctor says she is okay, that is good enough for me. What exactly are you worried about? She already told me all about how you and Maureen have been pressing her to sell up, just because Maureen daftly sold her house and invested in your scheme.'

'Yes, I guessed she could not wait to pull you onto her side. We have heard a load of bull from her, and now it's time she was reined in Romy. It's for your sake too old girl, we are going to get nothing from Dad's estate, and we have rights, you know.'

Rosemary laughed out loud. 'Frank, we got our inheritance already, remember? We have our trust funds and you also got the dealership, which you have added to, isn't that right?'

'But Romy, there is this place too and it is rightly ours, when she goes, right?'

Rosemary shook her head, 'This is our mother we are speaking of; she always said the place would be ours when she goes. Who else would she leave it to? Anyway, she is not going anywhere yet, and she paid for Ravenswood with her own funds, it seems.'

'Ah, but can we believe that? I have not seen the deeds, and neither have Dad's solicitors.'

'She has her own solicitor and why don't you ask her to show a copy to them, if it is bothering you so much?'

'Romy, I need the money now, I have over committed to an investment and yes, I know, I should have been less hasty, but all will come right, I promise you,' he smiled at her.

Rosemary implored her brother to leave Mavis in peace. 'She has been through so much recently, with Maureen parked here and making life difficult for her.'

Frank spread his hands and confessed, 'I need a quick injection of cash Ro, can you draw some of your trust fund down for me, please?'

Rosemary looked at him and patiently explained, 'Frank, I have finally found the man I want to marry and will need that money that Daddy left me. If you spent all yours, well, what can I say? It's tough, but it was your decision.'

He looked at in disbelief. 'You have found a man, Romy? How amazing! That was fast work indeed, who is the lucky man, do I know him?'

Rosemary rose to her feet. 'No, you don't know him, Frank. We are both lucky, I think.'

Frank did not give up so easily. 'You are the only hope I have, Romy. I am in deep trouble to be honest, if I can't get help from my sister, who can I turn to?'

She turned sad eyes on him and said, 'Frank, you are my brother, and I would help you if I could. You can surely get a bank loan? What about all those influential friends you are always talking about? You work, don't you, and you have assets? James and I want to buy a modern house and start a family soon.'

She left him sitting open mouthed.

He could not believe what he heard. His dowdy and schoolteacher sister had found herself a man and would not help him, her brother, out of his dilemma. His face grew dark with anger and he vowed they would both be sorry for treating him like this.

Upstairs, Mavis heard the front slamming shut and wondered where Frank was going. Was he returning to Dublin? She hoped he was. She listened but could not hear his car. She read three pages of her calming book and slept.

The next morning, before Mavis went down to the kitchen, she went into the sitting room and looked out the window. Frank's car was gone. Breathing a sigh of relief, she went down to the kitchen and made her breakfast. She planned to do some gardening today and needed to spend time in the tunnel. The tomatoes were slowly ripening and there were flowers on the courgette plants.

Rosemary came down at ten o'clock with a pile of washing to put on. She felt fresh after a good night's sleep and was also glad that Frank had gone. She and James were going for a hike up the mountains today. She smiled to herself as she put the washing machine on; the three girls were very interested to know how things stood between herself and James. There was a local football match on in the village this evening, then they were all going to meet at the local pub.

She had her breakfast sitting outside on the patio. The sun was shining, and her mother was singing up in the vegetable patch. She could hear her. She brought her cup of tea up and sat on a raised bed, watching Mavis remove weeds deftly and thinning out carrots.

They chatted about the holiday she had just returned from and Mavis was interested in everything the girls did and saw. She had been to Italy when she was young and had loved it. The heat, the colours and the excitable Italians; also, the food and the wine, which they both loved.

Rosemary left her mother and prepared herself to go hiking with James. She was going to pick him up at eleven thirty, and on the way do some shopping for a picnic lunch.

Mavis worked until twelve thirty and decided she had done enough stooping and bending. She needed a cup of coffee. She heard the phone ringing before she entered the kitchen and just as she got to it, it stopped. So annoying, when that happens, she thought. She put on the kettle and took down the jar of coffee. The phone rang again and this time she took it on the first ring.

It was James and he wondered if Rosemary was still at the house. Mavis told him that she had gone, as she had shouted to her mother as she left, saying that she would see her for dinner. He wanted to know what time that was, and she replied, about eleven twenty. She could hear the worried tone of his voice and told him that she was probably at the shops getting food for the picnic. She asked him to let her know when Rosemary arrived at his house.

She sat and drank her coffee. The phone rang again, and she smiled as she reached for it. Poor James, he was the protective type and she hoped he

,

was not the over-protective type. Rosemary was a free spirit in many ways. But it was not James, it was the hospital in the town. Rosemary had been in an accident and would she please come in as soon as possible. Mavis could not believe what she heard. It can't be Rosemary, she thought. It must be someone else. Why did they ring her? How did they get her number? The phone rang again. She prayed it was the hospital to say they had made a mistake. It was James, he was worried as Rosemary still had not showed up. Mavis told him about the telephone call she had just received, and she heard James' sharp intake of breath.

'Mavis, I am coming up to you now and we'll go to the hospital together.'

Chapter 28

Mavis never remembered later, the journey into the hospital with James. The two of them were numb with shock and did not speak. The sixteen kilometres seemed to take such a long time. When they rushed into the A&E department, a nurse immediately brought them into the office. A doctor was there, sitting at a desk. He rose and shook hands with them and said he was sorry for the shock they must have received. Rosemary had crashed the car into a wall on a bend and the car had overturned. She had head injuries and at that moment was in the X-ray department. They would know in a short time how serious her condition was. He took them to a room next to the X-ray department and reassured them that everything necessary was being done and that Rosemary was in good hands.

'I just can't believe it, James. We were just speaking ten minutes before she left. She was so looking forward to hiking with you.' Mavis was too shocked to even cry, but she was shaking all over.

James leaned over as they sat together and put his arms around her. 'Rosemary is strong, almost as strong as her mother. She'll make it, I'm sure.'

Rosemary was unconscious for a few hours. Mavis and James did not leave her bedside as they waited anxiously for her to open her eyes. The X-rays showed no permanent damage however, and they were relieved about that. At four o'clock Rosemary came around and opened her eyes. She quickly took in where she was, and her eyes locked on James and her mother sitting at her sides. It hurt to turn her head and the pain in her head was intense. Mavis quickly leaned into her and stroked her hand.

'You mustn't try to talk yet, Rosemary. You've been in an accident and you're in hospital, but you are alright, no damage done.'

She desperately wanted Rosemary to relax and understand what had happened. James on the other side of the bed also held her hand and tried to smile at her.

Rosemary frowned and opened her mouth to ask. 'How?'

James told her not to wonder about anything just yet. 'Try to relax and breathe gently, no questions for a day or two, okay? You have hurt your head and it needs peace and quiet.'

Mavis said that she would leave her with James and later she would be back with some items she might need. James nodded in appreciation and told Mavis that he would ring her when he was leaving.

James came up to the house later that night after Mavis had left the hospital. Rosemary was sleeping and had been given medication earlier. They chatted in the kitchen. Both were subdued and still shocked. James had seen the car and told Mavis that it was a write-off. They both realised that Rosemary had been amazingly blessed to survive the crash. They agreed that she was a careful and cautious driver and wondered how it happened. James did not think that she would have been on her phone while driving. He had been expecting her at eleven thirty and had no reason to contact her before that. Still, someone may have called her just at that moment and she answered it and lost concentration. It happens. They sat drinking tea. James refused a whiskey as he wanted to call into the hospital before going to bed. He set off at eleven and told Mavis that he would ring her if there had been any change.

Mavis poured herself a whiskey and sat in the sitting room when he left, pondering the day's events. She still had trouble believing all that had happened. She now understood the feeling that parents had when they got that awful phone call. She made her way to bed wearily and wrote in her notebook all the happenings of the day. She made a list of what she must do tomorrow and shopping she should do for the coming days. She did not want to have to run to the shops every day. She would need to concentrate on Rosemary. She talked to Dennis and told him she needed his help and so did Rosemary. She slept uneasily but despite everything dropped off quickly. The phone woke her and for a moment she was disoriented.

'Dennis?' she said into the phone, unconsciously.

'Mother, it's Frank, are you in bed? I did not mean to disturb you.'

Mavis became alert at once. What would Frank think of her saying her husband's name. She was annoyed at herself. 'Yes, I'm in bed, Frank, where else would I be? It's after midnight you know.'

'Oh, I just wondered if it would be alright to stay a few nights this week?' He sounded detached and a bit dopey himself.

'Of course,' Mavis said shortly. When did he ever ask for permission before? 'Good night, Frank.' As she finished the call, she suddenly remembered Rosemary in hospital and became fully awake. I forgot, she thought. How could I do that? I never told Frank! What sort of mother am I?

She rang the hospital first thing the next morning and was delighted to hear that her daughter had passed a peaceful night and had slept all night. She breathed a prayer of thanks and said 'good boy' to Dennis too. She made her breakfast and sat outside in the sunshine to eat it. She had a call from James who relayed the same news and the two of them were light-headed with relief.

Before she left for the shops, Jenny rang. The poor girl was distraught and told Mavis that she had decided to go away for a while and leave her mother in the house, as she could no longer live with her. The firm she worked with, had their headquarters in London and she was going to go and take up a rental apartment there for a few months. Mavis was disappointed for the girl but understood. Jenny was leaving immediately and told Mavis not to have her mother back to stay at Ravenswood under any circumstances. She felt that her mother was bordering insanity, as nothing pleased her, and Jenny could do nothing right. She thought she needed a good sharp shock to bring her to her senses. Even the neighbours were terrorised by her ranting and raving which she did at every opportunity.

Mavis laughed at that. She decided not to worry Jenny with Rosemary's news, since it appeared not to be too serious. The girl had enough trouble in her life with her mother. She told the girl to keep in touch and if she could help her in any way, to let her know. She had her mobile number and would keep her appraised of her mother's doings, if she heard anything. She hoped in her heart that she would not hear from Maureen for a long time. Maybe she would get fed up of Dublin and go back to Cork where she supposedly had friends

Mavis did her shopping and came home to put her goods away. She thought she would have an early lunch and then go into the hospital and find out how her daughter was progressing. James rang to say that he had been in to see Rosemary and that she smiled and seemed rested. They were doing more tests on her today to see if she had full motor function, but he was very optimistic. Mavis could hear that in his voice and was herself feeling confident because of it. As she was about to get into her car to go to the hospital, she was surprised to see Frank's car coming up the drive.

'Hello Frank, I did not expect you until evening,' she smiled at him.

'Oh, I had time off and decided to enjoy the countryside. Everything okay with you, Ma?'

Mavis decided to sound casual, she wanted no drama with Frank. 'Oh fine. I am just visiting Rosemary she had a little accident yesterday and they are doing some checks in the hospital before letting her out.'

Frank paused before closing the door of his car. 'An accident? When? Did she have a fall or something?'

'No, it was in the car, Frank. But do not worry, she is fine. I'm going to visit her now and bring in some items she may need if she must stay longer.'

'I'll come with you Mum. I can take the car and get it fixed up, no bother. Otherwise, we can use parts that are undamaged and get her something else. I'll go with you now.'

For some reason, Mavis thought this was not a good idea. James would be there, and she was sure Rosemary would not want a crowd around the bed.

'Not just now, Frank. The doctor has allowed me, as her mother to attend, but she should really be quiet and have no people fussing about her. I'm sure you understand. I'll let you know how things are when I get back in an hour.'

He looked like he wanted to pursue his desire and go with Mavis, but her tone had a finality about it. He watched as she got into the car and drove off.

Rosemary was much better looking today and was not in as much pain, though her neck still hurt a lot and she was wearing a collar to keep it immobile. Mavis put fruit and some items of clothing in her locker. James had already been in and would be returning later. He had spoken to the doctor and the staff; they were pleased with her progress. She had responded well to all the tests they had performed on her and seemed none the worse for wear. Mavis felt as though a huge boulder had been lifted from her shoulders. Mother and daughter chatted although it was Mavis who did most of the chatting. She did not want to wear out her daughter. She stayed for thirty minutes, then after relaying Jenny's news, which made Rosemary laugh, she left and told her that she might call back later.

She called into the nurses' station and asked the sister-in-charge how her daughter was progressing, and she was told that everything seemed normal, apart from bruised ribs and neck strain. She would be kept in for a couple more days probably, just for observation. Mavis left, a happy woman. She went down in the lift and on getting out, bumped into

James, who was standing waiting for the lift, with a big bouquet of flowers in his arms. He looked so abstracted that he did not recognise Mavis until she went up to him. Mavis told him what the sister had said and how relieved she was. She was surprised that he did not respond in the way she would have expected and looked at him quizzically. He shook his head and frowned slightly.

'Mavis, I need to talk with you, as soon as possible. Can I call by after I leave the hospital?'

'Of course, James. I'll be at home. Come for dinner if you like.' Then she remembered Frank was there. 'Frank is home as well for a few days, unexpectedly as usual.'

James looked at her. 'Did you tell Frank about the accident, Mavis?'

'I played it down, to be honest, I don't want him fussing around Rosemary and upsetting her.' She sighed as she thought about the evening ahead. The last thing she needed now was pressure to sell and any talk of money.

James looked a bit downcast. 'I just want to talk to you, Mavis. Maybe another time, soon though. This will not wait.'

Mavis knew that this was not like James at all. 'Will I call to your house then, instead, and we can forget dinner. I will make dinner for myself and Frank and then come to your place, if that is okay?'

James thought for a moment and then nodded. 'Come around eight, I'll be home by then.'

Then he got into the lift and was gone. Mavis was intrigued. What was up with James? Had he heard something different to what the sister had told her? Immediately she began to worry again and be fearful that something bad was going on in Rosemary's condition that they wouldn't tell her.

Mavis drove home slowly. She owed Sadie a visit but maybe next week when she felt able to talk about non-important things. She could not face poor Sadie now or the thoughts of bringing her out for afternoon tea. It would wait, she decided. Rosemary would hopefully be allowed home in a couple of days.

Frank's car was there in its usual place. She could hear movement upstairs in Dennis's office and could hear Frank's raised voice. He sounded impatient and worried. She stood for a few minutes in the hall, unashamedly eavesdropping.

'No, no, I can't do that, I'm sorry. I'll try everything else. I promise! Something will turn up. It might just take a little more time.'

Mavis tiptoed down to the kitchen and put on the kettle. She decided to do a simple and quick dinner; steak and chips, she thought.

After a while, Frank appeared in the kitchen. 'Ah! You are back again. How is my sister now?'

Mavis smiled and said, 'Everything is fine, and she should be home in a day or two.'

'I'm very relieved to hear that. I got quite a turn when you told me. She should be more careful. I might go in now and visit her. Does she need anything, do you know?'

Mavis shook her head. 'I brought her all she needs for the couple of days. Anyway, James is with her all the time.'

'Who is James, may I ask? Is he the new man in her life?' Frank sat at the island and stared at Mavis.

'Not entirely new, Frank, she has known him a while now and I know him from a long time back. I could not have wished for a better man for her.'

'Is this serious then, do you think?' He looked at his mother anxiously.

'Oh yes! I would say quite serious. Your sister is cautious you know, not one to plunge headlong into anything without due consideration. We should be happy for her.'

Chapter 29

Maureen was not happy in her new situation. Her daughter had gone off to London, for 'an extended period', she said, whatever that meant. She could have invited her mother to go as well. She had lived in London once and liked it. There was a lot of activity there. Never mind, she thought to herself, she would give her a week or two to find a place and then go over for a holiday. Living alone here in Dublin did not please her very much. The neighbours were too quiet; no dinner parties or bridge parties; nothing, in fact. Cork was even better than here, at least she knew more people there. She longed for intellectual conversation and cultural events; she yearned to be looked up to and her opinion sought, as it once had, a long time ago.

She decided to give Mavis a call. Even though she was still annoyed by her attitude and her mad statements, it would be nice to know how things were going. She was still waiting for her investment to mature and knew that she would have to exert some pressure on her nephew. Maybe she should call to his place of work and confront him there. She knew where the garage was, that way she could let him know that she was serious and in need of her money.

She rang Mavis's landline several times but got no answer. She searched everywhere for her mobile number but could not find it. She found Frank's mobile however and rang him one morning after breakfast. His mobile rang out and she did not want to leave a voice message. She was thoroughly fed up with Frank and his mother. She decided, then and there, that she would drive to the garage and see where Frank was.

The business looked prospering and there were many new cars in the showroom. She entered the reception area and looked all around, critically. An attractive blonde woman walked over to her smiling. Briefly, Maureen introduced herself and demanded to see the owner.

She was told to take a seat in the plush area behind the reception area. Annoyed at having to wait to see her nephew, she intended to give him a piece of her mind. When a strange man approached her, she glanced at her watch and gave him a supercilious look that took him in from his shoes, to the top of his head. He stood in front of her smiling and a quizzical look in his eyes. Impatiently, Maureen shook her head and stood up.

'I clearly asked to see the owner of this garage, nobody else,' she intoned loudly as if he might be a little deaf or vacant.

He continued smiling patiently. 'Yes, madam and here I am, at your service. Now what can I do for you?'

Maureen gaped at him. 'I mean my nephew, Frank Joyce, who is the owner of this garage, started by my brother, Dennis.'

Comprehension dawned in the eyes of Paul Kavanagh. 'Ah, I see madam. Did you not know that he sold the dealership to me a couple of years ago? I don't think he made you aware of that, did he?'

Maureen was still looking at him with her mouth open. 'Sold it?'

Paul Kavanagh nodded slowly, still smiling at her.

'But where is my money then, that I invested in his business ventures?'

Paul shook his head, frowning. 'I am afraid that I know nothing about his business now. Have you asked him?'

Impatiently Maureen cut him short and said, 'Of course, I have, many times. Where can I contact him, do you know?'

'Sorry, I have not seen Frank for quite a while, we are not close friends, you understand?'

Maureen looked distraught and unbelieving. 'I cannot believe it.'

Paul said, 'If I do happen to bump into him, I will certainly inform him that you are anxious to meet with him, is that alright?'

Maureen turned on her heel and walked out of the showroom. Angry and disgruntled, she sat in her car and wondered what to do next. This should not be happening to her of all people. She trusted Frank with her money and now could not contact him. It really was too much. She decided enough was enough. She drove back to Jenny's house and packed an overnight bag and headed back onto the motorway. His mother would have some influence over him she felt. This is going to be sorted, once and for all.

Rosemary was relaxing in the garden and glad to be home. Her ribs still hurt, and she still wore the collar. She was told to keep it on until her strained neck healed. Her mother had been up in the tunnel earlier in the morning, singing her heart out. She knew that the woman was happy to have her back. She also knew that Mavis was under some sort of tension and strain. James and herself were often huddled together talking and she wondered why. The pain killers made her drowsy and not as quick to respond so she asked no questions. She loved the attention James was giving her, although she felt a bit guilty, for making them both worried. Frank, on the other hand was not worried at all and even had the nerve to mention her trust fund again when he visited her in the hospital. Tired and frustrated at what had happened to her, she had confided in James about her brother's request. She was surprised when he passed no comment. The summer days were passing pleasantly, and she looked forward to being able to go walking with James again.

Today, her tranquillity was brought to a sudden end when Maureen made an unexpected appearance. She breezed in, hardly saying 'hello,' and asked where her mother was. Mavis was out at the time seeing Sadie. James was expected for lunch and she longed for his presence. She felt complete when he was there and knew that there was no way she could live without him now. She thought of her father and felt James had been heaven sent.

'Well, hello Maureen. How are you?'

'Very annoyed if you must know. I need to see Frank and fast. Did you know that he has sold the garage?'

Rosemary paused before answering. 'I think he and his friend have gone into a sort of partnership, at least that is what he told us.'

'No, that is not what the new owner told me. Is he around?' Maureen looked about the garden as if she would see Frank behind a tree.

'He was here last week for a short time.'

Maureen suddenly seemed to see her niece. 'And what on earth happened you?'

'Just a slight accident, Maureen. In my car, which is thoroughly wrecked, I might add.'

Her aunt clicked her tongue and shook her head.

'To think that I had imagined you were a sensible young lady. You and your brother both, careless and inconsiderate people.'

Rosemary wondered if her aunt had imagined that her accident was deliberate. She sighed and hoped Maureen would go before her mother returned. That was probably too much to wish for.

Maureen went into the kitchen and made herself a coffee and sat down, ignoring her niece.

James arrived next and brought some tapas and goodies from the delicatessen in town. He was surprised to see Maureen but greeted her civilly. She stared at him, trying to remember who he was and then recalled the 'mature pupil', whom she had warned Mavis about.

'What are you doing here? Coming for another music lesson?' She glared at him.

Rosemary had made her way slowly into the kitchen when she heard the exchange. 'Maureen, this is James, my boyfriend, James, my aunt Maureen.'

James and Maureen looked at each other, neither making any attempt to shake hands.

'We met before, Rosemary, when I came for a piano lesson. Your aunt thought I was a tradesman and did not want to let me in.' He laughed heartily at the memory.

Rosemary laughed uncertainly but on seeing James' face, she grinned at him, 'that's a hoot, I'm glad she didn't see us all at the Debussy debacle!'

James laughed loudly and took out plates from the cupboard and laid them on the kitchen table.

'You sit yourself down Rosemary, not too much exertion for a couple of weeks, remember?'

Maureen stood staring at both and said nothing.

James proceeded to arrange food on the plates and put on the kettle.

Mavis arrived as the kettle was boiling and James made a pot of tea. Her face lost the carefree look when she saw Maureen standing by the kitchen door with a face like thunder.

'Well Maureen, this is a surprise.' She did not say anything else but put some oranges and bananas she had bought into a bowl on the island.

'I need to talk to you both, in private,' she said as she looked pointedly at James. 'Family business.'

Mavis calmly washed the apples she had bought and said, 'I am going to eat first, Maureen. We can talk later, do sit down.'

'No thank you, I shall wait upstairs in the sitting room. I prefer plain food, as you know.'

'Will I make you a sandwich, Maureen?' offered James. 'There is ham and cheese you know; you don't have to have the tapas.'

Maureen sniffed and said, 'I am capable of making my own thank you and will do, after you have all eaten.'

She flounced out of the kitchen and they heard her marching up the stairs to the sitting room and banging the door. The three sat in silence and looked at each other in dismay.

James calmly said, 'Mavis, this is your house, and you should dictate how people behave. That is one rude woman.'

Mavis sighed. 'Yes, I suppose we are now going to get an earful. I had hoped that she would not darken the doorstep again after the last onslaught.'

Rosemary covered her mother's hand with her own. 'We are not going to stand for her rudeness anymore, Mum.' She could see the unexpected visit had knocked the wind out of her mother's sails and was upset for her. They both knew it would be about her investment with Frank.

When Mavis and Rosemary joined Maureen in the sitting room after lunch, they got the expected storm of complaints and demands. Mavis tried to be as calm as possible and let the woman get it all out of her system. Gradually she grew silent and stared at them.

'Well, what have you to say about all this?'

Mavis spread her hands and said quietly, 'What is there to say Maureen? I know nothing about Frank's business deals and he only passes by occasionally.'

Rosemary added, 'His business dealings have nothing to do with us Maureen, just as you would have nothing to do with Jenny's. He is a grown man. Why don't you contact your solicitor about the whole affair?'

Maureen raised her voice and said, 'Why should I have to pay any solicitor about all this? Frank is responsible.'

Rosemary nodded and replied, 'But every business deal or investment should be witnessed by a solicitor and should be a legal transaction, not a verbal agreement. You were unwise, Maureen and now you are beginning to realise it.'

Maureen glared at both women. 'I will go to the police and then we'll see who has been unwise.'

Mavis nodded. 'Yes, you could of course do that, but what evidence do you have to give them that you did indeed invest money with Frank, if there are no legal documents to prove it?'

Rosemary had to smile at the idea of Maureen ranting and raving in the police station.

Maureen saw and shouted, 'What do you think you are smiling about, hmm?'

Rosemary coughed and apologised for smiling. 'I'm just trying to imagine what they will think of an elderly woman, who gives away the money she made from her house, in a hare-brained scheme that was supposed to make her ultra-rich.'

Maureen glared at Rosemary but said nothing. She began to imagine the scene in the police station. Instead, she muttered, 'Who are you calling elderly? You and your so-called boyfriend of mature years! A bit on the old side for someone your age, don't you think?'

'

Mavis stood up resolutely. 'That's it, Maureen! We have put up with your rudeness for years now. It's time you left and please do not come back. When Frank calls again, we will tell him to contact you. I do not wish to have any further contact with you.'

Mavis left the sitting room. Her sister-in-law looked stunned and continued sitting. Nobody had ever spoken to her like that before. Rosemary got up slowly.

'I think you had better go now, Maureen. Sorry it should end like this, but we obviously annoy you terribly. You will be better off living alone'. She also left the room.

As the three sat on the patio in the sun, they heard Maureen's car speeding down the drive.

Chapter 30

Since James' conversation with Mavis, she was not sleeping well and was worried all the time. She had gone over the conversation dozens of times in her head and still she could not believe the implications. He had checked with his garage and the insurance people. There was no mistake. The brakes of Rosemary's car had been tampered with and a vital connection sliced in half. They agreed that nothing would be said to upset Rosemary. The insurance company were pursuing their own investigation and the police might be involved yet.

James had asked Mavis for advice and they had considered how best they could protect the girl, if indeed, she needed protection. Why would anyone want to do such a thing? When James told Mavis that he was suspicious of Frank, Mavis laughed. It was too incredible. What had Frank to gain from hurting his sister? When James told her that he had been pressurising her to draw down her trust fund in his favour, she began to consider the matter again. This time it did make sense, unfortunately. Frank was desperate for funds from any source. That was when she decided that she must act to help him. She did not tell anybody. She went into the city and saw some people in the planning office and then she consulted an engineer and an architect.

She would have to sell one of the fields. She thought about it every night and prayed for a solution. She remembered her vision of all the houses where the wood now was, and she was determined not to lose her wood. Men came and tramped all over the fields and submitted plans and drawings. There would have to be an entrance from the side road, where the wood was situated. An entrance could be made without taking too much of the wood, leaving it pretty much as it was now, with only an avenue at one side taking part of the wood away. She could live with that.

Maureen would have to be reimbursed, that was clear. She had no idea what sort of money would be involved. She hoped it would be enough to clear her son's debts. He couldn't owe too much, could he?

It was now August. Rosemary would be going back to work at the end of the month and was now out of the collar and able to hike again. She and James went off for a week to Kerry to walk and have a bit of private time together. She had not seen Frank since the accident and wondered what he was doing.

She lay in bed trying to sleep and remembered her calming book. She got up and found it. After a few pages she was drowsy, and her body totally relaxed. She smiled as she thought about the love birds in Kerry and hoped plans were being made. James had said he was going to ask Rosemary to move in with him until they could arrange a marriage. Mavis did not object. She knew that the man was crazy about her daughter and she trusted him completely. In fact, she would feel a lot more secure if she were living with James, after what he told her.

She was soon sleeping and gently snoring. A sudden movement in the room brought her back to an alert state and she opened her eyes. Someone was in the room. She sat up in bed at once, wide awake and reached for her light. As light flooded the room, she saw nobody, but her door was slowly closing. She got up, suddenly nervous and locked her door. She thought she had put on the alarm to home. Surely, she had. She stayed standing at the door and listening for any sound from the house. She could hear nothing. After fifteen minutes and getting quite cold, she went back to bed. That was the end of sleep for her that night.

The next morning, she gingerly made her way downstairs, still feeling nervous. No, the alarm was not on. She felt annoyed with herself. Last thing at night, the alarm routine was always followed, unless Rosemary was out. She was slipping again. Her imagination was playing tricks. How could anyone get into the house anyway? She had imagined it. If she was going to go like this, she had better sell up and move to an apartment. The thought chilled her.

She had a phone call from John O'Dea's office after her breakfast asking her to come for bloods to be done again. She said she would come in. The receptionist asked if she would come at twelve-thirty and be free to have lunch with John. She was delighted to have something to take her mind off the night terror.

Her blood pressure was up, she was told, and her medical dose would be slightly increased. John was not worried about that at all as she had been on a low dosage. He was worried about the tired and jaded appearance of the woman he had known for so long. She seemed agitated and her usual calmness was missing.

Over lunch they chatted about various local news. He asked her about how she was getting on and if she had seen her accountant and solicitor. Before she knew it, she was spilling everything out to John, who listened silently. She told him about the withdrawn money, Rosemary's accident and James Regan's suspicions. Then she recounted the previous night's scare and wondered if she was finally losing her mind. Of course, in daylight, her fears seemed childish and unreal, and she felt a bit embarrassed telling John everything. He was such a good listener and a dear friend; she knew that he would understand. He suggested that she get a chain attached to both back and front doors and lock her bedroom door in future. She looked at him in horror.

'You don't think that I am in danger, do you?'

'Better to be safe, my dear. If Frank owes money to ruthless people, they could cause you harm. It is not unknown.'

She had never thought of that. He might be part of something that he could not control. That silenced her. John saw that she was really frightened now and wondered how he could help this friend. He asked about James and Rosemary and when they were returning. He also suggested that James move into her house instead of Rosemary moving down to the cottage he lived in. Having a man in the house might be better, he suggested. She sighed in relief. That was the solution, she felt. She would certainly feel safer if James were there.

It was with a lighter heart and step that Mavis left John. He could see that he had offered some valuable advice and was thankful. Meanwhile, he was going to do a bit of digging and nosing around.

Mavis was singing as she worked in her tunnel. Rosemary would be back at the end of the week and she could hardly wait to put the idea to them. Of course, she must be prepared for them not to want it. If James were hesitant at all, she would not ask again. It would not be fair to the couple. But the house was large enough to absorb them. They could have the second floor all to themselves. She gathered tomatoes and courgettes and lettuce for her evening meal and felt quite proud of herself.

She was relaxing in the sitting room after a shower when she heard the doorbell. Wondering who it was, she got up and looked out. It was Paul Kavanagh, Frank's schoolfriend.

She brought him into the sitting room, and they sat and briefly talked about the weather, as they always do in this part of the country. She asked him how business was, and he said it was good considering that it was still summer. He expected the winter to be busier. They then talked about Frank. Paul admitted he was a bit worried about him and had not seen him for a while. Had Mavis seen him? She admitted that she had not and was also a bit worried about him. She told him about his aunt selling her house and investing the money with him. Did he know anything about this? Paul shook his head and smiled.

'When it comes to Frank, he is his own man and is the sort who doesn't let his right hand know what his left hand is doing.'

Mavis laughed out loud and said, 'How right you are Paul. You know Frank very well.'

She asked Paul if he would like tea and he said he would, but he insisted that he would make it.

'I know where the kitchen is Mavis, you just sit there and put your feet up, I won't be five minutes.'

She was happy to do that. He returned in five minutes with two mugs of tea. She was suddenly starving. 'Paul, would you mind terribly if I send you back, to get some chocolate biscuits from the cupboard beside the fridge?'

He went straight away, smiling. 'I happen to love them too.'

Then she noticed the spoon in her mug. Oh no. I hope he didn't put sugar in. She took out the spoon and deftly changed the mugs around. She sipped hers. Lovely, she thought, just the way I like it, good and strong.

Paul came back with a plate of biscuits. Mavis happily sipped her tea and dipped her biscuit into it. He smiled at her obvious enjoyment.

'That's the way my mother used to eat chocolate biscuits,' he said. He took a biscuit, and like Mavis, dipped it into his tea. Both sat in companionable silence munching biscuits and sipping tea.

'You make a fine cup of tea, Paul. A cup of tea that is made for you, always tastes better than the one you make for yourself.'

Paul told Mavis, as he left, that he would try and get in touch with her son and find out if there was anything they could do, to help sort him out, if he needed it.

Mavis thanked Paul and felt heartened by his concern. She wished her son could be as thoughtful as he was, she watched sadly as he drove away.

That night, Mavis mindfully locked the front and back doors, put on the alarm and locked her bedroom door. As she put her daily entry in her

275

notebook, she smiled to herself. She knew that she was in a better place now because of her meeting with John O'Dea. What would we do without good friends, she thought? She would ask James to put chains on the doors when he came back. He might think she was daft, but she was willing to risk it.

She slept like a baby and woke full of energy and a song ready on her lips. She decided to go up to the wood and take a flask of tea and have breakfast there. Dennis and herself often did that in the summer, early in the morning. There was something beautiful about the stillness at that early hour, the slight breeze murmuring through the summer leaves and summer still there.

The day was still, and sunshine came through the leafy trees delicately, spreading light and gradual warmth along the paths. Mavis sat deep in thought, with the flask cup in her hands. She wondered how she would divide up the field. The architect said she would easily get three detached houses with an acre and a half to each one, in the top field. The entrance, servicing the site would not take too much off the whole site and it would be a lovely tree-lined avenue leading to the houses. She tried to imagine how it would look. The architect was quietly excited and said he would bring her a more detailed map of how the area would look with houses built.

She considered the other plan the architect had suggested. He was an older man and knew the area

,

well. He said that if he were in her position, he would sell the main house, which was too big for one person and move into a modern and easy to keep, well insulated smaller house. She could have solar panels and be as snug as a bug. She had laughed at his suggestion at the time. Now it seemed to her, on consideration, to be totally rational. Why did she need a big house if Rosemary was going to move out? The house would have to be valued of course, but, according to the architect, it should fetch a considerable amount that would cover the building of three houses. It was up to her to sell the sites if she wanted or build the houses and then sell them, keeping one for herself, and he thought that many people would jump at the chance to buy.

She did not tell him about the money that she would have to give Maureen and mentioned nothing about her son's debts. That was private business. She would sell the big house and build a small one for herself, what was left over would, hopefully cover the debts incurred by Frank. If she needed more money, she would sell the other two sites. She would not have to sell the second field, just rail it off from the old house and gardens. She would also be able to keep her tunnel if she so wished. All the boundaries were her choice. She felt quite empowered by all the options she was given by the architect. She could hardly wait to discuss the situation with James and Rosemary. She felt that they would approve of the decision to sell.

.   Life seemed worth living now, she thought, as she got to her feet. She decided that she needed to play the piano. It was some time since she had played Bach, and this was how she would start today. Maybe a bit of gardening later before calling to Sadie to see if she would like afternoon tea out somewhere.

That afternoon, she and Sadie went out for a drive. She mentioned casually to her friend that she was thinking of moving to a smaller house. Sadie smiled and agreed it was a good idea.

'The older we get, the less we need, Mavis. Things get in the way and clutter up our lives and heads.'

Mavis was surprised by her rational thoughts today. 'I agree, Sadie. We don't need much to be contented, do we?'

The two ladies drove all the way to Clonmel and visited the hotel Mavis had heard about. The Moineir Hotel was splendid and rather grand. The two went in and had a gorgeous afternoon tea. Both women were impressed. Mavis thought she and Rosemary should come here sometime. When they were returning home, Sadie told Mavis that she would love to come here again. Even though it was a long drive, she said the afternoon tea was the best she ever had.

Chapter 31

Rosemary telephoned her mother on Friday night with the news that Mavis was hoping for. Both were so excited and extremely happy. An engagement had been announced and her daughter was over the moon. Soon after, the calls came from Rosemary's friends. They had just heard and were also thrilled. They wanted to organise a small welcome home party and Mavis agreed. She asked them if they would hold it at Ravenswood and they agreed but said they would do all the preparation and decoration; Mavis must do nothing. Of course, she would not agree to that and said she would provide a special cake from the delicatessen and champagne. They would contact other friends of both James and Rosemary. The couple were returning on Saturday evening, so there was not much time to get ready.

Saturday dawned bright and sunny and Mavis was up and about at seven, she had hardly slept with excitement. She rang the delicatessen at nine and ordered the cake and other delicacies. Then she rang John O'Dea and invited him to come as well. As she drove to town to get the champagne and other beverages, she called into Sadie. Margaret O'Neill was there, and she asked Sadie if she would be up to a party? Would she? The old woman's eyes lit up and a big smile spread over her lined face. She loved a party. Mavis invited Margaret also.

At noon, the three special friends of Rosemary arrived and started decorating the big front reception room. They were like excited and giddy schoolgirls and Mavis got a bit infected with their excitement. The activities went on until four o'clock, with a break for a sandwich lunch. One of the girls went to town to collect the cake and then, all was ready, and they waited for the unsuspecting pair to arrive.

John arrived at six and he and Mavis strolled around the gardens and then she took him up through the fields to the wood. There she revealed her plan to him and looked at him for approval. He grinned broadly and thought the plan was great and just what was needed.

'Now I won't have to worry about you rattling around in that big house, alone,' he confessed. 'I could have suggested that ages ago, but you were not ready for the move, I think.'

'No, I don't think I was, John. Even when Kevin the architect mentioned it, I was not ready to consider such a big move. Now I can't understand why I did not think of it myself.'

When they returned to the house more friends of the couple had arrived and Sadie and Margaret too, and Mavis was delighted to see that there was room for all. The food was laid out in the dining room that they seldom used, and all looked good. When the couple arrived at eight o'clock, they were shocked at first to see all the people present, who started singing "Congratulations", as they entered the front door. The next two hours were noisy and full of laughter and fun. Balloons were floating everywhere, and the party spilled out into the back garden. The evening was balmy and by ten o'clock the young people were sitting around on the patio drinking the champagne that Mavis had plentifully provided. John had left around nine along with Sadie and her carer, Margaret. Mavis was fatigued but would not consider going to bed and leaving this happy occasion. They all sat outside and chatted. Someone then asked James when it was, that he knew Rosemary was the one. He thought about it for a minute with his head on one side.

'I guess it was all to do with Debussy and his "Golliwog's cakewalk," he smiled over at Mavis and they both laughed.

Of course, nobody else had heard the story, so Rosemary related how they had been forced to dance together by Mavis, while he was there for a piano lesson.

They were all laughing at this and Mavis was topping up glasses when there was another visitor. She saw James' face changing and looked in the direction of his glance and there was Frank, advancing towards them.

'It appears there is a big celebration. May I please join you?' Frank smiled at everyone and appeared quite at home. He was dressed to kill in a new linen suit and looked at if he had dressed for the party, which of course, he knew nothing about.

Rosemary brought over a glass to him, and Mavis filled it with champagne. She looked at him and said, 'You would have been invited if we knew where you were. James and I have got engaged.'

'Wonderful. Here's to the happy couple.' He raised his glass and smiled at everyone.

He came over and kissed his mother on the cheek. 'Sorry I have not been in touch; business booming and all that, and I've been out of the country too. Just got back tonight.'

The young friends of Rosemary were all busy chatting and did not give Frank too much attention. They were busy organising the next big walk and James was giving directions to some of the lads who were new to walking.

Eventually people drifted off and said their goodbyes. James and Rosemary were left alone now with Mavis and Frank. James started gathering up the used glasses and bringing them into the kitchen. Frank sat drinking and looking at his sister. She felt his gaze on her and felt a bit guilty about him not being invited. Mavis was explaining that it was an impromptu party, organised by the friends today. They had only heard the news of the engagement Friday night.

'I have to admire you, Romy, you are a fast worker. Engaged! How about that? When is the big day, may I ask?'

'Nothing like that is planned yet, Frank. We have only just got engaged; yesterday, in Kerry.' Rosemary, remembering the nasty things he had previously said, made up her mind that she would not let him spoil her day.

'That is wonderful Romy, I hope you and James will be very happy together.' He said this smiling at James as he returned with an empty tray.

Mavis said quickly, 'How are you Frank? Are you working hard?'

'I am indeed Ma, never harder and business is bustling, I'm run off my feet these days.' He looked very fit and well groomed.

Mavis felt something had now occurred in his life and that he was somehow back on track and was more like the old Frank they all knew. James was quiet and sitting beside Rosemary holding her hand.

'Where have you been Frank? Maureen was looking for you, and Paul Kavanagh called and said that he had not seen you in a while. Were you hibernating somewhere?'

He laughed gaily and said he had certainly not been in hibernation.

'The opposite Mum. I have been scouting for business abroad and am now in a much stronger position than before. My problems are over, and Maureen is thrilled with her nephew.'

This was so startling that Mavis wondered if she had heard correctly.

'That is wonderful news, Frank. It's a relief too. When did you see Maureen?'

'Oh, we have been having phone calls the past few days and I think that she is a very happy lady again.' He beamed at them all and winked at his mother mischievously. 'She is in Cork right now, ending her lease.'

Mavis was transfixed, Maureen was happy, could that be possible?

Rosemary looked at this brother of hers who could change like a chameleon and pondered out loud. 'Maureen has got her investment then, has she, Frank?'

'Something like that, old girl. She knows she is going to recoup it all in time. She will be happy to get it little by little and is already wanting to invest again. Needless-to-say, I will not be taking her on again. She is too volatile. With investments one must be patient.'

Mavis was astounded at his news. James rose to his feet and said it was late and the party had been wonderful, but he needed his bed. Rosemary also rose and walked into the house with him. Mother and son sat in silence and they heard James' car drive away.

Frank got up and checked a bottle on the garden table. He brought it over and filled up his glass again and offered it to his mother, who shook her head. He put the bottle down by the side of his chair.

'I have had more than I should, Frank. It was all so unexpected but hoped for. I am so happy for James and Rosemary; they make a lovely couple and I'm sure they will be happy together. I hope you will feel the same.'

'Yes, it's time she settled down and she was damn lucky to find a man at her age.' He said this quietly and seriously.

'Honestly, Frank, you are only two years older than her, and nobody thinks or says anything like that to you, do they? Why are men such chauvinists?'

He laughed harshly and swallowed the rest of his drink and stood up, a bit unsteadily, to get another half-finished bottle from another table. Mavis thought that he must have already had drink taken before he arrived.

'Did your friend Paul get in touch with you then, and pass on the message?'

'Paul, my friend?' He chuckled and shook his head. 'Ah, poor Paul. He was not exactly my friend and had a lot of problems. Poor lad died of an overdose, they think it was, a few days ago.'

Mavis was horrified and shocked by this news. 'He can't be dead. He was here talking to me a few days ago and said he had not seen you in ages. Was

285

,

worried about you, in fact. Oh Frank! That is terrible news. I can't believe it.'

She was upset and numb at the news, at the same time, she was shocked at Frank's attitude and lack of sympathy.

Frank nodded his head. 'One man's loss is another man's gain, as they say.' He tossed off the remainder of his drink and walked unsteadily towards the kitchen.

'See you in the morning Ma. Sleep well, I know I shall,' he called over his shoulder.

Mavis sat looking after the stumbling figure of Frank sadly. Had she ever known him, this man who was her much loved stepson?

Chapter 32

Rosemary and Mavis were having a leisurely breakfast. Frank joined them at ten thirty and announced that he was going to drive to Cork to see his aunt Maureen and offer her a job. The women stared at him with widened eyes. He smiled at them and nodded his head vigorously.

'I think she will be very interested in a PR job, and my guess is, that she will be very good at it.' He helped himself to bacon and sausage from the dish on the table.

Mavis asked nervously, 'Frank, are you sure you know what you're doing? Maureen is a bit deranged at times. Jenny had to flee the country because of her.'

'Deranged yes, but when you know and talk to Maureen, she is the essence of respectability and probity. She would inspire confidence in customers and businessmen. She could be an important asset to me, surprisingly enough.'

Both women were gob-smacked and could offer no reply.

'Is business really back on track then, Frank?' Rosemary asked this doubtfully.

'Absolutely. I am in sole ownership of the garage now and a lot of my debts are now extinct, thanks to old Paul dying.' Frank was utterly unmoved by his so-called 'partner's', death.

Rosemary had not heard this before as her mother had not wanted to start the day after the party with bad news. Frank told his sister how Paul had been found dead in bed and an overdose was suspected. Frank did not know whether it was suicide or an accident. He had been so relieved to find he was the total owner again of his inherited property. Again, Mavis reiterated her unbelief that he could be dead so soon after his visit to her. She asked Frank when it had happened and Frank thought a while and mentioned a date.

'Why, that's the date he visited here, Frank. It was such a pleasant visit. I thought that he wanted to talk about you. He even made me a cup of tea.'

Frank looked at her in disbelief. 'He never said he was coming down here,' he muttered.

Mavis rose to her feet and said she must get ready for church.

Her mind was racing as she made her way upstairs to her bedroom. Paul had said he did not know where Frank was and had not seen him in ages. Here was her son, downstairs, saying that Paul had not told him he was going to Ravenswood. She was confused. She got dressed distractedly and went downstairs. Rosemary was coming up against her and as they passed each other, Mavis suggested that they have dinner at the garden centre if possible. She was delighted to hear that James would be there too. When she went to her car, she stopped abruptly at the sight of the car that was parked next to hers. It looked brand new and very expensive at that. This must be Frank's latest acquisition. Well, things had certainly changed a lot.

She was not able to concentrate at the church service too well. Her mind was all over the place. After Mass she looked around the church. There he was, the old reliable, John.

She went over to his pew and asked if they could have coffee again briefly. He nodded and got up. Over coffee she relayed the latest news, starting with the good news about Rosemary and James and going on to the sad news about Paul and then, Frank's renewed fortune.

John as usual listened in silence and eventually said, 'Now Mavis, you will have a bit of peace, at least for a while. He will not be pushing you for money. If possible, mention the sums which he owes you. If he is flush with cash, now might be the time to get it back. You don't know what the future holds, it all sounds too good to be true.'

Mavis was well-aware of that too. There was something wrong about this whole business and poor Paul's death, and this job for Maureen. She told John that she would do just that, as he was in such obvious financial sufficiency, if not affluence.

When she returned to the house, Rosemary was ready to go out to the garden centre and James was already there. Frank had left almost as soon as

James arrived. They had a nice meal at the garden centre and chatted about the holiday in Killarney. They steered away from Frank's business and mentioned nothing about it to James.

At five o'clock, Frank arrived back at the house, a big happy grin on his face.

He came straight into the kitchen where Mavis was sitting doing a crossword in the Sunday paper.

'Told you so, Mater! Maureen is feeling extremely honoured to be invited to join the company and is starting tomorrow.'

Mavis folded her newspaper and smiled at her son. 'Good. I hope she will enjoy her work. Might be just what she needs, she has too much time on her hands, that was always her problem'.

Frank was busy filling the kettle. Mavis decided to plough on with John's suggestion.

'Since things are back to normal, Frank, I wonder if you could repay me the money that I loaned you, and replace the amount of money taken from my account?'

He looked over at his mother. 'I think that is now possible, mother mine. I will never have to borrow again, I promise you.'

Mavis felt a huge relief wash over her. It seemed like her son had returned from whatever dark land he had been inhabiting. She smiled at him and told him she was glad he was clear of debt again and hoped he would not make any more mistakes.

'Once bitten, twice shy, as they say, Ma. Frank is going to be a very careful boy from now on.'

Mavis could not resist getting up and hugging her son. Every prodigal son should be welcomed back she thought, recalling that Sunday's gospel.

'Frank, you are precious to me, you must know, as is your sister. I may not be your birth mother, but I consider you my natural children and I love you both very much.'

He looked a bit embarrassed and hugged his mother tightly. 'Sorry for all the shit I gave you. You deserve better and I know it.'

Mavis was moved to see tears in his eyes and immediately forgave him everything.

James was not so certain about Frank's sudden conversion but did not want to dampen Mavis's relief and delight. Rosemary was also cautious in her hopes for her brother. Of course, they all wanted his life and business to be on course again and all dangers of ending up on the rocks banished, but the doubts remained both in James' and Rosemary's minds.

The insurance company was pressing for a police investigation into the damaged brakes and James was on the alert all the time. He wished Rosemary would move in with him as soon as possible and he would feel better. He broached the subject with Mavis after his next music lesson. She repeated what John

O'Dea had said, about him moving into her house. She knew that it would go against the grain; James was a proud man and would not want people to think he was taking the easy option. Mavis then revealed her plans to sell the house and build on the upper field. She was not sure in her mind that it was the right thing to do. When Rosemary was told of the plan, she was very excited about it.

The architect's drawings had arrived and the three of them pored over them intently. Rosemary was very animated. 'That is the type of modern house we were planning.' She looked at James, grinning.

James nodded his head. 'Actually, it's exactly the type we were planning. I thought we would knock my parent's old cottage and build there, if we could get permission.'

Mavis shook her head. 'No, my dears, you will have one of the three sites, I'll build on another and there is one for Frank. He can do as he pleases with it. I hope to have money left over to pay off Maureen in case *he* can't. If I need more, there is the other field.'

James and Rosemary both said together, 'Mavis we are not going to take a site for nothing, we are well able to buy it from you.'

Her mother shook her head and said that the three of them would share the field, and that was that.

Rosemary was almost jumping up and down. 'With my trust fund we can build it without having to borrow any money, probably.' She punched the air in delight.

James laughed at her exuberance. He looked at Mavis, his eyes twinkling, and said, 'You have it all worked out, haven't you?'

'Not exactly, but I am hoping the house will fetch a good price to let me do all I want to do.'

They had a celebratory drink to seal the deal and Mavis then told Rosemary that James should move in until they finished the house, whenever that was. The second floor was theirs and there was room for the three of them. She did not think that Frank would be bothering them as much now. It was agreed that James would move in over the next weekend.

Mavis was most surprised to find Maureen on her doorstep at ten o'clock the following morning. Remembering how she had left previously, and her hope that they would not meet again, she was amazed by the woman's audacity.

She greeted her coolly and Maureen swept in past her as if she was an expected visitor. Rosemary was just coming down to breakfast and could not believe her eyes.

'Well ladies, I have just dropped in on my way to Dublin to my new position. I suppose Frank told you that he needs my expertise in PR and asked me to take up a senior position in the company now that he is in control again?'

She looked at them expectantly and then asked, 'Would it be too much to ask for a cup of coffee, do you think?'

Mavis said calmly, 'Not at all. Please come into the sitting room and Rosemary will bring one up to us.'

'Oh, I don't mind sitting in the kitchen, Mavis. It'll be like old times, won't it?'

'No Maureen, we'll keep things formal, if you don't mind. Too much has happened and too many unkind things said.'

Rosemary went down to the kitchen without saying anything and Mavis led the way into the sitting room.

Maureen looked a little disconcerted by this reception and followed Mavis into the room. They both sat on opposite armchairs and Mavis waited silently for Maureen to say what she came to say. She gave her no help or introduction and was pleased to see the haughty woman opposite her at a loss for once, on how to begin.

Eventually she relaxed a little and asked Mavis if she had heard about Frank's good fortune and the regaining of his business. 'Of course, he should never have lost control of it in the first place, but it was not his fault. He was a bit too trusting I think.'

Mavis nodded and told her that Frank had told her about it all.

'

'I, of course, always knew that Frank would come right, I just knew his investments were perfectly safe and my trust has been proved correct. He has already repaid me three thousand euros, and the remaining monies are safe, and in other investments which will mature shortly.'

Rosemary came in with a tray and three cups of coffee.

'I knew your brother was a gem, Rosemary. It's just a pity that neither of you were brave enough to do what I did. I hope you will not regret your caution.'

Rosemary smiled at her aunt. 'No, I regret nothing Maureen, I have got my inheritance safe and will use it wisely.'

'Of course, I will have an apartment close to my place of employment and Frank has assured me that it will have all the modern equipment I am accustomed to. I will be working a five-day week although my hours will be at my discretion. I think Frank will be a wonderful employer and we will complement each other perfectly.' She smiled as she finished her coffee and looked at Mavis smugly.

Mavis suddenly woke up apparently. 'I think it's a wonderful chance for you Maureen; you have been unemployed for so many years, it will keep you fully occupied. It's so important for mental health I think, to be active and to feel useful, in whatever way possible.'

,

Maureen listened with her head on one side, smiling. Then not quite understanding the gist of what Mavis was saying, her smile faded, and the two women could see her trying to process mentally what Mavis had just said. Mavis stood up then, as did Rosemary.

'You will have to excuse us, Maureen, we have a busy morning ahead. We are in the process of selling the house.'

'Maureen gasped. 'You have no right to do such a thing. It's my family home,' she stammered.

Mavis told the shocked woman that she had every right. She had bought the house after all. It no longer belonged to the Joyce family. It was lock, stock and barrel completely hers.

They escorted the not so confident woman to the hall door and said their goodbyes.

Chapter 33

September was here and the weather was still warm and sunny. An Indian summer was forecast. Mavis was busy. Her tomatoes were prolific this year, despite their uncertain beginning, and the yellow courgettes producing, like a factory. The onions and garlic were all dried and stored in the garage and all the other vegetables were doing well and providing meals every day. Her roses had been and still were, looking beautiful. Rosemary joked that it was because of the nutritious fertiliser that Mavis had spread.

Nobody had ever been charged with the murder of Billy O'Brian and Mavis often thought of the lad and wondered if anyone ever would be. It seemed so unfair. She saw Margaret and Brigid regularly and of course, Sadie. Life seemed to roll on as before and all was calm.

Today, Margaret was bringing Sadie and Brigid up here for afternoon tea, as a change. Mavis had made a sponge cake with homemade raspberry jam in the middle, and strawberry meringue nests, with cream. She loved being able to use her own garden's produce.

James was now installed on the second floor with Rosemary who had become a more confident, and calm girl. She still went line dancing on Friday with her friends and James, and they all had a salad after their swim. Susie had met a nice man in Italy, from Kilkenny and gradually life was changing around Mavis. The foundations for her bungalow were already down and Rosemary and James were ready to begin theirs. The old house was on the way to being purchased by a family from another county and Mavis realised that this would be her last summer there. Part of her was sad. Sometimes she wondered if she was doing the right thing but deep in her heart, she knew this had to be done. She spoke to Dennis last thing at night and often asked if he minded her selling his family home. The bank had given her a loan on the strength of the pending house sale and the builders were local and eager for business.

Frank had not visited in weeks and Mavis and Rosemary took this as a good sign. They heard nothing from Maureen, for which they were grateful. Rosemary was busy at school and James worked from an office in town. In his spare time, he was decorating the old house and intended to rent it out, as it was quite habitable. He also felt sad at leaving his father's house, where he had grown up and later lived in with his wife Mary. He knew that a fresh start was better for himself and Rosemary. He was excited at the prospect of having a modern house which would be easy to maintain and would be well insulated.

Mavis and her guests sat under the canopy of rambling roses that almost covered the pergola. They had enjoyed the sandwiches and cakes and many cups of tea. Now they were just relaxed and enjoying each other's company without having to make too much conversation. Occasional comments would be made which would cause a flurry of talk, then a period of quiet and calm would descend. It was all so civilised. Sadie was lucid enough and enjoyed making the ladies laugh. Mavis decided to reveal her news of her new house and the old one being sold. They were surprised that she would want to sell such a lovely residence. Mavis explained that as she was getting older and as Rosemary would be marrying quite soon, she needed a smaller place with less overheads. Margaret nodded her head in agreement. Sadie asked where she would be moving to, so that involved more explanation. They were all delighted that she was not moving far away.

'Of course, now I understand,' stated Sadie, smiling. 'Patsy said that Dennis told him you were moving nearer to me, and sure you are, even if it's only five minutes nearer.'

The ladies laughed at this, quietly. They did not want to offend Sadie. Mavis though was curious and said, 'I'm glad you said that Sadie. I was hoping that Dennis would not be shocked, if he were alive, to see the old place go.'

'Not at all Mavis, he often speaks with Patsy. It's a great comfort to me, so it is.'

Margaret changed the conversation to who the new owners were, could they be local, she asked?

'They are people who were working in Abu Dhabi and are now returning home, and they have four children who are of school going age. It will be six months before they arrive and they are happy to buy some of the furniture as well, which is fine with me. Old furniture does not usually go well with modern houses.'

Sadie leaned forward slightly. 'I almost forgot Mavis. Patsy said you must make your living room big enough for the piano that Dennis bought you.'

That silenced all three women. Mavis laughed and said to Sadie. 'You are a gem Sadie, and you must always pass on the messages and not forget them.'

Margaret looked at her watch and told them that is was time for them to go now. Sadie was due her evening medicines soon and Margaret wanted everything done before she handed over to the next carer. They all got up and Mavis had a bag of tomatoes and courgettes and lettuce for each of them; the produce of her tunnel she said, nodding up at the polytunnel. As they all looked up, Sadie became a bit agitated. She sat down again and said, 'I'm dizzy.'

Margaret and Brigid produced her bottle of water and said that she had got up too quickly, and it was just her blood pressure playing up. 'We'll wait a while and then you must get up very slowly', they told her.

Sadie nodded and did as she was told. As they walked towards the house, she muttered to herself. Mavis heard her quite clearly; 'Poor Billy, why was he here?'

When they left, Mavis walked up to the top field to check progress on the house. She did this every day and was always pleased. She rang the architect later and asked him if her baby grand piano would have enough room in the living-room she had planned with him. She just wanted one big room on the south-facing side where she would cook, eat and relax. She was finished with lots of different rooms and always liked the idea of a big open-plan living area.

He told her there was lots of space and that he would point out the layout the next time he was at the site. He was a friend of John O'Dea and a lovely man; nothing was too much trouble. He was going to help with the layout of James and Rosemary's house. They were planning a family and would want things a bit different to her house.

After dinner, James had to go out to a meeting and Rosemary accompanied him. Mavis was tired after the social afternoon she had and contemplated an early night. As she went into the hall from the sitting room, she saw the lights of a car coming up the drive. She went to the front door to see who it was. It was Frank's flashy car. He parked quickly and came into the house.

'Frank, good to see you,' she reached out to him for a hug.

'I'm not staying Mum, in an awful hurry. Must get a couple of things from my room that I left behind. Maureen just told me you are selling up. Hope you get a good price.' He ran up the stairs, to the first-floor room he always used.

Mavis stood where she was. She felt a sick wave of disappointment wash over her. Her boy was gone again. She recognised the agitation that he had displayed for a while now. She waited and heard him moving around the room upstairs. He came down carrying a hold-all.

'Sorry about the rush, Ma. I'll be down soon again, I promise.' He practically ran out the door before she could say anything else.

She continued up to bed, sad at heart and wondering what was happening in Frank's life.

Later she heard James and Rosemary return and heard their steps pass her room on their way to the second floor. She would have liked to have asked their opinion of Frank's behaviour, but felt it was not fair to burden them with her troubles. Perhaps it was her imagination, after all. All she wanted for them all, was a quiet life and no dramas. Little did she know that her life would be more dramatic than before.

The two lovebirds were already gone to work by the time Mavis went down for breakfast. She had slept late again, not having slept until dawn. She hated when that happened.

She brought her tea and toast to the sitting room and put on the television. Rain was pouring down outside and there would be no gardening today.

The news was on and she watched it vacantly until she heard Greenways mentioned. She quickly rewound it and listened intently. Two young men, in their teens were found last night in a field not far from Ravenswood. They had been murdered apparently. Mavis sat with her tea untouched. Not again, surely. What was the world coming to? The only information given was, that drugs were suspected. Their names were not released, and Mavis was full of dread in case they were from the village. She found it difficult to settle to any activity today and was anxious for James and Rosemary to return later. She did not even go and see what the builders were up to. They would be working inside now. It was a timber framed house and once up, it had assumed the appearance of the house she would live in.

Later in the afternoon, she went into the front room and tried to play some Bach. After half an hour, she had to give it up. The choir was starting next week, and she knew that they would be lucky to get a few rehearsals for Christmas which was only twelve weeks away. With the move into the new house, she would have to settle down a bit first before resuming the practices. She suddenly felt tired of it all. She decided to look for someone else to take over the choir. Perhaps James would help her out. He was capable, she knew.

She prepared a vegetable curry for the dinner and lit a fire in the sitting room. It was chilly this evening and still raining. When Rosemary came home first, her mother asked her if she had heard the news? Rosemary nodded. Everyone was talking about it she said. The two men who were only about nineteen were not from the village but from the town. She said she suspected they were involved in crime and had fallen foul of a gang. It was happening all over, she said. James repeated the same thing when he came in from work. As he worked in the town, he had heard the names of the two lads mentioned. The three of them had never heard the names before and somehow, that brought relief. When parents or relatives were known, it always seemed worse. James could see that Mavis was visibly depressed. To lighten the mood, he asked if she would look over their house plans. They would value her input on the interior layout. Mavis was glad to have her mind taken off the gruesome murders which was now on the news.

Their peace was shattered at nine o'clock when the doorbell rang. James went to answer it and the two women were surprised but happy to see Jenny being led in.

'Jenny, what a lovely surprise,' chirped Mavis, getting up to enfold the girl in a warm embrace.

Jenny's eyes filled up and she tried to smile at them all. 'Sorry for barging in like this Mavis, and Rosemary. I did not know what else to do.'

The girl was told to sit down, and a glass of wine was put in her hand. They waited patiently for her to begin. She looked shattered and had dark circles under her eyes.

She had just landed in Dublin that afternoon. She thought she would give her mother a surprise, not having seen her in so long. However, it was Jenny who got the surprise. On arriving at her house, she found it full of people. They had looked at her in amazement when she let herself into her own house. There were four girls who appeared to be living there, none of them Irish. They shrugged their shoulders when Jenny asked where her mother was. Their English seemed to be sadly lacking. The men who had been sitting around smoking, suddenly seemed to evaporate. Jenny pointed to herself and indicated that this was her house. One of the girls shook her head. She had two words of English apparently, 'Frank' and 'Maureen'.

Jenny shook her head. She could get nothing more out of them and at this stage was tired and needed a shower and bed. What was going on in her house? Had Maureen sold it?

The three listeners were astounded by the story. Mavis knew that Jenny was past being distressed and told her she must go and have a bath and then something to eat. There was plenty time to discuss this and get to the bottom of it. Jenny looked relieved and nodded.

'I'm a total wreck, Mavis. I've been going over this on the way down and I just can't think straight anymore.'

Rosemary took the girl upstairs and ran a bath for her. Mavis went into the kitchen to see if there was enough curry left to reheat for her. James sat silently in the sitting room, watching the television, but it was clear that he was not really seeing it.

When Mavis came back in and the three were again sitting down. James looked up at Mavis and said, 'I hope that I'm wrong Mavis, but it sounds to me as if Jenny's house has been turned into a brothel.'

The women squeaked in protest. How could Maureen be a party to anything like that, they wanted to know?

James shook his head, 'Maybe she doesn't know. After all, she is now installed in a fancy apartment, isn't she?'

Mavis was indignant. 'It was not her place to rent the house out. It belongs to Jenny and it's in a lovely area. Surely it can't have been put to that sort of use.

'

We will have to contact her, as much as it pains me to do so.'

James thought a minute and then suggested, 'Maybe if you contacted Frank first, he might know something about it? Those girls mentioned the two names. He might be your first call, Mavis. I can't imagine Maureen agreeing to anything so dodgy.'

Rosemary agreed. 'Maureen would never agree to anything immoral, bad as she is. I would say that she knows nothing about it. She might have thought that renting it out was a great idea, but wouldn't know what sort of people she was letting in.'

Jenny came down in Rosemary's dressing gown and looked a lot better. She had a plate of curry and they insisted that she go to bed and try and put everything out of her head for now.

Chapter 34

Mavis let Jenny sleep on and crept quietly down the stairs. James was at home today, having done his job for the week. He usually spent all his free time now, down at his parent's house and was decorating it himself and sorting it out for either sale or rental. They had not made up their minds about it yet. She had rung Frank's number several times, but it was obviously turned off.

In the kitchen they quietly talked about the story Jenny had told them. Could they be mistaken about the house being used as a brothel? James had heard stories about landlords who knew nothing about what their premises were being used for and thought it was a real possibility. There was plenty of people trafficking going on, that was well known. It must be a lucrative trade for someone.

Mavis could not stop thinking about the poor women involved. Did their families know how they ended up? What happened if they fell sick? It was too disturbing to think about really.

It was afternoon before Jenny decided to ring her mother and find out about her house. Her mobile was just ringing out, so they looked up the number for the garage and rang. It was the foreign girl, Sonja who answered the phone. Her English had improved a lot. In two minutes, they were put through to Maureen.

'Jenny, you have returned! I wish you had let me know.'

'Mother, I have already been at my house and there are at least four females living there. I am so upset.'

'Now Jenny dear, don't be put out by it. It was a great idea that Frank had. You are not out of pocket I can assure you; the rent is all up to date. Frank put me into a rather gorgeous apartment, in keeping with my new position'. She laughed.

'Mum, there were girls there and lots of men too. I think the place is being used as a brothel.'

Maureen laughed shrilly. 'Jenny, you silly child! Of course it's no such thing! How on earth do you think such mad things?'

'Mum I need to get back into my house, now. I am in Ravenswood, after arriving back in Ireland yesterday, I am going to Dublin later and I'm going to chuck them out.'

'Now, Jenny. Frank will be back in a couple of days and we will speak to him and he will sort it all out, you can be sure. In the meantime, I'm sure Mavis won't mind you staying with her.'

'Not good enough, Mum. How would you like to be put out of your house like that? I kindly allowed you to stay with me when you moved from Cork, it's a very strange way to repay me.'

Maureen sighed. 'I thought you needed money for the mortgage, and I thought that this was a good way to get it.'

'Where is Frank anyway, why is he not there?'

'He is in Holland until tomorrow. We can sort it all out then, my dear. I'm afraid I must go now as I have a call waiting.'

Poor Jenny was distraught and did not know what to do. James wondered whether the girls were trafficked women and that made the poor girl feel worse. Mavis thought she knew what to do but said nothing.

Upstairs in her bedroom she searched in her notebook for the number she had got from the detective, Aidan Savage. After frantically rooting about in her desk drawer, she found it and rang the number. She was delighted when the man answered it. Briefly, she gave him the details of what happened at Jenny's house and James' concern about the women. He listened patiently and said that he had people who would look into it straight away. Mavis was relieved. She then asked about Billy's murder and if a suspect was found yet and was it connected to the two latest murders in the same area. He paused before answering and Mavis thought for a moment that they had been cut off. He told the woman that they were gathering lots of evidence and were sure it was all gang related. He promised Mavis he would contact her about the residents of Jenny's house; it might all be above board, although he thought that Maureen was a strange mother to do that. Mavis told him that he did not know the half of it.

She went downstairs and told them what she had done, and they wondered if that was the right thing to do. Jenny wondered whether her mother could get into trouble.

'Why should she? She rented it out in good faith, didn't she? How would she know anything about where they came from or if they were illegal immigrants? Let's wait and see what transpires, shall we?'

James went down to the village to work on his old house. Mavis brought Jenny up to see the house she hoped to move into soon. Jenny loved it and thought that her aunt had made a wise decision. When Rosemary came home from work the four of them had dinner together and Jenny felt a bit better. Rosemary offered her the study to work in, and it meant that Jenny could continue her work without disruption until she could return to her own house.

James and Rosemary took Jenny out for a drink later, to distract the girl. Mavis sat with her feet up and wondered how her life had suddenly become so hectic. The doorbell rang and she found her old friend John O'Dea outside. He had been out walking he said and wondered how the building was progressing. It was still light enough out, so Mavis brought him up to view it. He was impressed with the spaciousness and loved the open plan living area she had decided on. They returned to the house and had a whiskey. Mavis told him the latest instalment of her active and exciting life. He could hardly believe that Maureen would do such a thing, without consulting with her daughter. Frank should have known better. Jenny had only gone abroad temporarily and Maureen herself was just a visitor, not paying any rent. Was she quite sane, he wondered?

He made so many funny remarks and observations that Mavis was soon laughing her head off.

'If you saw something like this on the telly, you would say it was too far-fetched.'

He agreed and told her that in a few months it would be all behind her and she would be able to relax in her new house and not see anyone she didn't want to see.

'I expect you will be inviting Maureen to stay for a while, will you?' he asked jokingly.

'Ha! That's not likely John. I just hope Frank gives her the rest of her money so she can buy a house, far away from here.'

John said, 'It sounds as if the job was made for her. She may never retire, hopefully!'

Two days later the phone rang at nine o'clock in the morning, and it was Maureen. She was incoherent at first. Mavis gave the phone to Jenny, mouthing 'Mum'. Jenny held the phone away from her ear as her mother shouted into it. Jenny remained silent and let her mother rant and rave for ten minutes. When she paused to draw breath, Jenny was still silent. Her mother asked if she was still on the line.

'Yes, I am still here. You were raving so much I could not get a word in. Anyway, what do you expect me to do about the police visit?'

Maureen went off on another long list of complaints. Eventually, Jenny said, 'Sorry Mum, I'm working here, on my computer and have a call waiting. I'll get back to you later.'

Mavis sat mesmerised as Jenny recounted the story. The guards had arrived at the garage and asked to see both her and Frank. It concerned the housing of illegal immigrants in a house that Maureen had been living in. The girls had been taken away to someplace safe and it was understood that the house had been used for immoral purposes. In fact, they told her that the house had been under observation for some time. They wanted to speak to Frank. She told them that he was travelling back from Holland and that they would have to wait until tomorrow. She was highly indignant and told the guards that her nephew would not be at all pleased and that he knew people who were very high up in the force and that they would be hearing more about this intrusion.

Mavis could not suppress a smile. It was so like Maureen. On her high horse and having no idea what her stupid action had caused. Jenny was relieved that the drama was over. Now she could go back to her house, couldn't she? Mavis thought that she should get Frank to repaint the house and see to any damage that may have been done. They both wondered why the guards had been keeping the house under observation. Then Jenny guessed the answer.

'It must have been my neighbours, God bless them. They would surely have wondered what was going on and perhaps guessed, like James did. I told them I had to get away for a while from Mum.'

Jenny was now relieved that her house was vacant. She was also concerned about the condition it might be in. She decided to drive up the next day to inspect it. She asked Mavis if she would come with her and her aunt agreed. She went upstairs to work in the study, humming a tune. Mavis went into town to get brochures of paint colours for the interior and exterior of her new house. She also looked at tiles and bathroom fittings in her local stores. She was now actually enjoying all this activity. She had never had to choose these things before, and the plumbing would be very modern compared to the older house. She felt years younger and quite care-free. She would give a house-warming party for all her friends, she thought. She did not want to set a date in her

,

head as she knew that builder's dates changed all the time. It was something that she could plan slowly and thoughtfully.

At lunch time she made sandwiches for Jenny and herself. They sat in the kitchen and looked out at the leaves beginning to fall. The garden still looked stunning to Jenny who had never had any time to cultivate hers. Now she thought, when I am back home, I will get Mavis to come and help me design an easily maintained garden that I can enjoy. She knew Mavis would be good at that and enjoy it too. No use asking her mother. Maureen thought all that sort of work was below one's dignity and that is what landscape gardeners were for.

Chapter 35

Mavis was alone in her sitting room with a pile of sheet music on the small table in front of her. She was finally getting ready for the choir practice on Friday morning this week. The same music would be used for the Monday night practice. She had managed to build up some enthusiasm for the whole thing again. As she sifted through the sheets, she had the television on for the nine o'clock news that evening. As she adjusted the sound, a strange feeling came over her; something like the déjà vu she had experienced before. She paused and listened hard. The presenter was reading about a raid the guards had made on a lorry coming in from Holland. Mavis stiffened. She knew who was involved without any further announcement. It was her son. The presenter was talking about the amount of cocaine found and the four Vietnamese girls also found huddled in the back of the lorry.

Mavis sat numbly through the rest of the news bulletin. She rose slowly and turned off the television. When the others came in an hour later, they found her sitting in the dark.

Rosemary knew at once that something had happened and gently sat beside her mother and questioned her. Mavis told them that Frank had been caught by the police in a raid. James put the television back on and went to view the recording of it. The evening news was always recorded for convenience. After watching it, they turned to Mavis and pointed out that nobody was named in the bulletin. No mention of how many people were involved only the number of migrants being smuggled in and the drugs. Jenny thought that her aunt had jumped to conclusions just because Frank was driving in from Holland.

'He doesn't even drive a lorry, Mavis,' Jenny pointed out.

'Sadie said she saw him driving one, ages ago,' replied Mavis.

'Oh Mum, you know poor Sadie, she is hardly with it, is she?'

Mavis said firmly, 'I know it was Frank, and now he will go to prison, what can I do?'

James said stoically, 'If he is convicted, there is nothing much you can do about it, Mavis. You might be able to rehabilitate him by your support, I suppose.'

Rosemary looked annoyed. 'You can't just jump to the conclusion that Frank is involved, this is ridiculous. Just because he was travelling from Holland. Is this your sixth sense again Mum?'

The phone rang and Rosemary got up to answer it. It was her aunt, Maureen, again barely coherent. She stuttered that Frank had been arrested and the guards had visited the garage that afternoon and had told her and Sonja and the two salespersons, that they should go home now until further notice, first having taken their personal details and work description. The area, they said was now a crime scene. Maureen was at this point nearly hysterical.

Rosemary tried to calm her and said it was probably all a mistake and just do as they said: go home and relax and wait until Frank was in touch.

Jenny then spoke to the distressed woman and told her that she was coming up the next day to see what shape her house was in; at least Maureen had the fancy apartment to go to. At this, Maureen became hysterical again and she told her daughter that her apartment was also barred to her, and people from the Criminal Assets Bureau had seized it, and she was told to take all her items of clothing out and leave the premises. It was just too much she said, to take in. She had spent the rest of the afternoon packing her clothes, as much as she could and loading up her car. What was she to do? Jenny told her to go to her house and they would see her tomorrow about midday.

The four sat down and pondered in silence what was happening. They all felt helpless under the circumstances. Jenny had always envied her cousin, the lifestyle he had and the expensive cars and designer clothes he wore. Now she understood: his hard work in the garage did not provide this.

Rosemary sat and wondered whether she should have drawn attention to the cocaine she had seen her brother using, that time. James sat and knew that he was right to suspect Frank of trying to hurt his sister. Frank was in trouble up to his neck and James felt very sorry for Mavis. He looked over at her. She had aged ten years since this morning.

Mavis sat and thought about the vision she had once, of a prison. How long will he get, she wondered?

All four of them there, knew with certainty that Frank was not innocent. They sat there, hardly speaking and Rosemary asked Jenny and Mavis if they wanted her to accompany them to Dublin the next day? Jenny thought there was no need. She just wanted to see her house.

The next morning the two women left as soon as they had finished their breakfast. The motorway was not too congested, and they were in Dublin under two hours. Maureen's car was parked in the driveway of Rosemary's house and she answered the door as soon as they arrived. She must have been watching for them from the window. She stood aside wordlessly as they entered.

'Well Mum, what's the place like?' She started to look in the kitchen and then the sitting room, which was a long room, running from east to west. She took in the stained carpets and cigarette burns to the coffee table.

319

Maureen said, 'Jenny, I'm so sorry. You are going to get a shock.' She was wringing her hands, something that Mavis had thought she would never witness.

Jenny ran lightly up the stairs. She came down a few minutes later, her face pale.

'Well, the mattresses and all the carpets must go and probably the curtains. The place needs painting all over, and I just hope I will feel inclined to move back in. It's a disgusting mess, that's what it is. I just cannot fathom how Frank could have rented the place to those people.'

Maureen, straight away said eagerly: 'that's just it! He thought of the idea, it was nothing to do with me.'

Jenny turned impatiently to her mother and told her that she should never have left the house in the first place. She had placed her in a caretaking position, and it was her responsibility entirely. Why did she have to leave when she had everything she needed there?

'That was Frank's idea too, Jenny. The apartment is nearer to the garage and he thought my job deserved it. It is an executive position.'

Jenny laughed dryly, 'Indeed it is or rather, *was*, a very superior job, working for a criminal business. I hope you feel as proud now, knowing what everyone knows.'

Maureen then turned on Mavis. 'This is all your son's doing Mavis, do you see what you've reared? A proper thug, that's what.'

Mavis remained calm and detached. 'That is not what you thought when you invested your money in a dodgy investment. Who is the fool now, I wonder? You will probably have to help the police in their investigations into all this. For all anybody knows, you might be the brains behind the whole thing.'

Maureen blanched and held her hands tightly together. 'They can't possibly think that, can they, Jenny?'

Her daughter shrugged and said, 'It will surely look suspicious that his aunt is in such a high position.'

She and Mavis exchanged a quick look and Mavis could barely keep a straight face. 'Let her stew', was in both their thoughts; it might teach her a lesson.

Then poor Jenny calculated the cost of refurbishing her house and groaned out loud.

'What did I do to deserve this? I wonder if my insurance will possibly cover anything?' she muttered distractedly, running her fingers through her hair.

Mavis put her arm around the girl. 'I'm sure it will, Jenny. That's the first thing to do. We will go home and ring them and then organise for the damaged mattresses and stuff to be removed.

'No, Mavis. My mother will stay here and organise that. She is extremely good at organising things, aren't you, Mum? You can sleep on the sofa, as you obviously did last night and start ringing around for a removal van to take the things away. You can also organise a painter and decorator to come as soon as the insurance people have seen the place. I have work to do and cannot take time off. Time for reparation Mum. I'll ring you when to start, just as soon as the insurance people tell me that it's alright.'

Jenny and Mavis left then, leaving Maureen looking as though she could not believe her eyes and ears. They drove to a café just before the motorway for a cup of coffee. Mavis was surprised that Jenny was so matter of fact about the affair. She had expected tears from her and tantrums from Maureen.

'The big question now Mavis is, do you think we should have a doughnut?' asked Jenny.

'I think we deserve at least one,' said Mavis, and the two of them burst out laughing.

After that, they drove home in a lighter frame of mind and started to see the funny side of things. Poor Maureen, she certainly landed herself in some queer places and situations. At the same time, Mavis felt pain in her heart about her son. What would happen to him? He never had to endure any type of hardship in his life, would he survive prison?

She had a phone call from him later that evening. He was being held in custody and was denied bail as the charges were serious. He told Mavis he was sorry. He got pulled into something that he could not control and there was no getting out of it. He told his mother to prepare for worse disclosures. He had a solicitor whom he knew, and he had faith in him. He felt that he would not be subject to the full rigours of the law as he was not the man at the top, but a very small player and if he played his cards right, the solicitor said, he might get off altogether as he was in a position to be of great help to the police with his information. He sounded so proud of himself that Mavis could only shake her head. He had no idea of the way criminals operated. If he cooperated with the police with information, his days were numbered.

She tried to warn him. 'Frank, these are very vicious men, do you think that they will allow you to live, with the knowledge you have of them? Be careful and cautious of everything you say, son.'

Chapter 36

The news was all over Greenways and Mavis was subject to some curious looks when she went shopping. She let it wash over her. There was nothing she could do. She distracted herself by playing the piano and concentrating on the choir practices. Nobody there said anything to her, but as they came in, they all went up and gave her a hug or patted her on the back. She was so grateful for their concern. She knew by their attitude that they were worried for her but were not morbidly curious or judgmental.

She and Rosemary went to Dublin and saw Frank for fifteen minutes. He looked thinner and pale but was grateful for their visit. Mavis assured him that she would always be there for him and that he was her son. His solicitor spoke to them and asked Mavis a few questions about Frank's upbringing and background. He told her that he would do his best for Frank.

There was a surprise visit from Detective Savage later in the week. He called one morning when Mavis was alone. Rosemary was at work and Jenny had returned to Dublin the day before. She was renting a small flat while her house was being decorated and refurbished. Her mother had returned to Cork.

He brought some disturbing news to Mavis. She knew it would be bad as soon as she saw his face. It involved the murders that had taken place. The police now had the Moloney brothers in custody; they were the leaders of the gang along with Paul Kavanagh. Billy had, they thought, kept back money, and drugs went missing. They organised the murder and although that did not involve Frank, he must have been aware of the violence that they were capable of. The two other young men also, fell foul of the gang; they tried to cut into their territory and thought, in their naivety, that they were in the same league as the Moloney brothers.

Mavis suddenly thought of the money she had dug up, and the drugs she had spread on her garden and felt sick. Her face showed her shock and the detective immediately told her that none of it was her fault. She had brought the money to the police station straight away and the drugs were not her fault either. How was she to know what they were?

Mavis did not feel much relief. She would never recover from this, she knew. She asked Aidan why the money and drugs were in her tunnel? He explained that at that point in time, Frank was distributing drugs and thought it was a simple and straightforward scheme; Billy would collect the drugs and leave the money and all Frank had to do was drive down, leave the drugs and collect the money; what could be easier for both of them. There would be no witnesses in the dead of night.

'Poor Frank, what a shock he must have got when I dug up the money.'

'What a worse shock when he learned what happened the drugs,' replied Aidan. 'He could hardly tell the bosses what had happened, so he kept silent. He must have been scared when he heard what happened to Billy. He must have known that he was responsible.'

'How many years do you think he will be in prison for, Aidan?'

'It's hard to say, Mavis. He is not in the same place as the big boys, so maybe not too long, I wish I could reassure you, but I just don't know.'

As the detective left, he said, 'One thing that I find strange, is the fact that Paul Kavanagh the really big fish here, committed suicide. One just wonders why, when he was not under suspicion at that stage at all and it looked like he had everything going for him.'

Mavis nodded. 'I thought at the time it was such a waste, I really thought he was a lovely fellow. He visited me the day he died, in fact. He was so nice to me, chatting about Frank and even made me a cup of tea. I'll never forget him for it.'

She thought that Aidan gave her a strange look as he got into his car and drove away.

Her house was progressing well and her furniture that she was keeping, would be moved in the following week. Rosemary and James had started their house and would live in James' cottage until it was completed. She hoped to be celebrating Christmas in her new home and felt that it would be a fitting time to start the next chapter of her life.

She was clearing out her tunnel when Rosemary arrived one afternoon. She was obviously excited, and Mavis caught the aura she emanated.

'Well Mum, guess what? James and I have decided to have a very quiet wedding in February, round about my birthday. We have decided it would be the perfect time as it' half term at school. What do you think of that? We are of course sad that Frank will not be able to attend.'

Mavis leaned on her garden fork and smiled broadly up at her daughter.

'That's great news and your house should be ready for you by the end of January. I'm delighted for you both.'

Rosemary hugged her mother tightly. 'I guess I'm a very lucky girl.'

Mavis asked her seriously if she was sure that James was the right one for her? Rosemary rolled her eyes and told her there had never been anyone like James before and they were totally suited, just like she and Dennis were.

Her mother sat down on one of the raised beds and took off her gloves.

'You know? When I married your father, I was not *in* love with him, not then.'

'

As she saw Rosemary's shocked face she started to explain.

'I was looking after my best friend's children and I knew how they needed me and then I could see that Dennis also needed me. He was so relieved when I agreed to marry him. I knew that I was marrying him because I was so needed. It was only after a couple of years that I discovered that I loved him madly. So, out of need, love was born. I know Dennis also grew to love me with passion as he had with Sylvia. First there was need, though.'

Rosemary listened raptly. She knew that there were no half measures with her mother. She had always loved her and of course, could not recall Sylvia at all. She knew that the marriage she had witnessed was to her, a perfect one and she hoped hers would be the same.

'You don't have to worry about me at all, Mum. I am not at all naïve.' She smiled at Mavis as she recalled Frank's comments to her.

'Good Lord, you are certainly not that and never were. Cautious yes, naïve never.'

'Guess where we are going on honeymoon, Mum.' Rosemary was so excited.

'You will have to tell me love, I have no idea,' Mavis beamed at her.

'James, as you know has not been anywhere too exotic since Mary got sick. He is thinking about a two-week cruise starting in Rome and taking in

Venice, and the Greek islands. What do you think of that?'

Mavis paused and felt a twinge of weakness overtaking her. Her daughter looked at her anxiously, seeing her mother's pale face. 'What is wrong Mum, are you okay?'

'No, I mean, it's not that, what I mean is, please don't tell me you are going on a cruise.' She had her hands clenched in her lap.

Rosemary was alarmed at the sudden change in her mother. 'Mum, what's wrong with you, do you have a chest pain or what has suddenly come over you?'

She sat down beside Mavis and put her arm around her shoulder.

Mavis looked at her daughter and said, 'You are going to laugh at me I know, but the past few weeks I've had a strange dream, not every night, but every few nights, which I generally forget in the morning. When you said the word cruise, it came back again.'

Rosemary said, 'That's alright Mum, we all have strange dreams, now and again.'

Mavis shook her head. 'No this is different; there is a black cloud on the horizon it seems, and it gets bigger and bigger, then the word 'cruise' comes in somewhere. Now that you mentioned that word, the picture is there in my mind again. It could be a warning I think.'

Rosemary looked at her, disbelieving that her mother was speaking like this.

'I am not joking love, I think my dreams are a warning sometimes, God knows of what. I have no idea.' Her eyes looked pleadingly at Rosemary.

Rosemary shook her finger at her mother. 'Is this your sixth sense playing up, Mum?'

Mavis nodded and said, 'Yes, it is, it really is. I am scared.'

'How have you always known certain things, Mum, without being told I mean? Do you believe in a sixth sense?'

'Oh yes! What else do you call intuition or those feelings of warning when there is danger, or even just being able to, more-or-less guess, what is going to happen or be said next? It's just a part of us. We don't question our senses of smell, taste, touch, sight or hearing, do we? So why should we not believe that we possess another sense, a more spiritual one, if you like to think of it like that?'

Rosemary considered what her mother said. 'I suppose that is a good explanation. We probably don't pay enough attention to these feelings.'

Mavis agreed. 'I think that we are so active and surrounded by too much noise and energy. Our other sense is impeded somewhat by those things. Years ago, there was never constant music blaring and televisions belting out advertisements non-stop. Even the shops are full of loud music, have you noticed?'

'Do you think your friend Sadie really sees her dead husband in the garden?' Rosemary smiled. She thought that Sadie was hilarious.

'Why not? The dead are not far away, I believe. Not that I have seen Dennis prowling around the garden. But then, he was never a gardener, was he? I talk to him of course and he sometimes lets me know things. I always ask for his help when it's needed.'

She got up and hugged her daughter again. She apologised for dampening her daughter's good news.

Rosemary said she should try not to worry. Nothing had been decided and she would tell James about her foreboding. He had belief in her, she said, and he would not think her mad.

'Come on, let's go and get something to eat. I'm starving and I didn't have much lunch.'

The two women walked down the garden and went into the kitchen that would not be theirs for much longer.

The coming week was hectic with all the packing of the things that were being moved to the new house. Now that the time had arrived, they were excited like young children, and not too sad about leaving. The house had done its job, now it was time for new life to come and make the rooms ring with laughter and hopefully the new family would enjoy their lives there as much as Mavis and her family had.

,

After exchanging contracts with the new owners, Mavis understood from the solicitor that there would be enough money to pay for the building of her new house and for the settling of her son's debt to Maureen. They did not know of other debts, but the solicitor told her that it was not her responsibility and that she was being very generous to her sister-in-law.

The days were getting shorter now, darkness came earlier. All the trees looked bare, but Mavis could see beauty there too. Every season, she thought, brought something special. She sat in her sitting room watching the fire burn brightly and listened to James playing the "Gollywog's cakewalk" on the baby grand in the front room.

Rosemary came into the room just then and she laughed out loud when she heard what he was playing. 'That's how it all happened, in that room with that music.'

The next morning was crisp and bright with a clear blue sky. Mavis had her breakfast and as it was early, decided to walk in the wood before visiting Sadie, who wanted her to bring her to the hairdressers. She passed her new house on the way up. In a month it would not be possible to get there from the old house.

The fencing was going up when she was installed in the new house. She paused and looked at the site and knew that she would have to start making plans for a new garden.

,

She had lots of ideas and looked forward to going around the garden centres picking new plants and shrubs. She felt excited about it, not daunted by it at all. She knew she would need outside help with the heavy work, but that was all fine.

Her wood was busy with birds sounds. The ground was carpeted with leaves now and it looked so beautiful. She did the round of the wood slowly and then came and sat as she usually did, on her bench. A little robin perched on a log nearby and looked inquisitively at her, his head on one side.

She closed her eyes and breathed in the fresh cold air. She liked listening to sounds with her eyes closed; the peace of the place enfolded her gently.

After a time, she felt the familiar slipping away, into another dimension. Opening her eyes, she looked around. It looked the same, but it was different somehow. Then she heard a sound she remembered from long ago. A childish gurgling laugh came from the direction of some trees to her left and she watched in wonder as a chubby little toddler ran uncertainly into the clearing where she sat. She leaned forward. She recognised that form. He was like Frank when he was about two and a half years old. She leaned further forward and opened her arms. The child ran straight past and did not even appear to see her. He ran laughing and she turned to her right and saw him being swept up into her daughter Rosemary's arms. She too was laughing

,

and twirled around and around with the child, who had his head back laughing up at his mother who was pregnant, as Mavis could clearly see. Mavis walking towards his family, the broad smile on his boyish face. A black labrador dog followed them happily, sniffing at everthing as he came. He paused by Mavis and stood for a moment, nose pointing at her, still sniffing, then wagging his tail, he scampered off. The happy family were unaware of her presence and were totally engrossed with each other.

Then the scene slipped away as easily as it had come and Mavis was alone, sitting in wonder at what she had seen. She felt a sea of emotion wash over her at the circle of life around her, and lifted her face to the sky and whispered, 'Oh Dennis, oh Dennis, life does go on, doesn't it, my darling?'

Printed in Great Britain
by Amazon